Readers love
The Kai Gracen Series by RHYS FORD

Black Dog Blues

"I'm in awe over this Urban Fantasy world that Rhys Ford has created and I want more!"

—Rainbow Book Reviews

"This story is everything a fantasy should be."

—Love Bytes

Mad Lizard Mambo

"*Mad Lizard Mambo* is an outstanding sequel. Once again we are drawn into this crazy world author Rhys Ford has so lovingly created and carried away on an adventure beyond our imagination."

—Joyfully Jay

"Go get this book RIGHT. HECKIN'. NOW. It's a visceral urban fantasy adventure (with the barest flavor of future romance) set in a fascinating world peopled by compelling characters."

—The Novel Approach

Jacked Cat Jive

"…it's a wildly awesome ride every step of the way."

—Reading Reality

"…*Jacked Cat Jive* is just as full of life as the other titles, and I didn't mind getting hooked all over again one bit."

—That's What I'm Talking About

By RHYS FORD

Wonderland City

INK AND SHADOWS
Ink and Shadows

THE KAI GRACEN SERIES
Black Dog Blues
Mad Lizard Mambo
Jacked Cat Jive
Silk Dragon Salsa

Published by DSP PUBLICATIONS
www.dsppublications.com

RHYS FORD

SILK DRAGON SALSA

DSP PUBLICATIONS

Published by
DSP Publications

5032 Capital Circle SW, Suite 2, PMB# 279, Tallahassee, FL 32305-7886 USA
www.dsppublications.com

Silk Dragon Salsa
© 2020 Rhys Ford

Cover Art
© 2020 Chris McGrath
www.christianmcgrath.com
Cover content is for illustrative purposes only and any person depicted on the cover is a model.

Trade Paperback ISBN: 978-1-64405-871-8
Digital ISBN: 978-1-64405-870-1
Library of Congress Control Number: 2020937614
Trade Paperback published July 2020
v. 1.0

Printed in the United States of America
∞
This paper meets the requirements of
ANSI/NISO Z39.48-1992 (Permanence of Paper).

This is for the Five. Because always.
And Donald Kingsbury for writing my favorite book, *Courtship Rite*.

Acknowledgments

To my wondrous, glorious Five—Penn, Tamm, Lea, and Jenn. I love you all. Even as monstrous as we all are.

And Bru, Ree, Ren, and Mary. May your rice come out perfect every time.

Thanks will always go to Dreamspinner—Elizabeth, Naomi, Liz and her team, and everyone there who polishes what I send them. Thank you for being there.

Also a special thank-you to Chris McGrath for bringing Kai to a gorgeous vivid reality.

And to Greg and Michelle, who have loaned me both their cats for inspiration even if they did not realize it. The Newts in all the worlds thank you for your kind words and sweet souls. Remember to love your cats and obey all their wishes. Belly rubs for all.

Merged Earth Glossary

THE WORDS contained in the Kai Gracen series have a base in current language and serve as representative words in Singlish, a polyglot common tongue spoken in the book. While many have retained their original meaning, some have experienced a lingual drift and have developed alternative definitions.

aʻa: spiky, black lava (Hawaiian)

áinle: multi-use word, can be hero, champion, angel or if used in certain context, wild cat (Gaelic)

ainmhi dubh: black dog (Gaelic)

ampolla: vial, blister; slang: piece of shit, waste of a person (Spanish)

arracht: monster or 'scary monster' (Gaelic)

bao: an Asian-centric bread, usually a soft white yeasty bread (Chinese origin word)

bebé: baby (Spanish)

bonito: handsome, masculine pretty (Spanish)

chi wo de shi: eat my shit, damn it (Mandarin)

chikusho: damn it, fuck (Japanese)

deartháir: brother (Gaelic)

diu nei ah seng: fuck your family (Singapore slang)

fruteria: fruit store or rolling cart (Spanish)

gusano: worm (sometimes found in tequila) (Spanish)

hibiki: resonance, echo. Also a reference to a type of death-seeing witch. (Japanese)

hondashi: dried bonito (fish) flakes, mainly used for soup stock (Japanese)

Iesu: Jesus (Hawaiian)

Indios: indigenous Austronesian peoples living in Southern California / Mexico regions

jan-ken-po: rock, paper, and scissors (Hawaiian slang of Japanese phrase)

kimchee: pickled, spicy cabbage pickles, national dish of Korea. Also spelled kim chi or kim chee. (Korean)

kreteks: clove-and-tobacco cigarettes (Indonesian)

kuso: crap (Japanese)

li hing mui: dried fruit preserved with a mixture of salt, sugar, and other spices. Usually plums but other fruits like lemon and mango are used.

Sometimes even gummy bears or sour gummy worms. Also used to refer to the spice mixture itself. (Chinese)

malasadas: deep-fried yeast doughnuts rolled in granulated sugar (Portuguese)

meata: gone bad, turned rotten (Gaelic)

mija: daughter or younger female, spoken with affection (Mexican / Latino slang, Spanish origin)

miso: soybean paste, commonly used in soup (Japanese)

muirnín: beloved, sweetheart, darling (Gaelic)

musang: wild cat, civet, feral cat (Filipino-Tagalog)

nori: seaweed, usually pressed into sheets (Japanese)

paho'eho'e: ropey, smooth lava (Hawaiian)

peata: pet (Gaelic)

Pele: Goddess of lava, volcanoes, passion and general bad-assery. Not someone to be fucked with. (Hawaiian)

saimin: Local Hawaiian word for noodle soup dish based on Japanese ramen, Filipino pancit, and other Asian noodles. Possibly based on Japanese word ramen/sōmen or Chinese words xì and miàn.

shoyu: soy sauce (Japanese)

siao liao: crazy, out of your mind, insane. (Singapore slang)

Sidhe: fairy folk, also Seelie. Considered the "good" court of the Underhill faerie/elves. Pronounced she. (Gaelic)

sláinte: health, salute (Gaelic)

sucio: filth, dirty things (Spanish)

tik-tik: bulbous triangular taxi cab, single driver car with wide back to accommodate passengers, suspended above roadways by upper rails and trolley lines, resembles a rounder version of a 1976 Ford Pinto (Indian origin word)

Unsidhe: fairy folk, also Unseelie. Considered the "evil" court of the Underhill faerie/elves. Pronounced un-she. (Gaelic)

wana: sea urchin (Hawaiian)

One

"THIS HAS got to be one of the stupidest fucking runs you've ever dragged me into, boy," Dempsey spat at me from across the driver's seat of the old Chevy Nova. "But it sure as shit beats staring at the same bunch of walls. Just hurry it up. I've got some stories to watch this afternoon. Swear to all the Gods and Holy Marmots, if I miss that wedding, Kai, I'm going to take it out of your stinking cat-bastard hide."

I wouldn't say I loved the man who won me off of a Sidhe guard late one night during an ill-advised poker game, but I owed Dempsey not only my life but my livelihood. When he found me, I was a feral savage run through with iron rods and broken bones, a chimera of the two elfin races, an abomination, a blend of the Sidhe and the Unsidhe—nothing more than an arcane soup conjured up by Tanic cuid Anbhás, Lord Master of the Wild Hunt and more or less my father. At least by blood and bone.

Dempsey gave more to me than Tanic ever did... well, other than pain and misery. Tanic had a fucking lock on that. No, Dempsey fed me, clothed me, and put a knife in my hand. Then the son of a bitch taught me how to use it. It was something we argued about constantly. He liked the clean bleed of a kill over his hands; I liked blowing things away with a sawed-off shotgun and a pair of Glocks. Preferably from a distance. In case I had to reload.

Even among the miscreants and crazies who lived and died as SoCalGov Stalkers, we were an odd pair—a grizzled old Irishman who had injured himself out of a license and the elfin kid he dragged up to adulthood despite the wars and hatred our species threw at each other following the cataclysmic merge of our two worlds.

Dempsey was slowing down, riddled with bad blood and human diseases no healer could pull out. His stringy lank hair was ripe with gray and long enough to touch his collar in a frizzy bush someone who didn't know what the hell they were doing took a scissors to since the last time I'd seen him. His eyes were somewhat unfocused and watery, faded down to the gray the sky took on at the edge of the desert before a storm rolled

1

in, but they were still honed sharp enough to stab me when he looked at me through the passenger-side window.

He was smaller than he should have been, the strength of his brawny body sucked clean from his marrow, and unlike Thor's goats, I didn't see him springing back up every morning once the sun's rays hit the edge of the sky. His full face now hung down on his bones, jowls speckled with nicotine stains from the cigars he wouldn't give up and rivers of pink flushes coloring his cheeks and nose. But he was still a powerhouse of a man.

Or at least he was to me.

"You said you wanted to go on a job. This one came up. You take what comes up on the list," I parroted his words back at him. "Or are you too big for small-change jobs now? You that rich? You think I'm that rich?"

He was silent. The only sound from that side of the truck was the wet smack of his lips against his chewed-on, half-smoked cigar. I hated the things. Or at least the cheap-ass ones Dempsey seemed to prefer. He said the cheaper the better because it hid his smell from predators. I disagreed. The stink of whatever they used to stuff the damned things could make a dead cheetah's eyes water, and I was pretty damned certain it was an aphrodisiac for *ainmhi dubh*—the Unsidhe's black dogs—because the bastards seemed to find us every time we went on a run.

Okay, that last one could also be because my bastard father sends them out to hunt me down, but I blamed the damned cigars.

The wind was kicking up over the black lava fields covering the rolling hillocks near Pendle and its dragon-infested mountains. We were in the highlands, tucked between the craggy peaks scraping at the sky's steel-gray belly and the softer boulder-strewn crags bristled up against what was left of the 15. SoCalGov had made some effort to restore much of the inland freeway, but the coast-hugging 5 was shot to hell, and with the swarms of dragons swirling overhead with nothing much to do but eat and mate, no one was rushing to rebuild that stretch anytime soon.

No sense building a road where anything and everything would be picked off and munched on. It would be like giving the damned overgrown lizards their own sushi-boat buffet.

What we were doing was less dangerous than a Pendle Run. There really wasn't a lot of space for the larger wyrms to fit into the crags, and the smaller dragons liked the coast more. But in the nooks and crannies above Sparky's lay a cornucopia of Earth and Underhill creatures, and we'd

2

picked up a bounty to snag a couple to help the newly restored San Diego Zoo build up its attractions.

They weren't happy about losing their old space—Balboa Park and its sweeping long stretches of elaborate buildings and gardens—but that now belonged to the Southern Rise Court, and, well, the asshole Sidhe who'd somehow lodged himself into my life—Ryder, Clan Sebac, Third in the House of Devon, High Lord of the Southern Rise Court and my personal pain in the ass. No way Ryder was going to give up his Court for a bunch of animals, and when the zoo came over with their hat in hand to ask him to cough up a pair of the now-feral pandas wandering through Balboa's expansive forests, he told them they were welcome to catch them, providing they survived a heavily armed Crazy Gertrude, who took her panda protecting duties seriously.

They declined, so Ryder then offered me up as a consolation prize, forking over the money for a few animal bounties to fill their pens. Because that's the kind of stand-up thoughtful leader Ryder is—promising someone else's time so some idiots who live in San Diego's glass towers can spend a couple of bucks to go see beasts who'd sooner munch their heads off than eat the dead flesh tossed at them every night from the safety of a window at the back of their enclosure.

So now there I was, standing in the icy, biting wind cutting across the lava fields, hunting for fire hen chicks for the San Diego Zoo.

As a favor for Ryder, of course.

I was charging him triple of what I normally charged to get rid of a pair of black dogs from a meat-packing plant. Served him right for taking up the zoo's battle cry of restocking their cages just because he didn't want to catch any shit from Gertrude and her shambling black-and-white mounds of death.

"Go get the fucking chickens so I can get back to Jonas's to watch my stories," Dempsey rasped. "And we're stopping at the taco place on the way to the damned zoo. If I've got to eat one more tofu surprise casserole at that house, I'm going to puke."

A hint of sulfur curdled the wind as it swept over us, bringing with it the stink of guano from the nesting animals nearby as well as an undernote of rotting carrion. Something screamed deep in the hills behind me, but neither one of us flinched. We were long used to tackling larger things than whatever was complaining about life, the universe, and everything else. The scrub brush fought for space with rivulets of spiky black *a'a* lava, giving cover in the tangle of canyons and mesas, the wrinkled land providing cubbyholes and crevices for things that could give a hardened Stalker nightmares.

In a lot of ways, the hills were a lot like me and Dempsey—a screwed-up tumble of human and Underhill where up was sometimes down and even the normal no longer resembled anything sane. There were times I wondered why he took me. And there were also times I wondered why I stayed. But I knew the answer to that. It wasn't just that I owed him, it was because he'd taken a feral, wild-brained chimera of an elfin and fought to make me something more than a weeping mess of scarred and iron-riddled flesh full of hunger and fear. He was at the end of his journey—a broken-down human full of black blood and spite, aging right before my eyes while I still wasn't much older than when he found me.

So there I stood, tasting bird shit and spoiled meat on my tongue while Dempsey kept the Nova idling, waiting for me to go into the hills and grab a couple of fiery chicklets so we could pay for a few hundred bags of tacos and *elote*.

"You going to get those chickens? Or are we going to head back down to Jonas's?" His cigar flared up, a red dot on the semishadowed interior. "Because gas is wasting here, boy."

"Then turn the car off." I swallowed my unsaid words of worry when the red slipped from his face, leaving behind a gray, pasty stain on his flesh. "And pass me the tongs and asbestos bags. Sooner I get this done, the sooner I get some food in me. Just like the good old days when you were trying to get me to stop shitting in your sleeping bag."

Dempsey turned the car off, but the look on his face went from menacing to almost apologetic. He mumbled something under his breath that I didn't quite catch, so I leaned against the passenger-side door frame and stuck my head through the open window.

That was a mistake, because I couldn't hear him any better and I now had a mouthful of cigar smoke. After coughing slightly to clear my nose a bit, I said, "What was that?"

"We kind of don't have any tongs," he repeated a little bit louder, narrowing his eyes at me as if challenging me to give him a hard time.

Since I'd given him a hard time for quite a few years, I was about to change my tune. Sucking at my left canine—a habit I knew pissed him

4

off—I asked around my tongue, "Weren't you in charge of equipment for this run? Where the hell are the tongs?"

"Razor lost them. He had a fight with a salamander down in Calexico. Might have even been Carlsbad." Dempsey gave me a nonchalant shrug and scratched at the hardscrabble beard scruff creeping down his neck. "Guess it doesn't matter where, because we don't have them."

"How the hell am I supposed to catch these things without asbestos tongs?" Leaning harder on one of the Brents' many '77 Novas only dug the window rubber into my forearms, but the slight pain reminded me I shouldn't kill my mentor. If there was one thing he'd pounded into my head time and time again, it was that you didn't go on a run without proper equipment. "These things literally shoot fire out of their asses. Last time I looked, I was pretty fucking flammable."

"Najiri gave me these." He twisted around and dug out a plastic bag from behind the passenger seat. Once he pulled it free, Dempsey offered it up to me as if it were a pack of smokes and a couple of beers he was giving me for Christmas. "They should work out the same."

I snatched the plastic bag from his hand and opened it up, then looked inside. I then closed it and couldn't quite stop the growl crawling up my throat when I strangled my words through my clenched teeth. "These are fucking oven mitts."

"See?" Dempsey shot back, mashing more spit into his cigar end. "They should work good enough. You might get a little singed, but you've had worse."

There wasn't enough air in San Diego County for me to suck down to clear out the heat in my lungs. Opening the bag again didn't change what was inside of it. They were still floral oven mitts—big orange chrysanthemum blossoms on an ivory background with ruffles around the edges for decoration. I knew those mitts well. They'd been hanging on the Watts family kitchen wall for as long as I could remember—a gift from an aunt somewhere in Florida. Nobody ever used them because they were light on batting and couldn't even provide enough insulation for a boiled egg.

I would've been better off using the plastic bag they'd come in.

"Screw it. Pop the hatch, old man," I muttered at him, tossing the oven mitts back into the car. "Cari has to have something in the back I can use."

Cari had shit in the hatch of the Nova. I know. I spent a good five minutes digging through what little crap there was besides the spare tire and slammed the hatch down, tired and sweaty from digging around. Dempsey was chuckling when I came back to the front, his gnarled hand tightly gripping the potholders as he held them up for me to take through the passenger window.

"Go to hell," I muttered, snatching them from his clenched fingers. "When we get back, I'm going to make tongs out of Razor's ribs."

"You go right ahead and do that, kid," Dempsey gleefully shot back. "I'll even help hold him down for you."

THE HILLSIDE was rich with manzanita, California lilac, sage, and chamise, fragrant with their dry, dusty perfumes. There were a few large trees poking up out of the rocks, their twisted branches thick with scraggly pine needles, blue-gray bottle brushes scraping back and forth in the light wind. Outcroppings of lava jutted out from the canyon floor, the slopes dotted with bristles of black hematite flashing in the sunlight. There was movement among the vegetation—small flutters of wings and raspy serpentine shadows working through the tall grasses. None of that interested me. I was there for bigger prey, stupidly armed with only a pair of floral holders and my lack of common sense.

Working through the brush was fairly easy. I had a lighter step than any human, but gravity works the same on any species. All I had to do was make sure that wherever I put my foot down was solid, and the going was pretty easy. There were a couple of places where the sandy loam shifted beneath me, but nothing to send me tumbling ass backward across the strips of sharp pumice folded into the hillside's landscape. I'd never seen the place when it was either pure Earth or pure Underhill. I couldn't even tell anyone if I'd been born before or after the Merge. All signs point to before, but my dearly beloved father jacked up my genetics and growth so much there was no telling how old I was or even how long I would live.

But then I made my life as a Stalker for SoCalGov, and if there was one thing that could be said about any Stalker, it was that our life expectancy was about as long as a monarch butterfly. We weren't known for dying in bed with our boots on. I'd lost count of how many times I recognized a name listed on the Dead Wall at the Post where we picked up our bounties and contracts. It surprised the hell out of me that Dempsey hadn't bought it more than a few times in the past, but the old man had more lives than the proverbial cat, even though a knee injury had taken him out of the life.

Having him on the run with me was like old times, especially since I was the one doing the hunting and he was still sitting back in the car.

"Here, chickie-chickie," I muttered mostly to myself. "Come to Oppa."

I reached the section where the hillside was mostly lava, exactly the environment for the creature I was hunting for. The crenulation was deeper here—folds and ripples of broken-glass-edged rock throwing both sparkles and odd shadows about, making it difficult to read the lay of the land. It might have looked like small hillocks dotting the slope, but I knew better. There were deep crevices and caves with the occasional tumble of rocks from a collapsed tunnel just to keep a guy on his toes. The lava fields along the coast were riddled with different dragons, a holdover from their original hunting grounds in the Underhill. But while the grasslands belonged to mostly Earthly creatures, the canyons along the inner corridor were now home to nesting Underhill birds and relatively safe from predators due to the nature of their roosts—a fireproof sanctuary—which comes in very handy if you are a fire hen or phoenix.

I wasn't stupid enough to take on a phoenix without a lead-lined semitruck, a barrage of tranquilizers, and a group of people I didn't care if they survived, but the fire hen was doable, especially since I was only going after chicks.

I just had to get them away from their mama.

I got my first tickle from the telltale warble of an adult hen calling out to warn something off of her territory. Like most species, the female fire hen was the one to worry about. The males were generally smaller and really not very domestic when it came to sticking around to help take care of their offspring, but they sometimes hung around for scraps and to live under the dubious protection of a massive fire-shitting, angry, alpaca-tall female. Part of that was the stupid nature of the male bird itself, but mostly it was because a broody fire hen was possibly more dangerous than a full-size dragon. While both could shoot fire out of an orifice, the dragon would be more likely to snap your head off and eat you, where the fire hen would kick the shit out of you, pin you down, slowly cook your liver, and then nibble on it as you eventually bled out.

Luckily I was being paid to do this, because no one in their right mind would even approach the business end of a fire hen much less try to steal a pair of its babies.

There were two chicks—squat black-feathered balls held up by thin, blazingly white legs—digging at the edges of an outcropping when I snuck up on a promising crevice. They were about the size of a kiwi—the bird, not the fruit—and from what I could see, hadn't quite grown into their fire-starting capabilities yet. Or so I thought.

The slightly larger one twisted about, shoving her head down into her wing to put her ruffled feathers back in place, and I got a really good look at her back end. Her hind feathers were a veritable rainbow of reds, yellows, and oranges. It was a clear sign she'd been a good murder chicken and developed way ahead of nature's schedule. Her pink eyes were clear, not yet turned to the beady black of an adult, and she'd already picked up on her species' paranoia, scanning the rocks for predators and protecting the smaller blue-assed male by her side. Chances are they were siblings, but fire hens weren't known to be picky about their mates. So long as the male was willing to breed more little wildfire chickens, they were tolerated and fed along with any brood she might lay.

"Okay, no sign of momma hen," I muttered, craning my neck in an attempt to see farther down into the narrow ravine beyond. "Brace yourselves, chickies. You're coming with me."

Most people have a glamorized view of Stalkers. Pretty much everything anyone knows is something they learned from movies or vids. Books paint pictures of lone gunmen prowling the prairies and understreets, hunting down their bounties, be they human or creature. There's never any depiction of long nights slogging through mud holes and dusty caverns looking for a pack of black dogs who'd decimated a homestead or scraping off the remains of a fellow Stalker from your face after they'd been bitten in half by a prismatic dragon. The hero in Stalker stories always rode off into the sunset with a hot love interest and a bag full of money.

Reality never matched up to fiction, and I would bet every last penny I had that no movie or book would ever show the hero of the story tugging on a pair of ruffled floral oven mitts to scoop up a couple of fire chicks.

It was a good look—black jeans, an old blue henley, and orange-flowered frilly gloves barely wide enough to cover my hands, much less reach my wrists.

"And thank fucking Pele for that because I am never going to live this down," I grumbled, trying to shove my long fingers as far into the thin mitts as I could. "And if Dempsey takes a picture of me coming back with these things, I'm just going to leave the old man out here and he can figure out how to get back to San Diego all on his own."

The key to grabbing a fire hen—especially a baby one—is to wait until its head is turned. The problem is, like most birds, they tend to shit straight out their rear end like high-powered water pistols. *Un*like most birds, their natural defenses are actual flames. When small, along the lines of a butane torch. When fully grown, some have the range and heat of a small red dragon. And the adults were just too freaking big to grab, but some people tried anyway... usually ending up as fire-hen dinner. There's also the matter of the adults having powerful legs and sharp talons at the end of their hooked toes. They were cute enough when they were small—roly-poly feathered grumpy things easily scooped up if someone were careful and armed with a pair of asbestos tongs. But the adults were larger, more ostrich-shaped, and irrationally mean. I'd seen one go out of its way to bring down a pine tree that somehow pissed it off simply by existing.

I did not want mama bird to see me grab these two chicks, and I sure as hell didn't want to try to outrun her back to the car.

The male was easy, barely a peep when I grabbed at and tucked it under my arm, but the female—like most intelligent females—wasn't going to take any of my shit. As soon as my oven mitt closed down on her, she let out a banshee klaxon loud enough to warn Kansas of an incoming tornado. My ears were bleeding by the time I had her tucked under my upper arm, and despite the long sleeves of my shirt, she seemed to find a way to dig through the fabric with her beak and pluck out bits of my flesh.

And to make matters worse, I heard the warning cry of an adult fire hen gearing up for battle.

So I did the most sensible thing I've ever done.

I ran.

I was always fucking running.

The species as a whole is pretty, with sleek hematite feathers and multicolored ruffled bottoms. Problem with those feathers, as glossy as they were, they were slippery, and trying to keep hold of the chicks as I ran proved difficult. They slid about, crashing against my ribs and into the crook of my elbow. At some point the female cawed out loudly to her mother, either encouraging the older bird to sever my head from my neck or perhaps cursing her for being so lax in her duties that a lowly elfin was able to snatch her up from their hillside. Either way, their mother screamed back in return, shouting to the heavens what she was going to do to me once she caught me.

Thankfully, I didn't speak fire hen or I'd have probably run faster.

I nearly lost my footing on the sands as the loam slid away from my foot, and I must have squeezed the female a bit, because a second after I righted myself, she erupted with a warble of hot flames from her rear end, setting a sage bush on fire.

"Odin's—" My curse was cut off by the sudden drop of the hill underneath me. I hadn't seen the dip, and by the time I did, it was too late to adjust for it. I went down in a less than graceful tumble across the canyon slope, hitting every bit of chaparral and lava jut along the way.

The male squawked his displeasure when we finally came to a stop against a small boulder, but the female was furious and let loose a stream of orange-tinted flames from her nether regions, practically cooking the sand to glass. She struggled against my arm, pecking furiously at any part of me she could reach. Finding every tender bit of skin she could, she dug and twisted, sometimes going back for a second round on a particularly soft area just to make sure I knew she was pissed.

Their mother didn't sound too happy either.

Her cries were strident, more pissy than alarmed. She knew she could run me down once I got into the open. I could only hope for a long head start, because once we hit the flat land between the ravine edge and the blacktop road winding through the hills, I was screwed. Once upright, I clutched the chicks closer, not liking the spread of heat running down my ribs. The female was gearing up for another blast, one stronger than the ones she'd already given me, and if I didn't get the chicks down to the Nova and into the asbestos-lined kennel sitting in its hatch, she was going to turn me into a pile of elfin shawarma for her mother and stupid brother to feast on.

"Seriously, shut up," I scolded the chicks, and found my footing. The hillside turned from loam to gravel and back again every few steps, making the going tough, but the fire hen behind me didn't seem to be having the same problems. "Okay, hold on. We're going to do this ass first, because if we don't, your momma's going to snip my head off."

I flung myself down the rest of the way, praying gravity would push me down with enough momentum to give me breathing room between the car and the large bird barreling down on me. The fire hen was coming at an angle, so I could see her out of the corner of my eye as she ate up the distance between us, her long ivory legs flying up and down in a blur, talons digging into the ground and kicking up whirlwinds of dust with each loping step. She was a nightmare of a chicken, her elongated bright pink wattle flapping about her stretched-out neck, beak parted so her forked black tongue whipped back and forth as she ran. Unlike other birds, she had teeth—long ones. Probably a throwback to whatever ancient reptilian Underhill creature she descended from, but they were sharp and hooked, perfect for tearing into soft flesh and ripping out chunks to eat.

Much like her furious daughter was doing to my sleeved arm.

I tried to steer my slide as best I could, but my ass took a beating, seemingly finding every bump and rock along the way. The course was short—only a few seconds—but my weight was enough to get me up to a good speed and we flew down the slope, the chickens under my arms ruffling in the faint wind, framed by the floral horrors cupping their chests. The female blasted a short wave of flames along the way—a sputtering spray of embers and sparks—but it was mostly sulfurous gas and outrage. I didn't check on the male. He seemed content to be along for the ride, unconcerned about his fate and possibly believing he'd somehow gained the power of flight, a trait not shared by any other fire hen or cock in existence.

Not content with screaming at me, their mother stretched her body out, and it bulged, the sunset-hued feathers along her rump and underbelly going bright as she cut in closer. I swerved as best I could to avoid a chunk of lava, but it caught my shoulder, leaving a stinging scrape I would be feeling for a few hours. Glancing back quickly, I had just enough time to add my own screaming to the cacophony, some primal part of my brain believing that if I made enough noise, I could somehow go faster and avoid the inevitable storm heading my way.

Because while fire hens couldn't fly, they sure as hell could jump up like demented feathered ninja, fold their legs in, aim their asses forward, and blast anything in their path.

Unfortunately, the mother bird was fully engorged with fire and spite, and I was definitely in her fiery ass's path.

I hit the flats running, feeling the scorch of her blast at my back. The long grasses at my feet erupted into a smoldering fire, slowly catching, then rapidly dying out as the prairie sheaves quickly swelled with excess water to extinguish the flames. The dirt turned dry, its moisture sucked clean, but it was still packed tight enough for me to get a good purchase. Sprinting, I headed for the Nova, shouting for Dempsey to open the passenger-side door for me.

The car's gasoline–fuel cell hybrid V-8 engine was rumbling, but the door wasn't opening and I was getting close. The chicks' mother was still tight on my ass, probably gearing up for another flamethrower attack, but I couldn't spare her a glance. I needed to get into the car and gone before she reached the road or I'd learn firsthand what it was like to fall victim to her teeth and hooked talons.

"Dempsey! Open the fucking door!" I shouted, sucking in a mouthful of dry air. The chicks under my arms were squirming, and I almost lost the female when my right foot hit a rock hidden in the grasses. The male cheeped at me, thrilled for the little jog, or perhaps it finally dawned on him he was being taken away from his nest. "Momma's on my ass, old man!"

I was nearly twenty yards from the car when I finally saw Dempsey slumped over the steering wheel, his slack face turned toward me, a blob of pasty gray flesh dotted with silvering stubble and a large red nose. He wasn't moving, or at least not that I could see.

So I dropped the damned fire hens and pushed every last bit of energy I had in me to get to the car.

I didn't care about the bounty. Hell, I didn't even care if the mother fire hen caught me, so long as she let me go long enough to get to the old man. Panic clotted my veins, thickening the air in my lungs and shutting down my brain. Ice crackled through my blood, and I dove through the passenger window and slammed into Dempsey's limp body.

The glass scraped my belly, and I hit the center console hard, but I struck Dempsey even harder. His chest jerked, and his shoulder slammed into the door, but his open eyes only rolled to their whites and the cutting remark with its accompanying slap never came. His head lolled back and his chest stuttered when I hit him, his tongue swollen and pushing out from between his teeth, a pink mass held back by yellowed ivories stinking of cigar smoke and cheap whiskey. A silver flask fell out of his right hand, joining the dead cigar end on the floor by his feet.

"Come on, you old bastard." It was too cold all of a sudden and my teeth were chattering an imperfect rhythm, much like the one beating in Dempsey's chest. His breathing was shallow, and somewhere I heard a scrabble of thumps coming from the side of the car.

The Nova was cramped, and I hurt everywhere, bleeding in spots and seared along my ribs, but none of that mattered. Not even the enraged fire hen attacking the Nova's back quarter panel or the money I'd left on the prairie flat mattered. My world was suddenly only as big as the two front seats of a smelly 1977 Nova and the man struggling to breathe in my arms.

I tugged off the oven mitts, then threw them out the window, needing to free my hands. Pulling Dempsey's dead weight over to the other side of the car took me way too long, and I kept checking to see if he was still breathing.

If he was still with me.

"Stick with me, Dempsey," I muttered at him, kicking the flask out of the way so I could get my foot on the gas pedal while I threw the Nova into Drive. My eyes were burning, but I couldn't give in to their sting. The drive was going to be long and furious, and I couldn't waste my time on sentiment. Not now. Maybe not ever. "Hold on, old man, and when we get you all fixed up, you can kick my ass for losing the bounty and Najiri's damned oven mitts."

Two

NIGHT SEIZED the sky beyond the San Diego shoreline, but the city's sparkling lights held it back, a glittering cloak of flashing reds and steady whites, pushing away the edge of blue from its outskirts. From Medical's upper floors, I could see where the night surrendered to the sprawling metropolis's defiance, peeling back the darkness in waves of cloudy blue. An air ambulance whipped around one of the glistening glass towers studding the city's crescent, its red lights flashing rapidly as it approached.

"I've never seen one actually fly," Ryder said quietly, approaching me on silent feet. "Whoever is inside must be very important for them to risk it so close to Pendle. It's brave of them to pilot that, to risk being plucked out of the sky and eaten."

He wasn't wrong. Any type of air travel was dangerous, a far cry from the days before the Merge when giant planes skipped across the atmosphere, whisking people around the world. Now the air was populated with dragons and other airborne creatures with a healthy dislike for sharing the skies, and nothing said "quick meal" like a tube full of meat unable to defend itself from flying fangs and teeth. There were areas and times where a hasty flight was possible—between hatchings and mating seasons—but those were mostly along the interior regions, far away from the coast where dragons dominated the black lava fields separating San Diego County from the rest of SoCal.

"Nah, it's a safe approach. Coming in from the south side. Probably someone from the inner corridor." The heat of his body near mine was a welcome shift away from the cold shivers running over my skin. "In a couple of months, though, they'd have to go down the 8. Rocs' hatching season makes them territorial near Helix. One of those will take down a chopper just because it got too close to Junior."

The scattered clouds lingering on the horizon flickered with lightning, and my imagination worked dark shapes into their roiling forms—echoes of serpentine lines from somewhere in my buried memories. There were enormous cloud dragons who spent most of their lives slinking through the upper atmosphere, feeding on storms of white krill. Like Ryder and the helicopter, I'd never actually seen one, but I'd come across the shattered remains of what I thought was a cloud dragon's skeleton, fallen from the skies following a battle or perhaps just dying of old age. The story was they were the size of mountain ranges, coming to rest in the high peaks of the Himalayas once a year or so. No one knew their exact numbers, but the elfin confirmed their existence, telling tales of Sidhe and Unsidhe warriors losing their lives to the hungry crystalline hatchling they stumbled upon while climbing the Underhill's ice-swaddled mountain ranges.

"Here." Ryder nudged my shoulder with his, holding out a waxed paper cup with a sipping lid. "I brought you coffee."

I hadn't even noticed he'd left.

It'd taken me nearly an hour to get Dempsey down to Medical and another ten minutes for the emergency room staff to hear me out. The only thing that saved the nursing staff from me shooting someone was my neighbor and onetime long-held crush Dalia Yamada, who spotted me down the corridor where she'd been handling an intake. In the years since we met, she'd gone from a nursing student to a full-fledged resident, stopping briefly at being a triage nurse. She'd stitched me up more times than I could remember and took care of my cat, Newt, when I was called out on a run.

Now she took care of my… mostly father, pulling Dempsey into a maze of surgical arenas and testing rooms, leaving me to drift alone and in the dark in the waiting room outside of a door where my past lay dying and my future stood beside me.

The coffee was hot, a rich shot of bitter chocolate and cream followed by a punch of whiskey, a hit to my empty gut, and I smiled despite the shitty circumstances and took another sip to taste the smoky charcoal whisper on my tongue again.

"This isn't hospital coffee," I said softly, meeting Ryder's dark green eyes in our reflections on the wall of windows overlooking the city's southern face. "Doesn't taste like cat piss."

"What's the use of being a High Lord if I can't get a decent cup of coffee." Ryder saluted me back, his smile glimmering among the lights sparkling beyond the glass. Behind him, the people in Dempsey's life sat in sparse numbers, pulled together by calls gone out from the Post. Ryder glanced over his shoulder as if taking attendance on the useless vigil. "Where's Jonas?"

"On a run in El Centro. His husband, Angus, said he's handed it over to someone else." I sipped again, now wishing it was more whiskey than coffee, but I was glad for it anyway. "He and Razor are heading back now."

Neither one of us mentioned we hoped they made it in time.

Sparky was sitting with Dalia's boyfriend, Jason, a tattoo artist and master mechanic I'd known for a long time. They were an odd pair, her long-boned, desert-weathered, lanky frame next to his muscular, wide-shouldered, hunched-over body. Still, they were two peas in a pod, both engineers masquerading as grease monkeys, and in Jason's case, a fantastic artist. He'd slid into my inner circle, hooking up with Dalia and getting in tight with Sparky. The old girl needed someone who'd take over her business, letting her retire and move closer to the city, but we all knew that would never happen. Jason would set up a satellite shop in downtown somewhere, and Sparky would burrow down into the desert nest she'd made, working on monstrous vehicles for Stalkers to use on dangerous runs while renting out storage bays for their shit.

Until the day one of us found her up there, dried up by the sun and staring at the sky.

I had to get my mind off my macabre thoughts. I'd been surrounded by death since the first moment I took up a gun, swearing to sculpt away the filth of the world for a few pennies and a shiny Stalker badge. Death was a constant in our world, yet I was being tackled by its touch this time, dragged down by the weight of cancers eating through Dempsey's body. It was inevitable. We all died. We all gave up our last breaths to the hooded man with his sharp scythe. None of this was a surprise.

So then why the hell did it hurt so much?

"I might need more coffee to get through this," I muttered under my breath. "Never thought I'd be such a coward."

Ryder studied me for a moment. I knew this because not only could I feel his stare rake over my face, his glittering green eyes reflecting in the glass were pretty obvious about it. If there was one thing he was not made for, it was stealthy surveillance.

"Is that how you see yourself? As a coward? For feeling upset and unsettled because the man you think of as your father is dying?" He approximated as good of a derisive snort as he could, but I could hear him force it. His tone gentled when his shoulder pressed into mine, the push of his weight against my skin calming some of the gnawing in my stomach.

"I've never had anyone close to me die like this, but looking at everyone else in here, I'd say you're doing fine."

We stood shoulder to shoulder in silence for a long time. Or at least long enough for the night to steal more of the sky away from the city as lights were doused and the understreets began to glow brighter than the upper levels. There were shimmering waves punching through the gaps between the upper levels' roadways and concrete mesas, vibrant and insistent signs of the lives going on in the labyrinth of streets and alleys below.

It was hard to look at my mirrored self. I was still always shocked to find an elfin face staring back at me, and even worse, one that looked more like my true father every time I saw it. I was still gritty from the run, a bit of dust ghosting my black hair, but Ryder was, as usual, pristine in his long Sidhe Lord jacket, metallic emerald threads woven into the hunter green fabric to match his too-damned-cunning-for-his-own-good eyes. Every one of his golden hairs lay perfect against his skull, pulled back into a queue, probably to draw attention to his handsome face with its high elfin cheekbones and sweeping, pointed ears. Humans found him irresistibly attractive and charming, lulled by a melodic voice trained by centuries-old politicians and other lords.

To the elfin he was okay. Unfortunately for me, some perverse biological time bomb went off when we met, and I wanted to crawl over his whole body and leave my mark on every inch of his ivory-sheen skin. If I were honest, I'd admit it wasn't just that we were drawn to each other on some primal level. He'd grown on me, worked under my skin like a spill of ink from a tattoo machine's needle, but I wasn't ready to confess to that. Not yet. Maybe not ever.

I didn't like being told what to do, how to feel, but damned if Ryder wasn't making it hard for me to think.

"Have you talked to the doctors?" Ryder finally asked, breaking the stillness between us. "I sent healers in—"

"I know." Suddenly the coffee was flat in my mouth, sawdust with a burnt-charcoal chaser. "Thanks for that. There's just nothing for them to do. Dempsey's done. He doesn't want to… try anymore. So, now we wait."

"You going in to see him?" Another glance over his shoulder at the people gathered behind us pulled a sigh from his somber mouth. "Or is he keeping everyone out?"

"They just wanted some time to make him comfortable. I think they've run out of tests to do on him." I couldn't imagine what they could do to make the carved-in pain lessen on Dempsey's craggy gray-skinned face, but I hoped it would be enough. He'd nearly broken my hand when he woke up, racked with a rolling anguish tightening his bones. "Doc said he'd let me know when—"

It had been a long time since the sound of a door opening made my muscles clench so hard that my bones cracked. The memories I had of being in Tanic's cage were clouded by pain and starvation, living in a stew of bruises and iron hammered through my body. I still carried the mark of my father's House on my back—a cicatrix in the shape of a black-pearl dragon's wings, the ghost of its body traveling down my spine. The keloids were extensive and horrifically beautiful to someone who didn't know the elfin healed without scarring for the most part and that every bit of ridged and mottled skin was put there by shanks and bars of a metal so poisonous to the Unsidhe that Tanic wore gloves to handle it as he worked them into my body.

Back then a door opening meant I would be forced to live through another seemingly endless nightmare, nothing but a meat puppet made to dance on Tanic's strings. This time the double doors swinging apart brought a different horror, the grim face of a human doctor emotionally distancing himself from his dying patient with every step he took toward me.

"Mister Gracen?" the doctor called out, his hand on one of the doors to keep it open. He scanned the waiting room, eyes flowing over Jonas's extended family and Sparky gathered around a low table overflowing with paper cups and candy wrappers. The doctor finally found me, his eyes widening as if he'd forgotten I was elfin. Or maybe he hadn't and finally spotted Ryder the Great and Gorgeous to All Humans standing next to me. "Ah, um… you can come in now."

Sparky stood up, and then Sarah, the Post Mistress, followed, both of them shuffling through the maze of people and chairs, but a shake of the doc's head stopped them in their tracks.

"Just Gracen, please. Mister Dempsey is tired, and he's not always able to maintain consciousness." He met my gaze, twisting his mouth into a thin line. "You've got five minutes to visit with him, and you have to—"

"I'll take however fucking long I want," I growled back, baring my canines. "The only one kicking me out of that room's going to be Dempsey."

I knew the way, but I followed the doctor down the hall, forcing my feet to take each step. Dempsey's room was at the end of the hall—private but close enough to a nurse's station so they could get to him if he needed anything. I didn't want to think about how much this all was going to cost. I hated that it even flickered through my brain, but that's how he'd raised me. "Don't pay for someone to put you together when you've got duct tape, a needle, and some thread, boy," he'd said more times than I could count. "Nothing flows quicker in and out for a Stalker like money and blood, so don't be handing it out to some quack with a handful of aspirin and a stethoscope."

There wasn't enough duct tape for this. Never would be.

I don't know when the doctor slipped away, but it wasn't like I was expecting him to stab me in the back with a knife he kept hidden on him. He whispered away, leaving me behind with the smell of death and antiseptic clinging to my face.

Dempsey was awake, his eyes hooded and glazed. His once brawny body was now stripped of its flannel-and-denim armor. There were machines chirruping along in some sort of dissonant song, keeping track of every time his heart beat or his lungs drew in air. For all I knew, there was one marking each time he peed or shit. He hated being here lying in that bed, flat on his back and waiting for Death to come knocking on his door. I could see it in his eyes and the set of his stubbled jaw when he stared at me, drugged to the gills so he wouldn't feel any pain but not deep enough for him to sleep through his final breath.

I probably hated it as much as he did, but nothing was ever going to make me turn my back on him and walk out that door. The hospital was going to have to pry me out of the chair, and since I came in armed, I could take out anyone who tried.

"Tell me you've got a cheeseburger on you, boy," he coughed out at me, a bit of spittle sticking to his lower lip. "Bastards are telling me only liquids for now."

"I can get Ryder to get you something to eat. Fuck them," I replied, holding out my nearly full coffee. "Here. This is liquid. They can't bitch about that."

I had to shove a straw through the sippy hole and hold the cup steady until he could get his fingers around it, but once Dempsey took a hit from the so-not-hot coffee, he sighed happily. Clearing his throat, he struggled to bring up his other hand. He tangled his elbow in the plastic lines taped to his arm but eventually fought his way clear of them. I didn't move to help him. Hadn't planned on it because he still had one hand free and I was within slapping range. Instead I grabbed the plump upholstered armchair from the corner and dragged it closer to the bed.

The view from the hospital room was spectacular—a breathtaking sweep of San Diego's skyline with the ocean stretching out from its shores, the water glittering from the city lights, and the moons rising swollen and full, kissing the edges of the rolling waves. After dropping a quick thanks to Ryder and a plea to get Dempsey a Double-Double with extra-crispy fries, I closed my eyes and took a moment to finally breathe.

"Don't fall asleep there, asshole," Dempsey croaked, breaking through the singsong bell tones of his pet machines. "I've got a couple of things to tell you before I kick the bucket."

"Old man, I don't want…." I ground my teeth together, rubbing at the grit and dried tears tangling my lashes. My tongue tasted more of sulfur and chickenshit than whiskey and coffee, with a faint hint of resignation and fear ghosting around the edges. "Save your strength. Ryder's going to grab you that burger, and you're going to have to eat it, because I sure as hell ain't going to chew it up like a momma bird and spit it in your mouth."

His eyes glistened, either from the moonlight or maybe tears. I wasn't sure. Still, I was damned certain I was out of swinging distance just in case he was done with my sassing him and had rallied enough strength to clock me. Dempsey might have been dying, but he was still the same mean, irredeemable asshole who raised me.

"Just… shut up for a few minutes. I need to talk," he grumbled back, stopping for a moment to suck on the straw again and wheeze through another blast of oxygen. "There's shit you've got to know. And I've been holding this off for as long as I could because, well, it didn't seem like it mattered, but now… what with everything going on, you're going to have to deal with some crap, and you should know about it."

"You took a mortgage out on the property in Lakeside and I'm going to have to pay it off," I responded flatly. It would be just like Dempsey to saddle me with a debt I wouldn't be able to carve down for years, even if I took every damned contract the Post threw up on the boards. "Because if you did, I'm just going to sell that fucking place to the chicken farmers down the road. That damned place was paid off—"

20

"Seriously, I miss the fucking days when all you did was grunt and bite people," Dempsey shot back. He struggled to sit up more, but the pillows under his head kept him in place. "Help me here, then shut up. This is important."

I got the pillows arranged around his head and shoulders, earning myself a slap across my head as thanks. Flopping back down in the chair, I waited, refusing to rub at the smarting sting on my temple and the tip of my ear. I had to sit through him slurping up more of the whiskey and coffee before he put the cup down on the bed, gripping it tightly as he wiggled back into the plumped pillows.

Dempsey rolled his lips and held them there for a long second. Then he finally said, "There wasn't ever any poker game."

My first thought was his mind was going and maybe giving him whiskey on top of the painkillers had been a terrible mistake, but he shook his head when I reached for the call button gizmo dangling from a cord at the side of the bed.

"Hear me out," he continued. "I mean, that story I told you. Shit, the one I told everybody about winning you in that poker game? It wasn't real. None of it. There wasn't any guard who'd taken you out. I didn't palm any cards to cheat at the hand. It was all made up. Every single last bit of it.

"And before you start in on me, I'm going to tell you the truth and why I lied," Dempsey cut me off before I even said a word. "See, you were a contract. A *big* one. I didn't know when I took it that it was… you. It didn't come through the Post, and that was fine by me because the percentage they would have cut out of my take would have been huge, and, well, the Post would have asked too many questions. Questions no one at the other end of that contract wanted answered."

The slurping began again, and his hand trembled when he lifted the cup to his mouth. I reached for it before his fingers gave out and caught it before the dregs could spill onto the bed. I was trying to process what he was saying, but none of it made sense. Sliding the cup over onto the side table next to the bed, I asked, "I don't understand. What the hell are you talking about?"

"I was hired on a shadow-market contract to get a chimera out of Tanic's workroom. It lined up right for me. I was in Belfast and the Unsidhe Court wasn't much more than three days from where I'd been staying. Ireland's all Underhill now, but it was a good risk. The money was… I wouldn't have had to work another day in my life. All I had to do was get the chimera to Elfhaine and I'd be set forever." Dempsey shook his head, doing another lip roll. "The contact I had was a go-between, but he said the monster was small. About the size of a kid. What I didn't expect was for it to be an actual fucking kid."

His words eventually worked their way in, and I was left with a gaping hole in my being. Everything I'd known about how Dempsey found me, cheated at cards for me, was as solid as the clouds sweeping over the seas. The world was crashing around me, but I couldn't find anything to hold on to. There wasn't a single thing to grab at to steady myself—nothing but the old man dying in front of me.

"See, I brought a kennel with me, one of those folding ones to shove this creature into, and by the time I could get it hidden nearby, Tanic himself walked through the hallway and into that damned workroom. That's when I heard him call you Ciméara. Shit, that's when I finally figured out you were there, tucked into a cage beneath one of the worktables, matted hair, covered in fleas, and rebar sticking out of your back." Dempsey looked away, his attention fixed on the city outside the wall of windows behind me. "All I could do not to throw up, watching him do things to you, waiting for him to finish so I could hit my contract and get paid. It took him hours. I don't even know how long it was, but I can tell you I swallowed more vomit than air that night, and by the time he left, you weren't nothing more than a bag of flesh, whimpering when I got near."

"When did you decide you weren't going to fill the contract?" My murmur seemed to startle him, maybe because I knew him all too well, and he smiled at my question.

"Takes a long time to travel across oceans and continents now. And it wasn't like I could take you on a train. You were wild and injured, crazed out of your mind. By the time I got to Canada and bought that old truck of mine, you'd bitten me at least six times already. Almost lost a finger when I tried to feed you that first time. Stunk so much the boat captain thought I was smuggling ambergris into the States." He chuckled as if my childhood was a romp I'd skipped through and not the stuff nightmares were scared of. "Drove the first two days toward the border with you in the back of the truck. Had a cage big enough, and, well, a tarp covered most of it. Figured the rain would at least wash off some of the stink, but then it began to snow."

I didn't remember any of what Dempsey was telling me, but then again, my memory of that time was spotty. Tanic used me for his blood magics, stripping away pieces of my skin and flesh to power his spells and craft the ainmhi dubh he hunted with. I needed to throw up, to rid myself of the bitterness pooling in my stomach, but I couldn't find my legs, or at least that's what it felt like.

"Pulled up into one of those roadside motels with bungalows. I needed to get you inside because I knew jack shit about elfin, and for all I knew, you could freeze to death. Figured I'd take a stab at bathing you at least, because I swear I could smell you through the glass…." Dempsey swallowed, his Adam's apple working up and down his throat. "I got you in the bathroom and got my first good look at you. Then you kicked the shit out of me before I could even get you in the tub. You were ready to do anything you could to give as good as you got. You had balls. More than I gave you credit for. No way I was going to turn you over to those cat bastards in Elfhaine.

"You had too much fight, too much will to live. I sat and watched everything that fucking bastard did to you, and Pele knows how many of those times you'd already lived through, and you came out of the other side of it, bleeding and broken but ready to claw your way through whoever touched you," he said, his voice thickening with emotion. "He *made* you. Or at least that's what I understood. I was told you weren't anything more than a golem, like one of his blasted black dogs, and with about as much intelligence as a sea cucumber, but that's not what I saw. Not then. Not now. You were clever. Under all that hair, behind all of those fangs, you were going to survive, and if you got the chance, you'd kill whoever hurt you. *That's* when I knew."

"And not like the Post could ding you for not doing the contract," I said through the waves of numbness hitting me.

"Nope, not a fucking thing they could do." He nodded. "Thing was, I was kind of caught between a rock and a hard place. Couldn't go back to Ireland, not with the Wild Hunt Master looking for his pet chimera, so I headed back to SoCal, figuring I could keep you away from the elfin. Not like they left their sparkling white mountain. Scraped the blood and dirt off of you and taught you how to be a Stalker. Only thing I knew. Only thing I figured would keep you alive."

"Then Ryder came down to San Diego." It was the shift in my world Dempsey hadn't planned on. The arrival of the Sidhe into the city changed the dynamics, and the distant threat of Elfhaine was suddenly on his front porch. "That's why you kept hounding me to do runs. To keep out of the city."

"Figured that was best. I'd already gotten sick, and, well, we had a good thing going. Me out in Lakeside and you bringing in your bounty to clean up there. Things went to shit when the Post saddled you with that pointy-eared bastard. About lost my fucking mind when that asshole took you up to Elfhaine. I figured things would go to hell in a handbasket and we'd have to blow town but... then I got sick." He turned his head, meeting my gaze head-on. "Someone up there wanted you. Someone up there knew about you. Knew Tanic had you. Now, I don't know what they were going to do with you, but my guess is it wasn't going to be good. Ryder seems to be on your side, but I don't know if that's a lie and he's playing you or he's ignorant of what happened. Either way, I've done my best by you, and, well, it's time for you to step up and understand what's out there."

"Did Jonas know? Sparky?" I don't know why I wanted to hear him say they were as clueless as I was about all of the lies he'd told me, but I wasn't surprised to see him nod. The pain of it went deep, scoring down into my belly and guts. "Why? I mean, why did you even feel like you needed to make this shit up?"

"Because I needed to protect you. Or at least that's what it came down to later. In the beginning? And I'm going to be honest with you, boy, because, well, you deserve it. The fewer people who knew I'd taken you out from under Tanic's nose, the better," Dempsey said with a shrug. "There's an outstanding contract on you, and I more than a few times thought about turning you in because it's been a shit road trying to haul you up. Right now, lying in this bed, I'm glad I didn't, but it was close a few times. Especially when I was down hard."

"You'd have handed me over to...." I didn't finish it. I was a bounty Dempsey didn't finish, a contract remainder he'd been dragging around for decades, and the people I counted as my family knew about it. "So, what? I was like a piggy bank for everyone? Something someone could eventually smash open and cash in if things looked dire?"

"At the start of it, yes." He sugarcoated nothing, stabbing me deep with his bluntness. "At some point I began thinking of you as my apprentice, and then, well... my son. I did the best I could with you. And now that's all I can give you. Because mark my words, boy. You best be watching the horizon for ainmhi dubh, because the devil's coming for you and he's coming hard."

Three

LIGHTNING AND thunder rolled over the Presidio, the skies thick with dark, churning clouds glittering with sharp white electrical spikes. A heavy humidity settled over San Diego, pressing its weight down on everything until it was nearly impossible to breathe.

Or that could have just been me standing at the edge of a circle of mourners, waiting for either the gods to reach down and smite us for mourning a man some say was impossible to love or the damned priest to finish droning on about Dempsey as if he were some kind of angel come down from the Heavens to right every wrong set upon this Earth.

He clearly did not know the man, but apparently redemption and soul whitewashing were big in the Catholic Church.

People shuffled around me, their soft murmurs grating along my bled-raw heart. Ryder stood to my right, an odd glimmering blond comfort, and I was thankful for his silence. I couldn't absorb any more drops of false condolences and prayers for Dempsey. I was still reeling from the last few hours I'd spent with him, sorting through my emotions and the false truths I'd been told. It wasn't until the babble of harsh Latin stopped that I realized everyone was looking at me, expectant and impatient.

Oh yeah.

The brick.

I held it in my hands, too tightly probably, because I couldn't seem to open my fingers to place it in the outstretched palms of the Post's honor guard. The curved wall behind him was mostly hollows, but there were a few similar white bricks set into its winding arc through the Presidio's northern garden. It was a peaceful slice of greenery and flowers, with sweeping willow trees providing shade for water ponds and comfortable benches no one ever sat on.

The wall itself was a marble river winding down the gentle slope, its thick face punctuated with rectangular hollows meant to fit the square stone boxes the crematorium provided to the Post for the rare Stalker who died someplace their body could be recovered. It was the final resting place for very few, usually those without families or, worse, abandoned by all but other Stalkers. We were a curious, antisocial bunch, but no one could understand the destruction and gore we lived in like another one of our kind, so it was only fitting we would gather together in death as we did in life.

One such hollow was waiting for Dempsey, a brass plate already gleaming above the gaping wound in the marble river, a metallic black sleeve fixed into the space to lock down the brick once it was put into place. All I had to do was give the brick to the man standing in front of me.

It was just so hard.

I felt like I needed to tell the man in his dress blues what he needed to know before I could hand him my father. Important things like he hated for his eggs to be runny. Over hard was his preference, but he could never flip them, so he usually ate them scrambled. While he liked a good cigar, any type of stogie would do, and he'd pitch a fit if someone splurged on an expensive box but squirrel them away to smoke on a special occasion. His whiskey had to be neat, and his beer needed to be ice cold. The telenovela he liked came on at three in the afternoon, and he didn't need subtitles because he understood Spanish. The guard was going to have to make sure Dempsey cut his toenails or they would grow long and sharp enough to cut through his socks.

And most importantly, he always wanted to know what happened after every run. Mostly so he could criticize and tell someone how he would've done better.

"It's time, Chimera." Ryder's hand was at the small of my back, his long fingers brushing over my spine. "It's time to let go."

My knuckles hurt, and I choked on the anger boiling in my guts. I wanted to scream at him that I didn't get enough time. I never would. And the people who were around me who should've been a comfort were nothing more than a pack of liars who kept my own secrets from me, secrets I should've known in order to protect Dempsey. I was lost and drowning in a sea of emotions, my hands aching from gripping the brick too tightly and for too long.

"Goodbye, Dad," I whispered as I brought the brick up to my lips to give Dempsey the one and only kiss I'd ever given him. "May the road rise up to meet you and may you always hit what you aim for."

I placed the brick in the guard's hands, and somehow the absence of its weight made me feel heavier. Brushing my fingers down my left thigh reminded me I didn't have any of my guns, their cold hard comfort left locked up in my truck. The world was unsteady beneath my feet, and I couldn't find anything to anchor myself with. Not until I found Ryder's hand once again on my back, a spot of warmth in the blizzard raging inside of me.

"Let us bow our heads in prayer as we say goodbye to our brother, Michael Gray Dempsey, who, while he leaves this mortal coil, remains in the hearts of his family and friends." The priest's voice rang out, fighting to compete with the toll of the Presidio's often-silent bells. "Thus we consign Michael's soul to the hands of his God and the Heavens, where he shall rejoice in His eternal glory."

It was almost impossible to hear anything over the bells, but I heard Jonas well enough when he leaned over to whisper into my ear, "I'm sorry I wasn't here, son. Dempsey—"

"Don't you fucking call me son," I growled back. "Not after all these years. Not after all those lies."

JONAS CAUGHT up with me in the parking lot and grabbed my arm while I tried to get my key into the truck's door lock. I might have been stronger than most humans, but no elfin musculature was going to be a match for Jonas's pure brawn and mass. He flipped me around and had me up against the old Chevy's side before I could protest, my keys flying from my fingers and landing someplace near my feet. I didn't look for them. Not when Jonas stood nearly half a head again taller than me, his husky body blocking out most of the sun.

His dark eyes were filled with fury and confusion, and the small lizard part of my primal brain was happy to see it there because at least he knew how I felt. Especially now.

His deep complexion was made even darker silhouetted against the flashes of lightning still roiling through the clouds—an ebony statue looming over me with the same oppressive heat and humidity clinging to the air. There was no gentleness in his features, or what I could see of them. His breath was hot on my face, the words on his tongue thick with spit as he let them fly, splattering me with his anger.

"What the hell was that? You think you're the only one that misses the man?" Jonas stepped into my space, trying to crowd me against the truck. "You think—"

"Dempsey told me I was a contract." My words struck, cold jabs to Jonas's fury. "And all of you told him to complete it. To drop me off at Elfhaine. Even when he told you it didn't feel right to him. That his gut told him something was wrong. You. Sarah. Sparky, who found out afterward… who cut the damned iron out of my bones… and *still* said toss him to the fucking assholes on the white mountain. Because he's not one of us. Not *human*."

I'd held in everything, every damning secret Dempsey whispered to me in the rising tide of his death, the rattle in his throat clattering and clacking in time to the machines struggling to keep him alive for just one more moment. I'd listened, growing numb with each peeled-back layer of my past, exposing the callous man who'd taken me from Tanic's lair in Ireland to flee across the American wildlands with every intention of throwing me to the wolves once he reached California.

Except he hadn't, though every person in his life hammered at him to turn me over.

Including the man looming over me, a man I considered as much my uncle as Dempsey was my father.

There were people gathered behind Jonas, faces I knew in my soul, or at least I thought I had. If Dempsey's death left me unanchored, the truth of how he'd fought his closest friends to keep me left me adrift and hurting. Ryder was lost in the small crowd, and I didn't—couldn't—seek him out. Finding an elfin face among the all-too-human sea would have undone me, unraveled what little grip I had on my forged humanity.

"Deny it. Tell me how Sarah didn't leave him because he wouldn't give me up and then tried to block my Stalker license until he pressed the Post to issue me one. Or how about you coming in that night, with me mostly there and you offering me chocolate with one hand while whispering to Dempsey that you'd take me on north if he couldn't do it himself." My shoulders began to ache, the scars dug into my skin itching and crawling beneath my shirt. The storm had nothing on me. I couldn't stop talking, couldn't stop plunging my verbal knives into Jonas. My voice cracked, but I ground out, "Even Najiri. So go on, tell me how Dempsey lied to me. Tell me I'm wrong and he just decided to spend the last hour of his life fucking with my world."

There were tiny bits of gravel beneath my boots, rubbing against the lot's asphalt pour when I shifted my weight. The world past Jonas's shoulders blurred, an indistinct mass of people I was no longer sure about. I thought letting go of Dalia hurt, but it was nothing compared to the weighted blows of Dempsey's final words before he slipped off to the nothingness, his nicotine-stained gnarled fingers going lax in my grip.

Nothing sang in the trees lining the lot except for a sharp breeze picking through the leaves with a tight, discordant whistle. Someone behind Jonas said my name, but he jerked his hand out, keeping them back. I couldn't even tell who spoke, but no one drew closer, probably held back by the storm brewing in front of them, the one bubbling across the skies fading into the background.

I searched Jonas's face for even the slightest denial of Dempsey's damning words, but I saw nothing there but resignation. Even his ire slipped from his eyes, the fire slinking off under the regret ebbing in. His gleaming deep brown skin grew slack over his bones, and Jonas faded in on himself, his mouth diving down into a grimace.

"It wasn't... you've got to understand, Kai," Jonas began softly, his hands dropping to his sides. He still loomed. He was too large of a man to do otherwise, but he was smaller now, pushed back by what I'd said. "Things were different. For us, it was a long, hard time fighting... we lost so many of our own. And then Dempsey showed back up with—gods, I don't even know how to explain it to you. How damned hard it was to deal with having what was one of your worst nightmares dropped into your lap and be told by one of your best friends—"

"It was like he'd brought home a black dog and told us all, 'Look at the puppy I found. I'm going to keep it,'" Sarah cut in, edging in around Jonas. "That's what it felt like. We were still standing knee-deep in death and blood, and there he was, asking us to keep quiet about having an elfin in our circles. He chose to keep you over marrying me. For what it's worth, I spent years resenting you because you took away the life I thought I was going to have, only to find out you were a better man than he'd ever been. I still... it's not easy to change, Kai. It's hard to let that kind of hatreds go."

It was hard to imagine the older short-haired stocky woman who ran the Post as a loving fiancée to the man who raised me, especially since his taste ran to floozies and mean-spirited bitches, but Sarah didn't seem to be lying, and Jonas sure as hell didn't contradict her. She'd left off wearing her typical uniform of cargo shorts and a loud Hawaiian button-up shirt for the funeral. The shapeless black dress she'd pulled over her square body did her no favors, but her steely, honest gaze was firm, fixing me in place with a sternness I'd never truly challenged before.

I wasn't sure I wanted to now, but Jonas threw down first, and it didn't look like I was going to be able to walk away from the years we'd piled up beneath us. I just hadn't known about all of the shit being churned up, festering beneath my friendships, a bubbling poison growing more potent with every day of lies going by.

I'd spent the last couple of days in a blur, turning over everything Dempsey told me, picking through the bits I thought were the drugs talking and the half-truths he'd always been known to spin. There hadn't been time to examine everything. Or at least not until Jonas called me *son* and the dam I'd built to hold back my conflicted emotions surged forward, an unstoppable destructive force I would never be able to get back in.

"That's how you saw me? As one of Tanic's fucked-up creations?" Sarah wasn't wrong. Pele knew she probably spoke more of a truth than I wanted to admit, but it still stung. "Is that why you told him he might want to leave the iron in me? You remember that conversation, Jonas? Because he did. And he was at least honest about thinking you might have been right. Or at least back then. Because he wasn't sure what I would do to him if I weren't in constant pain, having that metal bleed into me, rusting through my bones and leaking into my blood. Did he tell you that part of it? About how I threw up most of what I could get down into me? Because I was that iron-sick, I couldn't even digest food. It's how Tanic kept me beaten down, leashed in tight and broken. I was a *kid*, Jonas. The man I thought you were would never have let anyone suffer through that, least of all a kid."

"You *weren't* a kid. You were a *monster*." Sarah shrugged off Jonas's hand when it settled on her shoulder. "As dangerous as one of those things whose skins we bring in for cash. And yes, Dempsey told you the truth. Because that's how we all saw you then. It didn't matter that you were as stupid as a brain-damaged turtle or that your back looked like a rusted chandelier with bits and pieces sticking out of it. You weren't… *aren't*… human."

"Kai!" Ryder shoved his way through the gathering at the edge of the lot. There was a bit of panic in his voice, a brilliant strident silver flash in the golden syrup of his Sidhe accent. He spoke my name with a familiarity I couldn't take at the moment—another complication in my already tangled life. "Sparky, let me go."

She'd grabbed hold of his arm, twisting it around to keep him back. They began arguing, but I couldn't hear much beyond the rumble of thunder breaking over the Presidio. The promise of rain thickened in the air, an earthy note to the sluggish wind ambling over the hillside. Ryder could take care of himself, and at the moment, I didn't want to add him into the mix. He was everything I'd run from, a clear symbol of the bloodlines and past I'd tried so hard to outrun, to hide from. I thought I'd been successful. After all, how many times had one of them cursed the elfin in front of me only to apologize and reassure me they didn't mean *me*? I wasn't one of *those* cat bastards, not one of the pointy-eared, fanged demons who'd poured over their fractured world, bringing with them horrific predators and unspeakable magics the humans had no way of fighting.

"I love you like you're one of my own, Kai," Jonas whispered, his face wet with tears. I couldn't look at him. Not and hold on to my anger. "And yes, it took me a long time to… understand you. Najiri and I prayed over my troubles, trying to find some place in me where I could stand to look at you. I expected one day to find myself across the table from an elfin, but to have one thrust on me so soon was difficult, and I'm going to be honest with you and say I thought you'd be better off with your own. We all did.

"You've got to see this as how it was. Back then," he continued, "you were a blacklisted job. One that would have set Dempsey up for a long time. He could have retired, set up a new life with Sarah and quit living on the edge. He threw that all away. For an elfin kid he pulled out of a shithole and didn't know one thing about. Everything about you was… you bit and fought, even when he was trying to help you. You kicked the shit out of him. Some part of that asshole respected that, and yeah, he said he had a bad feeling about things. Because why would a retrieval contract be blacklisted? We did them all the time. Just not for elfin. And not so far away. He knew he was bringing danger down on his head, and he was asking us to shoulder that with him. I'd just gotten married. Wanted to have kids. I knew what the elfin could do, and I didn't want that coming down on me because I'd gotten conned into protecting someone's stolen pet."

"That's what Dempsey was asking of us. Because I bet you he didn't tell you about the black dogs he had to kill along the way," Sarah said. "How many pelts did he rack up, Jonas? Thirty? Forty? The Wild Hunts were looking for you, and if we want to be all honest and shit, I'm going to say what I've thought all along—that you're the reason we have so many infestations.

"These packs are too far from their masters, gotten loose from their hold, and now they're breeding up as far as they can before their magics fall apart." Sarah's mouth tightened into a dark twisted line. "And then there's the Sidhe who contracted the job. Dempsey blew that exchange point, and they were looking for him, and it wasn't because they owed him money. Someone up there was… probably still is… hunting for you. I know. I helped him bury three Sidhe who'd come for us one night. That was the end for me. I wasn't going to be a part of hiding you. You weren't worth the risk."

"It's different now, Kai. Things are… we all are… different." Jonas stepped in close, edging in past Sarah, who snorted and eased away, throwing her hands up. "We know you. Know who you are. Just like I know after you sit and think about this, after giving yourself some time to deal with Dempsey's passing, you'll see the truth in all of this and know I've got your back. That I still hold you in my heart. We're your family, kid. Through thick and thin, we're tighter than blood in a lot of ways, and I count you as one of the best people I know. Just give it some time. Give yourself some time and I'm hoping you understand."

"Any time I've got right now is going to be put into getting drunk." Spotting my keys a few inches from Jonas's right foot, I bent down and grabbed them up. "Funny thing is, all my life with you guys… well, what I remember… everyone's always going on about how shitty of a person Dempsey is. Because as I see it, he was the only one of you with a heart and soul. He might have been a fucking bastard, but from pretty close to the beginning, he did right by me. And I'm sorry to say, it seems like he was the only one."

Four

DESPITE THE guns and gear I had in its trunk, my Mustang bucked and swerved in the unrelenting pound of rain. San Diego's streets weren't made for a '69 muscle car, especially not the tight turns near Balboa, and I was running out of gas, too drunk to change over the engine but not so trashed that I couldn't find my way to the one place no one from Dempsey's world could get ahold of me. The buzz I'd worked myself into back at my warehouse was gone, leaving behind the brain-numbing stillness I'd been filled with since the machines in Dempsey's hospital room chirped their final beat, dropping down to a keening, screeching flatline.

I shouldn't have been driving. Not in the rain. Not in a car the size of a rhino. And especially not with my cat, Newt, sitting in a plastic carrier strapped down to the passenger seat. But I had to leave the warehouse with its memories of Dempsey and the others living in every shadow pooled in the corners of my life. There was some kind of sick irony in Dempsey's steadfast reluctance to come down to the shoreline where I lived while Jonas spent hours there, helping me rebuild the Mustang and complaining he couldn't get an ounce of peace and quiet at his own house because his family was too loud and happy.

I didn't know what to do with myself. To make matters worse, I wasn't even sure who I was anymore. Everyone who had a hand in shaping my character had lied to me. I'd been so desperate for any scrap of affection, any hint of kindness after decades of torture and pain, that I'd taken their lack of physical violence as being welcomed into their hearts.

"Do you know what it's like, Newt?" I asked my cat, who was screaming his displeasure at being trapped in a beige plastic kennel. "It's like I am the pig they brought into the house to raise among the dogs so it grows up thinking it's a pet, and then one day they slaughter it for bacon."

I'd like to think he stopped meowing long enough to hear me, but I knew he was just taking a breath for another course. Still I took the brief silence as a thoughtful reflection on my words, but I knew better. Another deep inhale and his furry little chest was refueled, a brace of breath to power the siren pouring out of his tiny little mouth.

After the first ten messages from Jonas and Sparky, I turned off my link without answering their calls as I'd gotten Newt all packed up. When Cari's number flashed across the wristband screen, I waited until her message was done recording before listening to it, not trusting myself not to break apart if I answered. Instead of her smoky voice scolding me for letting the call go to voicemail, I heard Jonas's deep rumble telling me he was coming down to talk to me. Pissed off Cari let him use her link, I packed up the cat and left, hoping to go to the one place I knew I could find sanctuary.

And I hated like hell that I had to go there.

The darkness surrounding Balboa was a milky veil, the towering forest poured over the hilly mesa throwing up a coy barrier between the Southern Rise Court and the sprawling human city surrounding it. Before the Merge, the area had been a verdant park dotted with a constellation of museums set with a sparkling star of a conservation zoo. Now all that remained of San Diego's former crown jewel were the sweeping historic Exposition buildings built for several long-ago expositions and a scatter of wandering pandas cared for by a wild-eyed hermit named Crazy Gertrude.

The Court's towers were crystalline white stone spears nestled into the older human structures, taking on some of the Spanish and Mission Revival forms as if struggling to blend into the city's bones while maintaining their Sidhe essence. They were visible through the thicket as I crossed over the bridge to the cobblestone courtyards laid down by long-dead human craftsmen. The Exposition structures were ivory weathered, stone holding a bit of the sun in its façade, and even in the cloud-draped moonlight, it was easy to see where the Sidhe buildings were beginning to shift to match—a slowly encroaching tide of color washing over the too-bright walls pulled up from the land beneath the Court.

Southern Rise was very different from Elfhaine. The city against the white mountains to the north of San Diego was as ethereally foreign to me as the cloud dragons I'd seen the bones of. The towers in Balboa Forest were building themselves off of the remains of human structures, blending their newly risen edifices into what was already there, embellished by elfin forms and broad windows to soak in every bit of sunlight the city had to offer. The Court was far enough away to be safe from the sheer ravines to the east, a steep drop-off where a raging river cut the upper part of the city, yet the air was moist from the nearby waters, a filmy mist often rising up into the skyscraper-tall trees to pearl the elfin commune in glistening dew.

I didn't understand how the elfin built their cities. Or rather how the Court built *itself*. Ryder tried to explain to me. So did the stone crafters who spoke to the construction to guide it along its way. There were Sidhe stone-magics involved, but more importantly—or so the Sidhe told me—the Court decided for itself who spoke for it and its people and guided evolving and shifting structures to accommodate its inhabitants. Ryder, Clan Sebac, Third in the House of Devon and bane of my existence was the current High Lord of the Southern Rise Court, and I was tangled up with him in ways I also didn't understand.

The Court did. Or at least that's what it seemed like, because the bristling brace of new towers to the north of the main structure began to thrust up from the ground after we'd shared a single kiss.

Scared the hell out of me to think of what would happen if we ever went further than a kiss, and I sure as hell wasn't in any state of mind to contemplate *that*. Not when I was coming in hot and torn open as if I were still carrying weeping iron in my bones.

At some point the living stone decided I needed a place for myself, or at least that's what everyone told me, because not long after Ryder punched his way into my life, the Southern Rise Court began to shape a spire for me to live in, connecting it to Ryder's suite in the main structure. I tried to deny use at first, but I was drawn to its wide-open balconies and the curling metal dragon shapes the Court somehow pulled out of the earth to accent the broad spaces it made for me.

After parking the Mustang near the base of my tower, I wrestled with Newt's kennel and the supplies I'd brought with me. Whiskey still numbed my face and kept my legs a little shaky, but it was only four flights up from the side entrance, which kept me from having to speak to anyone in the main building. Some elfin rarely slept—usually the older ones—and I wasn't up to talking. I'd carried bigger kits while on runs, but never halfway drunk and dragging a screaming cat in a plastic box with me, but eventually I made it to the top. The door to my space opened easily, the knob practically turning when I reached for it.

The one thing the Court didn't provide was furniture or a litter box, so I was surprised to discover a bed the size of an ocean at the far end of the open space I'd claimed as my own, as well as a sectional couch that looked as soft as the bed and was about as large.

"Ryder," I muttered to my cat. "Hold on, bastard. Let me make sure all of the doors are closed. Last thing I want is for you to go roaming through the Court. I don't want to have to go pull your teeth out of someone's leg just because they've pissed you off."

Letting the small mottled gray ball of fury I'd found chewing on one of my kills out of his kennel earned me that bite on the leg I was trying to save others from, and after the damned cat got his bit of blood from my flesh, he sauntered over to the cat dish I'd put down for him and noisily chewed through the bits of tuna I'd dumped into his wet-food bowl. The litter box was his next stop, but by that time I was done with dealing with his needs and the last thing I wanted to do was remain upright.

I also needed to take care of the sobriety I seemed to be developing while making sure Newt was comfortable.

The cat had food and a place to shit, pretty much all he needed to keep himself happy, so I shucked off my boots, pulled off my shirt, and climbed into the middle of the humongous bed. The sheets were cool and smooth on my skin, and when I lay back against the pillows, my shoulders and back sank into their soft cradle, propping me up so I could stare out the open doors and on to the city beyond the Court's boundaries. Reaching for the bottle of whiskey I'd tossed onto the bed before I took care of the cat, I watched the lightning tear across the sky, and I tore off the black wrapper, then twisted off the cap and inhaled the sweet-perfumed sting wafting up from the open bottle.

"I'm going to miss you, old man," I murmured, saluting the roiling skies. "Thanks for saving my life and fucking it up at the same time."

There was half a bottle of Jack in me when I heard the suite door open and a golden light from the outer passage sliced through the dim shadows I'd pulled over me after dousing most of the sconces in the loft-like space. I didn't need to hear the silhouette framed in the door speak to know who it was. My body responded eagerly to Ryder's presence, invigorated by some uncontrollable genetically connected threads stitching us together, and for once I didn't fight the pull. Lying in a wealth of pillows on a bed soft enough to sculpt itself around my weight, I stared at him, drops of charcoal-rich whiskey sitting on my tongue as the city's lights sparkled across the horizon beyond the balcony and glass doors I'd left wide open to pull the rain-scented air into the nearly empty space.

He carried in with him a hint of popped-rice green tea and vanilla, his Sidhe skin whispering its scent through the metallic flavor the city storm left with its electrical splatters across the night sky. There had to be an open window somewhere at his back, sweeping a brisk gust through the open door. Silence hung between us, broken only by the clatter of thunder at the edge of the city. The clouds were churning toward us, their gray underbellies tinted tangerine and puce from the upper streets' lights. I knew I would eventually have to close the balcony doors to keep the rain out, but at that moment, I couldn't find my damned tongue, much less my legs.

"Hello, Newt," Ryder said, bending down to scoop my cat to cradle Newt's wiggling fuzzy body against his chest. "Let's go see how your daddy is doing."

Closing the door behind him, Ryder cut off the too-bright light from the outside hall, letting the shadows back in to creep across the floor. His feet were bare, and they made no sound crossing over the hardwood floors to the bed, where I lay sprawled, my half-empty fifth of whiskey propped up against my side, my fingers lightly gripping its ribbed neck as if it were a lover I wasn't sure whether I wanted to hug or strangle.

"I'm not Newt's father," I pronounced as clearly as I could, but my tongue was thick against the roof of my mouth and I couldn't seem to work it around my teeth. "We're more... roommates. Sort of."

"You care more about that cat than you do your car," he pointed out, pinning the truth down with his words. "You call the Mustang baby and coo at it. I think it's safe to say calling you Newt's ad hoc father is well within bounds."

I snorted, overcome by the irony of a mangy, clipped-eared cat being my kid. Newt and I shared the same notches in our ears—battle wounds neither one of us could remember Newt getting or at least not a story he ever told me. Ryder gently placed the diminutive cat on the mattress, and Newt bounded over to my right foot to attack my big toe with a playful fierceness he usually reserved for roaches or knitted mice.

Dressed in a loose pair of cotton pants and a T-shirt that looked suspiciously like one I'd lost on the last run we'd done together, he stood at the edge of the bed, looking down at me with a look of passive judgment I'd seen way too many times before. It was unnerving, mostly because I was too sober to deal with the churn of emotions raging through me and I didn't have enough energy to fight my fingers' itch to grab his shirt to pull him down onto the bed.

Because sex *never* complicated anything. I took a hit of whiskey and let the burn scrape my throat raw, wishing it would take with it the ashes of my friendships that were somehow lodged in a hard knot in my chest.

"I'm throwing a wake, so if you're going to be in here, you've got to help me drink this," I said, waving the bottle about slightly. "Because Newt sure as hell isn't going to do it."

"That stuff can peel the enamel off your teeth," Ryder said, angling his head slightly and studying me. "But sure, I'll help you drink it. It's the least I can do for a friend."

"That's what we are? Friends?" I waited until he was settled against me, his shoulder pressed against mine, before handing over the bottle. "It's hard to tell sometimes."

Unlike most people I knew, Ryder didn't wipe the mouth of the bottle with his shirt before taking a swig.

"*Morrigan!*" Ryder coughed, choking down the snort he'd gotten past his lips. "You sure that's whiskey and not what you put in that car of yours? Dear Gods in the Skies. I can't feel my tongue."

"Wimp," I muttered, putting my hand around the bottle neck to tug it away. "It's Jack. That's smooth. Next time I'll bring in some of that moonshine Jason and I cooked up at his place last year and see if you've got any flesh left on your tongue."

"Hold on, let me get some more in me. I might not be able to catch up with you, but at least let me try to get the taste out of my throat." He took another tentative sip, barely suppressing the shudder the whiskey pushed through his bones. "Gods, that's so foul."

"Keep drinking. When it starts tasting good, stop." I chuckled, recalling the first time Dempsey gave me that advice about whiskey. "That's when you know you're drunk."

"Seems… counterproductive? Is that the right word?" Still, Ryder took another healthy gulp, then passed the bottle over, making a face when he swallowed. "It feels like my bones are on fire."

"Wait 'til you can't feel your tongue." Savoring the burn on the roof of my mouth, I let the Jack sit to sear my cheeks. "That's the best part sometimes."

My head was buzzing with ideas I couldn't shake, and from what I could see, no amount of whiskey would quiet them. Cradled in the soft bed and leaning on Ryder's arm, I stared out at the cluster of low towers to the left of my spire, their windows bright with glittering lights. The forest surrounding the Court swayed around the serpentine flow of connected buildings, their curved shapes speckled with graceful turrets dotted with a complex weave of curling shadows and balconies.

Whiskey kept away any guilt I might have felt about not visiting our twin nieces, but they were barely out of lump stage, so I couldn't imagine Rhi and Kaia missing me at all, but Ryder always seemed to assure me they were delighted to see me. Mostly they giggled, played, and slept, their identical enormous emerald-ocean-and-slate eyes following every movement in the room. I liked them well enough, but they'd be a hell of a lot more interesting once they could hold a weapon for longer than a minute.

The Jack was also keeping me numb enough not to wonder what the kiss Ryder and I shared did to the Court, other than seemingly give it a hard-on to stretch itself out, pull stone and wood from the ground, and let itself be shaped by the damned magic-wielding Sidhe who crooned lovingly at every faucet and doorknob they could shape out of the wall.

"Is it me or is the damned place getting larger every time I blink?" The whiskey couldn't take away the shock resonating in my soul from the Court's avarice, its aggressive growth shoving the forest farther back toward the ravine. "And who the hell do you have living over there? I don't think the rooms were even painted the last time I was here."

"We've got a few families coming down from the Courts in San Francisco and Seattle," Ryder murmured, relieving me of the bottle. He held it against his chest, warming its amber depths. "The towers were done, so it made sense to put them there. There aren't that many of us, but you'd be surprised to find out how much room a Sidhe needs to live. Some of the Court have moved into the spaces as well, mingling in. You should go meet them all sometime."

"Why?" The stars were dimming again as the storm rolled in closer. A hot splash of metal hung heavy with water filled the space, and Newt mewled his displeasure at the thunder rolling over Balboa. "They don't know me from... Adam. Which would make more sense if you were human."

"You're a part of the Court, and yes, they *do* know you. Alexa is more than happy to extol your virtues to anyone coming through our gates."

Ryder reached out to Newt, who sniffed at the Sidhe Lord's extended fingers. "Do *not* bite me, gargoyle. I've got fish scraps in the kitchen with your name on them."

"He'd rather eat the fingers." Snorting, I nestled down into the pillows again, wishing the whiskey would numb every inch of me. There were parts of my soul I couldn't reach with its amber kiss, aching raw spots where I'd sliced apart my conflicted feelings for Jonas and Sparky. Maybe the booze made my tongue looser or maybe I just didn't give a shit anymore, but the words were pouring out of my mouth before I could stop them, spilling into Ryder's lap. "You know the shittiest thing about this whole thing? All this time, everyone's been telling me how much of an asshole Dempsey is— *was*—but he was the one who protected me."

"Why did he tell you these things about Jonas and the others?" Ryder spoke carefully, treading softly across the eggshells I'd laid down between us. "Wouldn't it have been better for you not to know how things were back then? I mean, they love you. I've never had any doubt about how Jonas feels about you, so why would Dempsey bring that all up now?"

It was a good question. I asked that as well. Grimacing when Newt's claws dug into my thigh, I responded, "Because he wanted me to know about how things were. So I knew what happened. How people thought. About me. About… him. I get that. I understand back then they never really saw an elfin up close unless of course they were killing it, and to everyone, I was probably the biggest monster they were ever going to face. It didn't matter that I was half insane from iron and about as feral as a mad lemming, because all they saw were the pointed ears and glowing eyes.

"He never spoke against any of them. He encouraged each of them to get to know me, to help make me *human*. Even with Sarah, who walked away from him. I was the reason they never got married. She didn't want to raise a cat bastard her husband retrieved on a run." I closed my eyes, willing the whiskey to stay down in my stomach. "I used to think people distanced themselves from Dempsey because he was an asshole, but the truth was, they were just avoiding *me*. He worked to bring Jonas and Sparky around, making them important to me, to my life, but even though he wanted me to understand how people changed—that everyone deserves a second chance—I can't get past the idea that none of them were willing to help save me."

Ryder remained silent, but he took the bottle from me and set it on the floor. His hands crept into mine, squeezing tight enough for me to feel his heart, but then I didn't need to touch him to be aware of his presence. There was a part of him that lived inside of me even if I wasn't willing to admit it, and in the flashing lights and angry shadows of the brewing storm, I couldn't help but feel him anchoring me.

"You know how much I love chocolate. My first real memory of Jonas was him giving me a piece of it. Apparently he'd come out to meet Dempsey to take me to Elfhaine. They'd made arrangements to meet up someplace near Ithaca so Jonas could help transport me. That's when Dempsey told him the deal was off. That he was going to take me in and give me a life, because he knew in his gut that if ever I made it to Anaheim, I would never see the light of day again." I took a breath, amazed at how hard it was to get my lungs to breathe. Pain pressed into my chest, sharp phantom daggers of whispered words piercing through my soul. "He'd given me chocolate to make me complacent, to make it easier to lead me to my slaughter in Elfhaine without a fight. So tell me, what's the difference between Jonas and Tanic? Tell me, what's the difference between the executioner with a carrot and the psychopathic Wild Hunt Master with a stick?"

"That's not who he is now," Ryder pointed out. "He thinks of you as his son as much as Dempsey did."

"That's because he doesn't see me as an elfin anymore," I said, suddenly missing the rest of the bottle. "You should hear them sometimes, talking about the wars and what they went through with the cat bastards they fought. And then there's always a little hiccup of space before they assure me they're not talking about *me*. That they don't think of me that way. Listening to Dempsey talk to me about how I was going to need to change how I felt about the Sidhe, how I needed to embrace being an elfin, was just lost in a bunch of buzzing noise, because all I could hear was how every single one of them wanted to turn me over, to make me go away so Dempsey could go on with his life. Even if mine ended."

"You don't know that. Maybe the contract to extract you was because your mother's family found out you existed and they wanted to bring you home." He moved closer, until the length of his body was up against mine, pressing against me in delicious and confusing ways. "Dempsey might have read it wrong. You don't—"

"The contract was for dead or alive." I felt his startled gasp more than I heard it. "He would've gotten double the contract if I were alive, but they were more than happy with dead. Greed kept my head on my neck long enough for Dempsey to get me out, and then after that, whatever good he had inside of him gathered up into a ball of stubborn and refused to give me up. He told me everything they gave him for the contract was left with his brother Kenny in New Vegas. The guy hates my guts, but I've got a handful of Dempsey's ashes to give him and his share of Dempsey's estate, providing he coughs up what's in that deposit box.

"Dempsey told me it was up to me about whether or not I opened it. He thought I shouldn't go chasing after ghosts, but it looks like shit is coming for me, or at least has been for a while. I just didn't know it. So not only do I have Tanic to worry about, but somebody living under Sebac's web wanted me dead." I was grateful for Ryder's hand, unwilling to let him go even when the cold wind blew through the open doors, leaving my skin icy. "He didn't tell me before because he didn't think I could hold my own. I was too young and inexperienced and pretty much hidden from view. Not now. Now everyone up north knows I exist, and Tanic is circling. Funny thing is he really wasn't sure if I would survive with just Jonas and the others at my side, but now there's you and the Court. He somehow thought you'd stand with me, although I don't know how much good that would do against anything. It's not your fight. And it sure as hell's not theirs."

"It *is* my fight. Wherever you go, I will be there," Ryder whispered. He leaned over, pressing his forehead against my temple. "I am your friend. At the very least, I am that, even as I want more. And having said those words, I will tell you I will go with you to give your respects to Dempsey's brother, and I should probably leave you to get some sleep."

"Yeah. Sleep would be good. I don't want to think about any of this right now. It's too much." I refused to let go of his hand. Despite not having another mouthful of liquor, I was getting drunker by the moment, and the thought of being alone hurt more than any betrayal I felt. I licked my lips, then said, "Stay. Please."

His eyes were as verdant as the forests surrounding the Court, his handsome face nearly expressionless, but a hint of a smile played at his lips. "As much as I would love to take what you have to offer, I don't think either one of us is in any condition or the right frame of mind. Besides, if I take advantage of you when you're drunk, you'd stab me when you woke up sober."

"I wasn't thinking about sex. Even though, you know, nothing beats a good sweaty tumble when you're pissed off. I just want…." I felt raw and scraped apart, peeling myself open for Ryder to plunge his hand into my guts to play with what he found there. "I just don't want to sleep alone. I'm just so… fucking tired of being alone, Ryder."

I couldn't read him. Not then. He was so still I wasn't even sure he was breathing.

"I can definitely spend the night holding you," he finally said, then glanced at the open doors. "Right after I close those. Or we'll freeze no matter how many blankets I pile on top of us."

He eased out of the bed, leaving Newt and me behind. Closing the doors softly, he stood in front of the glass, a dark shape outlined by the dimming city lights. I still had his warmth on my skin, more potent than the whiskey I'd gulped down to ease my hurt. He turned to pad back, then stopped at the end of the bed when I cleared my throat.

"I've never slept with someone holding me before," I whispered up at him. "It's not something I've ever done."

"Well then, thank you for letting me be your first, my Chimera," Ryder said in a teasing lilt, pulling the duvet up from the bottom of the bed. He slid into bed next to me, wrapped his arms around my waist, and held me against him. "I am honored."

"And just so you know," I muttered, shifting until I was comfortable, "you're probably a hell of a lot more than a friend, but right now, I can't deal with any of that. Not until I get my own head on straight, and sure as hell not until I find out who hired Dempsey to bring me in like a black-dog pelt. Not like I can go live my life when there's people out there who are damned determined to bring it to an end."

Five

THE STORM left a sodden forest in its wake, broad leaves torn from the canopy and scattered about the ground. The Court's governing population apparently began bickering at dawn that day about whether to clear the debris, with a great many arguing the natural lay of the leaves was the will of the forest. I'd walked in to find out where I could get something to eat and maybe a knife to cut my aching head off from my neck. The barrage of liquid elfin words made me wince, and I wasn't sure if it was a residual loathing left over from my father weaving spells or the whiskey, but either way, the stupidity of the people gathered together to talk about wet fallen leaves overwhelmed my vow not to get involved.

"At least clean up the damned walks and courtyards before one of you slips and breaks your dainty ass on the bricks. And Pele help you if one of the kids cracks their heads open, because if that happens to any of them, I'm going to come back and take the skin off of everyone who argued to leave that shit on the ground," I snarled, trying to quell the pounding in my head. "Now, is there any coffee in this place or am I going to have to go hunting for some in the city?"

Ryder barely hid his smirk as he pointed toward an open door, saying he'd meet me in the kitchen in a few minutes, then politely asking me not to eat anyone along the way.

After baring my fangs at him, I slunk off to the kitchens, keenly aware of the tense silence I left behind me.

This wasn't my Court. These weren't my people. I had no right to tell them what to do, and I'd stepped on every single one of Ryder's toes, but he said nothing when he joined me in the main hall's kitchen, making me a grilled cheese sandwich for breakfast as I brewed us a strong pot of coffee. We ate in silence. Then I fled to the courtyard where I'd left the Mustang to spend a good half an hour picking wet leaves off its body before I could begin tackling its wonky carb.

I was cranky and out of sorts, a cat with a kinked tail with no way to straighten it out other than to wait for the rocking chair to swing down on it again. Everything and everyone was rubbing me wrong, and after the twentieth or so leaf I'd pulled off the Mustang's once-gleaming red body, I snarled at the buildings behind me, baring my canines at them much like I'd done the council gathered around Ryder to talk about cleaning the damned sidewalks.

"You want to build me something?" I hissed at the tower dotted with metal and wood the Court grew for me. "Make me a damned garage so I don't have to get shit off my car every time I wander into Wonderland."

I had turned back to finish the job when I heard scraping and rumbling behind me. Refusing to look, I left the Court to whatever shenanigans it was going to get up to and sent a quick prayer to Pele that whatever it was going to drag up from the ground wouldn't block anyone's windows. The elfin had a thing about sunlight, and I already felt like an asshole for the tower it built for me absorbing all of the windows and balconies of Ryder's suite after the Court got a wild hair up its butt and decided I needed someplace to live among its menagerie.

Mock phoenix swarmed into a curving pink-and-orange murmuration around the towers, weaving between the pale-oyster turrets, leaving a swirl of sparkles in their wake before disappearing into the heavy forest canopy beyond the Court. Somewhere nearby something wild screamed in the damp shadowy depths beyond the courtyard and its long stretches of buildings. I could see the top of the organ pavilion down the way, visible through the red maple trees run wild over the grown-over paved roads cars once used to get from one part of the park to the next. The Merge stole bits and pieces of Balboa, replacing entire sections with Underhill forest while leaving other parts behind, including most of the wild animals living in the zoo below the 8 Corridor. Some had been recaptured while others found new living arrangements, like the lion colonies in Kearny Mesa. I wasn't all that concerned about anything other than the occasional panda and perhaps a black dog, but I'd not seen an ainmhi dubh since I'd tossed my half brother over the ravine and into the river at the west end of the Sidhe's territory.

But I was always worried about the ainmhi dubh. Especially since Dempsey assured me I'd pretty much knocked on the Unsidhe's front door and announced I was still alive. They would be coming for me, if only to make me an example of what happens to a piece of magicked flesh that dared walk away from its master. Tanic cuid Anbhás, Lord Master of the Wild Hunt for the Unsidhe, was definitely not going to just let me go. I didn't need Dempsey or anyone else to tell me that. I knew that in my guts. Mostly because his hands had played in my bowels nearly every day since he'd made me, and I remembered the pain of his dragging iron spikes through my flesh in every breath since Dempsey pulled me free.

I had the Mustang's carburetor torn apart and spread out over a tarp when I heard footsteps on the cobblestones behind me. The stride was hesitant, confident when far away but a stammering clop closer in. I ignored whoever it was, intent on getting the guts of the carb cleaned out for the run I still wasn't sure I would take.

Yesterday I'd woken up sprawled out on a strange bed, alone except for my cat, Newt, kneading at my bare shoulder and another pounding hangover dug into the inside of my skull. This morning my sheets were perfumed again with a hint of green tea with a whisper of cinnamon chasing after it, woven into the fine cotton threads as deftly as the scrolling Sidhe leaves embroidered along the linen's edges. Showering didn't get Ryder's scent off my skin, and I stumbled downstairs for some food later that day, whispers and soft smiles cresting in my wake.

I'd have punched the asshole if he hadn't been with our nieces when I found him, so instead, I spent the afternoon wincing when one of the mini-banshees let loose her ear-piercing sonic blast and trying to match their laughter when they giggled. It was alarming how tired I got chasing after a pair of barely sentient twin Sidhe babies, but I'd returned to the tower the Court made me, fed the cat, then face-planted on the bed, not bothering to take off my clothes.

I'd oddly gotten used to waking up in the middle of the night with Ryder wrapped around me and Newt someplace on my legs. In the half week since Dempsey's funeral, I'd fallen into a numbness, coming up for air only for a Sidhe Lord and the occasional feline demand for ear scritches and belly rubs.

Today was the first day I felt halfway normal and mostly… human, still shuddering a bit when the Sidhe chatter in the halls played havoc with my nerves, and my stomach knotting in anticipation for the glut of whiskey I longed to pour down my throat.

Drinking was out. It was a crutch too many Stalkers used to wipe away the blood, guts, and gore splattered over their memories. I'd pulled Dempsey out of more than a few bars, dragging his argumentative dead weight behind me before both of us got our faces punched in. During every single one of those times, I thought he was drinking to somehow dull the loss of his mobility and the end of his Stalker career. Now I wondered if it wasn't because of me. I was the reason he'd become an outsider in the only community that embraced his irascible, hardheaded personality. Three—no, *four*—days wasn't enough time for me to get over Dempsey's death, and I still hadn't wrestled with the demons left in my brain from his final words to me.

I couldn't pull a scent off of the person standing behind me, but the wind was toward my face and some of the elfin didn't always register with me, the light hint of fragrance from their skin too delicate for me to catch. The midmorning sun was a splash of warm amid the cool shade of the surrounding forest, and while the Court's main cobblestoned square often soaked in the heat, the retreating storm left it stripped of any warmth, dampening the bricks and the chill so deep they practically shivered in their mortar. If I'd been smart, I would've brought something to sit on besides the tarp, but the cold creeping through my muscles kept me alert and the tingles of pain along my nerves reminded me I was alive.

"Dempsey would've scolded you for sitting on the cold stone." Cari's voice wavered as she spoke. "He used to tell me doing that would give me hemorrhoids."

The carb's choke valve had been sticking, and I wanted to see if it could be cleaned or if I was going to be stuck with rebuilding the damned thing before I headed back out. Turning the parts over in my hand, I tilted them up one by one, ignoring Cari's approach.

Her legs appeared at my left side, and I caught a glimpse of her fingers reaching for my shoulder. "Kai—"

"What do you want?" I didn't trust myself to glance up at her. There was still anger in my blood at *everything*, including her giving Jonas her link to call me. She was my little sister, or at least the closest thing I had to a sibling, and something small and dark in me ached every time I thought of hearing Jonas's voice when I'd expected to hear hers.

"At least you give me credit for hunting you down and not asking how I found you." She crouched, her dark hair curving around her strong jaw.

I knew every inch of Cari's face, having watched her grow from a swaddled lump of crying meat to the woman she was now, and somehow I'd missed the faint lines beginning to form at the edges of her eyes. I'd blinked and the years were now in her face and hands, a stretched dryness along her skin, chafed red from the cold wind cutting into the courtyard's open expanse. Dressed in one of my old jackets I'd outgrown years ago, she'd shoved up the sleeves until they rode her upper arms, the worn leather scrunched up over her ropey muscles. She was still vibrant and strong, but there was an earthiness to her face and demeanor, one I'd missed her gaining over the years.

"You're a witch, remember?" I curled my lip at her. "Pretty sure you could have sliced open a pigeon and it would have led the way. Lots of damned pigeons around here. They like to crap on cars as much as the trees do."

"Like I'd waste the meat looking for you," she sniped back. "Still got that folding chair in the Pony's trunk? Because if I'm going to talk to you, it's not going to be crouched over like some auntie picking through peas."

I couldn't hold on to the kernel burning hot in my belly. No matter how much I tried. I'd learned how to be human with Cari, taking each mental footstep with her as she grew. I was still pissed. That wasn't going to go away, but her coming to poke at me was… so normal, and at the moment, I needed a bit of normal after quieting the raging shitstorm through my head.

There were more birds taking flight above the canopy, but they were too far away for me to identify. Not enough to alarm, but certainly something to take note of. I listened with half an ear as Cari wrestled the metal chair from the Mustang's trunk, gauging the size of movement through the forest beyond the Court. It didn't seem large enough to startle more than a few flocks, and I couldn't hear the telltale thunder of a heavy animal breaking through the underbrush. The woods around the Court were largely unexplored, left to grow feral and heavy with roaming wild animals.

"Still think something's going to come up and snatch someone from the forest?" Cari asked, shaking the chair out until the seat locked down.

"Lions' territories go out to more than a hundred miles sometimes. It's not that far from here to Kearny Mesa, even with the river cutting across the valley. And as far as I know, the damned pandas have gotten a taste for flesh after years of chewing down bamboo. No sense being stupid and losing someone when having a lick of common sense will keep everyone alive," I retorted, going back to scrubbing at the crevices of the Mustang's carb. She got settled, hunched over in the leather jacket, and gave me owl eyes from under its upturned collar. I snorted, too used to her wheedling ways. "Don't give me any shit, *mija*. Speak your piece—"

"You never sounded more like Dempsey than right now." Her words went in smooth, sharpened with the keen edge of someone who knew every single one of my weaknesses. I felt the cut down deep, but I had nothing more to give her. I'd bled out days ago, left white and lifeless in front of the Presidio's Death Wall. "Listen, I'm sorry about giving Jonas my link, but he's going crazy thinking you hate him, and I'm pissed as hell at Dempsey for dragging that stuff out when it didn't need to be. These are *your* people, Kai. *I'm* your people. Yeah, they were assholes for one little moment in your life, but they changed. If you can't see that, then you're more of an ass than they ever were. What the hell are you thinking? And why the hell are you hiding here? Don't tell me it's because of the food, because I've eaten with Alexa. They've got bug burgers. I spent five hours one time trying to pick some damned leg prickles out from between my teeth."

"It's sure as hell not for the bug burgers," I confessed, making a face. I'd eaten a lot of things over the years. There were times when hand-sized larva plucked from the insides of fallen trees fed me and Dempsey for a month while tracking down a large pack of black dogs in Colorado, but if I had to choose, I preferred my meat to have four or two legs. "I'm not pissed at you. Well, a little bit. I get why you did it, handing the link over, but sometimes, Cari, I need some space to figure stuff out. I just buried Dempsey, dammit, and there's all the crap he dumped on me that I've got to deal with. You all have to listen to me when I need time. You can't come picking at me until I'm ready to blink."

"But time to you isn't going to be the same as it is for us," she pressed, shoving her hands into the jacket's pockets, shivering when the wind picked up. "Dempsey shouldn't have—"

"Dempsey was a hell of a lot smarter than a lot of people gave him credit for, and behind that Irish-hick asshole mask was someone who manipulated the hell out of everyone around him, including me," I dropped in, putting the carb down. My knees were a bit stiff from the cold tarp, but they worked well enough to get me up on my feet and over to the Mustang. I tossed Cari a blanket from the back, then sat down in the passenger seat, stretching my legs out in front of me to ease the ache running through them. "I got drunk—shitfaced drunk—and in the middle of all of the haze, I realized Dempsey was trying to kick me back to here. To the Sidhe. Or at least to the Court. He wanted to shake my trees because it was his way to dealing with shit after he was gone."

"What? By yanking away the only family you've got?" She made a small mound of leather and plaid, the swaths of cloth burying any hint of the chair she sat on. "Jonas raised you. So did Sparky. They're always going to be here for you."

"Until they're not. Because they're going to be gone, and I'm going to need allies that are going to be around. This is the long game. I can't hide behind a ring of humans anymore. Sooner instead of later, Death's going to pick off everyone who gives a shit about me, and I'm going to be stuck in the middle of some stupid blood feud without anyone to back me up. Dempsey knew that. Shit, I wasn't listening to him when he told me, so he pretty much ripped me open until I saw it." I'd spent the past few nights lying in a bed big enough for an elephant to stretch out in, shoved to the edge by my little cat's sprawl. Sleep hadn't come easily while my brain picked apart Dempsey's final hours with me, and I'd had a lot of time to think about the old man manipulating me to find my way out of trouble. "Dempsey knew me. Coming at me with the truth wasn't going to get him anywhere, so he did what he always did—shoved at my weaknesses until I moved to where he wanted me to be."

"So what? He had to crack apart you, Jonas, and Sparky so you'd go dancing into the Court?" Cari gave a small snort that only lasted long enough to wet her nostrils. Her luminous eyes grew wide, and she looked around. "Hell, that's exactly what he did. Because here you are."

"Yeah, here I am."

I'd sprayed cleaner on the wonky parts and let them sit on the tarp, hoping it would do the trick and I wouldn't have to rebuild the whole damned thing. From how it responded in my hand after I tweaked at it, I didn't have a lot of hope for its quick resurrection. Finding a new one would be a bitch and a half, and I'd cut off my supplier with my anger. It wouldn't feel right to go hat in hand to Sparky and ask her to find me a new one, especially when I'd been the one to toss up the fence between us. Jason was an option, but I didn't want to put him in the middle of it. The fewer people in the stew, the better.

"So now what? You just sit here with the Sidhe and wait out your pissiness, or are you going to go do something about the crap you're sitting in?" Cari leaned forward, clasping her hands between her knees. She was shivering beneath the blanket, her cheeks turning pink from the crisp wind sweeping through the courtyard. It caught up a pile of sodden leaves, lifting up the edges enough for a few dry pieces to swirl around her feet. "They're sorry, Kai. And if you don't fix this, then you're going to end up losing people you've considered your family. Is that what you want?"

It wasn't. Shit, I was angry as hell at them, but also at myself for not seeing how my life was going to play out. I'd lived in the moment, a true Stalker, jumping from contract to contract, kill to kill without planning for any future other than a retirement filled with scars and aching muscles. Dempsey'd known better. He knew Tanic would come for me eventually, and I wouldn't be able to stand up against him and his Wild Hunt with only humans by my side.

I just hated like hell on how he decided to show me the truth. I needed some time to work through all of the crap in my head, and luckily I had an out to give me space to get my head together, a small Run up the interior to hopefully outrun some of my stray demons.

"What I'm going to do right now is take that handful of Dempsey's ashes to his brother in New Vegas, and when I come back, I'll talk with Jonas and Sparky." I shook my head, cutting off Cari's sputtering protests before she got too deep into her arguments. "I've got to do this, Cari. He's got some stuff of Dempsey's from back when he accepted the contract on me. After I'm done, I'll have a better idea on what I'm up against. Or at least what was behind me. Alexa said she'd watch Newt for me. Shouldn't take more than a week or so to get this taken care of. It's just something I've got to do."

"I'm coming with you," Cari argued, mad turning her eyes hot beneath her hooded lids.

"Well then, I'm calling shotgun," Ryder drawled, sneaking up on us with silent footsteps. "That's the expression, right? Shotgun? Because to borrow one of Kai's snarling expressions, there's no way in hell I am sitting in the back seat."

"YOU'RE NOT coming with me." I hadn't planned on taking up residence at the Court, so my duffel didn't have a lot in it. Just a few pairs of jeans and some T-shirts, but I'd learned my lesson years ago and packed enough underwear to withstand a siege on a city until someone rolled a wooden horse up to its gates. "You're the damned High Lord here. You can't just go wandering off into the desert every time you feel like it. You're like one of those starship captains on the telenovelas. 'Look! I'm the ship's leader, and I'm going to take every other important person with me to look at this dangerous planet. Let's leave the fry cook and that guy with the one wonky eye in charge. What's the worst that can happen?' Seriously, take the red shirt off, Ryder, and sit your ass down where it belongs."

From his nest on my bed, Newt gave a mewling snort and rolled over, showing me where his balls used to be, while Ryder leaned back against the door frame, crossing his arms over his chest. He looked comfortable. Smug even. And I flipped him off with a backward V, guessing he didn't know what it meant.

I was wrong.

"Don't take that tone of fingers with me. Alexa can take care of both the cat and the Court." He pushed off the wall. Then his long legs quickly nipped away at the distance between us. "*You* need someone right now."

"Lordling, I don't—" He was pressed against my side before I could finish the half-baked excuse sitting on my tongue. The Court wasn't ever noisy, not like the city a few blocks away, but I would have sworn at that moment it dipped down into a silence so pure I could hear the beat of his heart through his fingers as they clasped my wrist. "Ryder...."

My body remembered him holding me, my arms wrapped around his shoulders and waist, pulling him close to snuggle against while my soul grieved and my head pounded from too much whiskey. The scent of his skin filled my lungs—a tang of teas or maybe even maile and vanilla. I wasn't sure anymore, but my tongue ached for a taste of his lips, to slide across the plump of his mouth and leave teeth marks on them. This was more than some primal drive to become a part of the Sidhe Lord who called to my blood. He carried a part of me in him now, without even sharing anything other than a sheet and a curled-up cat, he was under my skin, and no amount of digging would get him out.

I wasn't ready for that kind of complication in my life, and I needed to tell Ryder to step back, to go away, to go hide someplace safe and dark and warm until I was able to come back without any strings or slavering black dogs on my trail. Right now I was nothing but trouble, and I would bring all of the Hells mankind ever could think up down upon his Court if he did more than touch me.

The gold-green flecks in his forest-and-emerald eyes told me he knew all of that and didn't give one shit about it.

"You do this all the time. I watch you. *Every* time. Whenever someone gets too close, you hiss and snarl like your gargoyle on the bed, pushing them away." He whispered, leaning in closer until his breath tickled my jaw, "You've just lost the man who pulled you out of a nightmare and gave you purpose. He spent what life he had as a human to prepare you for the day when the Wild Hunt Master would come for you, and he taught you to shove away anyone who could love you, because he knew you'd turn yourself over to Tanic rather than watch your loved ones be taken or killed. Because you know what Tanic will do to anyone who stands with you.

"You've had his hands on you, his pain in your bones, and I'm standing here right now to tell you, Kai, I will not sit down for that fight." In that moment, Ryder was as imperfect as I was, a bit of spit flecking over his upper lip as his canines flashed, his passion dusting a golden pink flush over his cheekbones. "And I'm not staying behind on this one either. You need to have someone by you. And I will be that someone. I won't let you talk me out of it like you did Cari. You don't get a say in this."

"And if you get killed? Who's going to go sit at the frilly chair they've got for you in the Court chambers? Alexa? One of the twins?" I rounded on him, but he wouldn't let go of my wrist, his fingers tightening down when I tried to pull away. We were still shoulder to shoulder, our faces close enough for me to finally take that bite, but I wasn't sure if anger or fear drove that creeping thirst in my belly. "Is there going to be anyone left to sit on it?"

"Alexa will. The Court calls to her as well. Not as much as it does you and I, but she can hold it. And she will if she has to. Cari will be here to help her. Someone else who wouldn't just let you fall either." Ryder jerked his head over toward the bed. "After all, Alexa has a fierce defender in her reserves. All she will have to do is put them between Newt and food to win any battle she might need to fight. I'm going, my Chimera. You will not do this alone. I'm not letting you shove me away like you've done others. It's time for you to accept I will not leave you. Even if I have to step on your shadow to do it."

"This is a simple ride to New Vegas. Nothing's going to happen. I'm going to find Kenny, hand him the ashes I set aside for him, and get whatever Dempsey gave him to hold. I don't need a babysitter." The ride would be long and mostly empty, past small townships barely big enough to see. I'd been dreading the silence, left alone with my thoughts, but I'd planned on listening to music loud enough to make my ears bleed and to find crappy motels along the way until I hit the glittering jewel in the middle of Nevada's wastelands. My mind whispered about all the trouble I could get into with Ryder in New Vegas, but I shut those thoughts down before they could take hold. "Besides, the place isn't like San Diego. I want to get in and out quickly. Stay too long in that stew and you begin to think you can live in it."

"Good, if the trip's going to be nothing, then we can go and come back without any trouble. But I *am* going." Ryder finally released me and peered into my duffel. "Although, from the amount of underwear you've put in there, are you sure it's only going to be about a week? Because if not, I have severely underpacked or you're lying about how spicy food doesn't affect you."

Six

WE LEFT before the sun cracked apart the black on the horizon. Draped in a glittering veil of lights, San Diego never truly went dark, holding back the night with a soft, gentle golden push, but to the east, the mountains were stygian, crags of blue against a scatter of stars. The marine layer was already moving in by the time I fired up the Mustang, its snaking tendrils undulating into the valley and canyons, filling in the Court's nooks and crannies until only the towers' peaks poked up out of its misty blanket. There was a promise of rain in the air, but we wouldn't be there long enough to see it hit the ground.

I pushed the Mustang toward the sunrise, leaving the remains of my life and family behind me.

Oh, except for the damned Sidhe lordling who'd decided he would be my green-eyed, pointy-eared golden shadow on a run I was doing for no money and pure sentiment.

It was hard to ignore Dempsey's harsh scold rising up out of my memories—*Only reason to burn gas and time is if someone is paying you to do it, boy. Other than that, someone's just trying to bleed you dry.*

"Yeah, well, suck it up, old man. I'm doing this for you," I muttered at the road unfurling out under the Mustang's high beams. "Anyone bled me dry, it was you."

Glancing over to see if Ryder heard me, I discovered he'd already fallen asleep against the passenger-side window, a small pillow tucked under his head. There was a brief moment of chaos tingling in my thoughts, and I itched to blast a thrash-metal mix out of the Mustang's powerful speakers but thought better of it. I needed a bit of alone time, and the brightening blue skies would be on us soon enough. For right now I wanted to simply fall into the black road snaking out in front of us and sip at the tumbler of creamy sweet coffee I'd gotten from the Court's kitchen.

I was pushing to get as far north as I could before stopping. The plan was to drive long days, running on cell fuel instead of gas, mostly because the cells could run for months without being recharged, and since we weren't going through Pendle, I wouldn't need the punch of acceleration from the combustion side of the hybrid engine. Truth was, it'd been more than a few years since I'd been up to New Vegas, and the gas depots along the way might have fallen on hard times, disappearing into the landscape like so many of the small towns did following the Merge. Unlike the constellation of ghost towns around it, New Vegas thrived in its mutated desert setting. The dying bones of a gambling mecca had resurrected itself and now glittered with wealth, a siren call to anyone with a spare credit or two, promising to make them rich beyond their dreams.

Perhaps it wasn't so much a resurrection as a desert vampire getting a new shot of blood to add flesh to its withered corpse.

The sun was pretty high up in the pale blue sky when the Mustang screamed past Rainbow, and Ryder woke up with a groggy smack of his lips. Disheveled and slightly perplexed by his surroundings, he blinked a few times before figuring out where he was. It was easy enough to see the comprehension dawning in his deep green eyes, reason returning to wash away the confusion he'd woken up in. I liked him asleep. It meant he was quiet and I could sneak a few looks at him as I drove, caught between the hate of wanting a Sidhe Lord in my bed and recognizing my own tangled thoughts on having him close.

There was too much change in my life right now, and I needed— longed—to keep things as simple as I could. But there was no going back to the life I'd led before. Dempsey was dead, the family he'd pulled around me was uncertain now, and I asked Ryder to stay with me, to hold me when I felt cracked open. There was no pushing anything back through those open doors.

"Where are we?" Ryder sat up, caught in the seat belt for a moment, then working his way out. Running his fingers through his hair, he straightened the gold metallic strands, pulling them away from his face. "I'd say this looks familiar, but it all kind of looks this way—big rocks, brown ground. More big roc, but these are flying and hopefully far enough away that they don't think we're lunch."

I ducked my head a bit to catch a glimpse at the birds to the right of the freeway. "Those aren't rocs. They're lesser golden thunderbirds. Usually fish eaters. Although I've seen one pluck a Minnesota lake monster out of the water like it weighed nothing. They're good for the lakes, especially around fishing villages, because they keep the big predators down. They don't go after anything smaller than six feet, so they leave salmon and trout alone. So long as I don't drive the Mustang into some water, we'll be fine."

Ryder stared at me for a long moment, then said, "You have an amazing retention for details about all of the wildlife we encounter. I never thought about it until just now."

"I've got Dempsey to thank for that." I tensed my thighs, looking for a telltale ache in my muscles to see if we needed to stop and stretch. Ryder was usually good for a long haul, but too many hours sitting down meant we would both be cramped up when we did finally stop. "There is a turnoff up ahead with a general store we can stop at to grab cold drinks. Take us about fifteen to twenty minutes to get there, but it'll be a chance to walk around. We've been going solid for about six hours now. I would've stopped sooner, but you were off in la-la land and I didn't want to wake you."

"Do you always deflect a compliment?" Ryder's attention was sharp, pinning me in place. Not like I had anywhere to go, seeing as I was driving a couple of tons of steel down an old asphalt freeway. "I've noticed whenever I tell you something good about yourself, you give credit to somebody else. Like Dempsey or Jonas."

"The animal thing is important if you're going to be a Stalker. You've got to know what's a threat and what isn't, and if it is, you've got to know what's going to take it down." I gave him a quick glance, but it didn't seem like my answer was good enough for Ryder, because he continued to stare at me. "And it's not like I keep *everything* in my head. SoCalGov has a lexicon, and there's people out there who have their own lists. If I run into something new or find out something's weakness, I sometimes add what I know. This isn't the kind of job where you can hoard your knowledge. That's as good as killing someone if they're out in the field and run into something they don't recognize. It's kind of one of the rules your mentor teaches you. If you don't know what it is and it's growling at you, get the fuck out."

Ryder laughed—a soft low sound husky and smooth enough to send a tingle down my spine. "I guess I never thought of you going back to your warehouse and updating a database about the monsters you run across."

"Like I do it every single time. Just every once in a while, and mostly only if I find out something new. The Underhill brought a lot of trouble with it, and things have gotten twisted a bit. I was kind of hoping Alexa getting her apprentice license would mean she could feed some information to the databases, but you guys seem to operate on an 'if it doesn't bother us, we don't look at it' basis. Which doesn't exactly help when something's trying to eat your face off and you go look it up, only to find out there's not a damn thing about the six-eyed, blue-tongued lizard living in algae in the shallows of a freshwater lake."

"You've run into something like that?"

"Yeah, about five of them. Bastards are about the length of my arm and can jump like five hundred feet from under the water. And they're all teeth and tail. Not sure if they can see well or if they're reacting to motion, but they sure as hell are fast, and a mouthful of flesh is a good hunt for them." I shuddered, remembering the job we'd been on. "They didn't get me, but I can tell you Nickel-Nose Ned didn't have that nickname before we took the contract. After that, I walked around the lake with a baseball bat and a twitchy right arm."

I was hit with a wave of sorrow before we went another few feet down the road. So much of my life had Dempsey woven into it, and the encounter with the snapping blue lizards had been one of the first times he told another Stalker they had to work with me or get off the job. Some left but most stayed. Dempsey had a reputation for taking on the very worst of contracts and earning high payoffs. I was just a condition of working with him, and soon enough, I could stand on my own name and pull in enough money to support us both.

"I never really understood your relationship with him. Dempsey, I mean. I'm closer to my mothers than my fathers, but I really don't know how Dempsey raised you." Ryder must have seen something in my face, because his voice gentled, the teasing falling away to something sweeter and poignant. "The two of you always bickered and fought, but it seems like you have a lot of affection for him."

I never thought about how my relationship with Dempsey might look to somebody on the outside of it, but then again, I hadn't really cared either. Shrugging, I replied, "Some people think it might've been a little bit complicated, but it was simple enough for us. He taught me everything I know and kept me alive. So when he couldn't be on the job anymore, I owed it to him to keep him going. Plain enough."

"I think there's a lot more to it than that, but I'm not going to push," Ryder said in a way that told me the pushing would come at a later date, when I least expected it. "I didn't know a lot about him. Maybe tell me about something good, something you and Dempsey shared, even. All I hear is how antisocial and bossy he was, but you've got to have some good times with him. I can hear your affection for him in your voice, and don't give me the excuse that he was better than Tanic, because your loyalty goes deep and I know it's hard to earn. So tell me something good about Dempsey."

"Something good about the old man?" I snorted, trying to figure out what angle Ryder was taking this into. "He was an argumentative asshole who pushed until you thought you'd break and then gloat when you didn't."

"He kept you safe," Ryder replied softly, then tilted his head. "Relatively. I'm not sure teaching you to be a Stalker was exactly the wisest profession you could have followed, but…."

"It's all he knew, and he was damned good at it." The sky was beginning to cloud, pockmarked with dark gray dots and a promise of more clinging to the mountaintops on either side of the road. I slowed down when the first heavy raindrop struck the Mustang's windshield, not knowing how long it'd been since the asphalt got a good soaking. There was always a chance of hydroplaning on a wet oil slick if the roads were left dry too long. "Like that thing about knowing the animals. We all operate within certain areas, so it makes sense to know the common threats or even the stuff that might look like a threat. People get all worked up about the creatures that came through the Merge, but there's a lot of stuff that was here beforehand that could tear apart a man before he saw it. It'd be stupid to go out there without doing your homework. The more you know—the more you study—the longer you'll live."

"One good thing, Kai." Ryder's chuckle was a soft roll of heat, tickling at parts of me I didn't have the time or inclination to scratch. "There must be something."

There were a lot of things—moments and times I didn't think a Sidhe lordling would understand. I knew nothing about *his* childhood, and here he was poking at how Dempsey raised *me*. Bringing that point up would have Ryder saying I was avoiding his question, and he wouldn't have been that far off the mark. Especially when the road seemed a bit filmy until I blinked against the sting in my eyes.

"He always made sure I had books." I grinned, remembering the excitement of discovery while digging through the boxes he would dump on my lap. "I mean, some of them were shit. Don't get me wrong. Like really crappy books, because he'd go through abandoned houses, places the black dogs or something else with teeth cleared out, and scavenge what he could find. Shit, a lot of my clothes when I was younger came from places like that. His too."

There'd been boxes of books stacked up behind the seat in the old truck we rattled around in. They took up valuable weapon and supply space, but he hadn't minded. I worked to keep the number I kept down to a minimum, and he kept shoveling more at me, forcing me to cull my collection. I thought about something personal—something I hadn't thought about in years—and debated sharing it.

Ryder was so earnest. So dedicated to—not trying to normalize me but trying to understand who I was and how I got there. First time I met him, I thought his sole purpose for meeting me was to use me. Meeting his grandmother and nearly dying under her clenched-fist magic didn't change my mind about the elfin being manipulative and selfish. If anything, it only confirmed my suspicions, but Ryder kept at me, aware of the growing attraction between us but not pushing at me. He worked instead to make sure we were friends at the very least. I'd never been friends with anyone I slept with. Relationships were a tangle I didn't need, and I never had any hope anyone would want me for longer than one or two nights.

I wasn't somebody you kept forever.

I'd never been somebody anyone really wanted in their life. Not that way. Never someone to wake up next to more than a few mornings in a row, and sure as hell not someone who became part of a daily routine, much less a presence in their hearts.

Ryder was asking for something different, and I shoved him away each time, keeping him at arm's length with my suspicion and doubts, but the truth was I was afraid—afraid to wake up next to him for two mornings only to find out I was unwanted on the third.

What he was asking for now was for me to trust him. To trust that someday—on the third morning—he would still want me in his bed.

And in his life.

I took a long breath and leaped into the unknown.

"After Dempsey got hurt and it looked like he wasn't going to be able to work, he asked me where I wanted to make our home base. The idea was always that he'd retire one day and I'd pick up the slack, supporting him like he'd supported me. That was *always* the plan. Just… the end date moved up a bit once his knees blew." Shrugging at Ryder's noncommittal hum, I continued, "So when that time came and he asked, I told him I wanted to go down to San Diego, because that's where the truffula are."

"What are… is the truffula?" Ryder shifted, wedging himself against the door and the seat, facing me as much as he could in the Mustang's bucket seat.

"They're plants. Real ones. Sort of. But the first time I heard of them was in one of the really old books Dempsey got me. The guy who wrote them was from San Diego, and when I heard that, I wanted to see them. Just to see the fields of truffula." I eased around a dip in the road, slowing the car down. A bit of crackling lightning sparked across the clouds to the right, and the clouds flexed and darkened, promising to unleash something onto the rough brush before pounding into us. "He wrote about these trees and flowers, fantastical things that couldn't exist but did. Or at least in some way, but he'd seen them as different and more than what they were. We hadn't really explored San Diego. Not really. I mean, visiting Cari's family down south and then Jonas when he moved onto the ranch, but not the outskirts. So there he was doped up to the gills with me driving, and we were heading to Jonas's place to stay for a bit when I made a wrong turn and we came across this hillside covered in pink-and-purple puffballs… the truffula.

"They weren't the flossy cotton-candy balls I'd read about, but the idea of them was there. I pulled over and got out while Dempsey grumbled that he was hungry or had to take a piss, but he understood because, hell… there were truffula all over the field." The rain began, dappling the car's windshield with a light kiss of water drops, but it wasn't heavy enough for me to turn on the wipers. I did anyway, mostly to give me something to do where I didn't have to look into Ryder's too-open expression. "They're flowers. Gomphrena. All different kinds of those, but they were truffula. I grabbed a handful of them and brought them back to the car, and you know what Dempsey said to me?"

"No," Ryder murmured gently. "What?"

"He lit up his damned cigar and said, 'Well, guess we're moving to fucking San Diego, kid. Now that you've found your fricking truffula flowers.'" I did my best impression of his garrulous voice with its harsh smoke-and-bitters lilt. "See, the thing was, I never talked to him about the flowers, about how they fascinated me. And once I found out they were based on something real, I wanted to see one. I didn't share any of that crap with him, but he knew. He knew how I felt like one of those damned things—halfway between real and imagined."

"Those dried purple flowers on the bookcase. The ones in the green case. Is that them?"

"Not the ones I picked that day. Jonas's goat ate them after it got into the truck, but those are the ones Dempsey gave me to replace them. They dry out nice. First thing he put up once I got the bookcases built. It sounds stupid but—"

"No, it sounds like home." Ryder laid his hand on my thigh and squeezed my knee. "We should put some around the Court."

"You're not going to tell anyone I told you this shit, right?" I eyed him, liking the heat of his hand on my leg but not trusting the warmth in his voice. "Because...."

"No. Something just between us, Kai. Something just for you," he assured me, giving me that smile he always had lurking somewhere, ready to gild me with its shine when I needed a lead out of the darkness I'd put myself in. "That way, whenever you see them, you know you're finally home."

Seven

A HINT of smoke drifted under the heavy scent of impending rain, probably a carryover from some distant wildfire eating through a nearby but unseen mesa. Hemmed in by thick threads of impervious black lava, the occasional erratic fires raged with intense heat, only to die off in mewling whimpers when their devastating flames met the *paho'eho'e* and *a'a* swaths brought on by the Merge. For all the trouble the Underhill caused, it effectively put an end to the devastating wildfire seasons, although I could have done with less rain.

Especially when it looked like the gathering clouds would ripen into lightning storms and we were too close to dragon territory for my comfort. Despite the mountain range separating the coast from the inner corridor, coppers could smell the crackle of electricity in the air for miles around, and I kept one eye on the sky, looking for any sinuous metallic shapes.

Nothing gets a dragon hungrier than playing with fire or electricity, and a quick-moving red flash in the shape of a muscle car was pretty much a guaranteed takeout meal to tide one over until it could find something bigger to shove into its maw.

Alexa would kill me if I got her cousin chewed up by a dragon, no matter how much the idiotic Sidhe worshipped the damned lizards and the chaos they brought.

We'd needed to stop and stretch our legs. Or at least I did. But the automat wasn't in the best location, sitting on a bend and perched on a jut overlooking a deep gulch. The passage wasn't as tight as some we'd gone through earlier that day, but the steep, crenulated mountains loomed in, their sides thick with brush and boulders bigger than a full-grown elephant. The terrain wasn't prone to slides, but I was still cautious. Who knew how long those massive stones had been sitting there, waiting for the right sparrow to land on a certain spot to send it tumbling down onto the highway below?

"What exactly is this?" Examining the coconut-marshmallow-covered cupcake I'd gotten out of the autoservers in the convenience stop, Ryder looked like he was about a second away from curling his nose up at the snack. He sniffed it, and apparently that was enough to wrinkle his senses. "It smells like hyped-up sugar."

"This is one of my favorite things to eat, so if you don't want it, feel free to pass it over. I'll be glad to take it off your hands." I carefully peeled off the marshmallow dome covering the cake bit, sighing contentedly when it came away in one piece. "Okay, seriously… either bite into it or eat those withered grapes you insisted I get you."

"At least the grapes don't look like they are made out of pure chemicals." He handed me the cupcake, pinching its wrapper closed with his fingers.

"Considering they stock this place probably once a week, there's no telling how long those grapes have been there. For all you know, they started off as raisins, and at some point during their incarceration, they absorbed enough condensation to plump themselves up." I stood strong against his disgusted glare. Rattling the package at him, I said, "At least these won't give you food poisoning. Best thing about processed foods? They taste the same no matter if it's day one or a hundred years from now."

"I'm not sure that's something you should brag about," he drawled. "Especially since you can't even guarantee that you would've digested it after a hundred years."

"Just remember, you eat those grapes and something happens to your guts, I'm just going to stop on the side of the road and let you out. No looking for bathrooms or anything," I warned. "There's not much between here and New Vegas on this stretch, so choose wisely."

He said nothing for a long moment, staring at the long rectangular building I'd pulled the Mustang up in front of. Despite my precautions, he peeled back the plastic wrap on the grapes' container and poked at their slightly wrinkled shapes. "There's a lot of food in there. In that… what did you call it?"

"An automat." It was hard to talk around the gummy marshmallow, but I didn't think Ryder was going to dock me manners points. He knew who raised me. Speaking with my mouth full was the least of my faults. "They used to be extinct, but after the Merge, places like these popped up along the roads. Easier than having someone work a counter. Just have a couple of trucks make the route a few times a week to stock up the place, and it runs itself."

The storm teased and licked at the mountaintops, but I so far hadn't spotted anything reptilian playing in its depths. Since the automat was pretty much a rectangular tin box with vending machines lining the outer walls and a few low aisles in the middle, we could ride out a hard storm if we needed to, but I'd rather be on the road with the storm behind us, leaving any potential to ending up as a dragon snack in the dust.

"Isn't it kind of... foolhardy?" Ryder smirked, probably satisfied he'd dug up that chestnut from his Singlish vocabulary to throw my way. "Reckless? To leave all of this without an attendant? What's to stop someone from cracking open the machines and taking everything?"

"No," I replied, peeling off the coconut fluff from the second ball in the package. "Any sign of someone messing with the machines, the box locks down and, well, sort of depressurizes. Seals up like a nun's chastity belt, and then knock-out gas is pumped through the vents. Takes about thirty seconds for the person locked inside to pass out. Sometimes less. An alarm goes off somewhere, and they send someone out to look at the place."

"Suppose the gas kills them?" The look of horror on his face was comical, because when it was all said and done, Ryder was an innocent babe in the woods compared to... well, an actual babe in the woods. "The food in there isn't worth someone's life."

"A lot of people would disagree with that. Besides, place is easy enough to blow a hole through the ceiling if you go in armed with enough shot and you're good enough to concentrate on a single spot. All you need is an open hole, and then you've got all the time in the world to pick through what you want." I nodded down at the stretch of highway awaiting us. "Most places like this are a good hour before someone gets here. You can clean a place out in less than ten minutes and be broken out before a guard even reaches the halfway point."

"And you know this how?" The grapes were forgotten, the one between Ryder's fingers smashed nearly to juice.

"'Cause humans can't hold their breath as long as we can. You and I can probably go for a good five minutes past the point they give up and have to suck in some air. Four or five shotgun blasts will tear open that box quick enough, and then it's just a matter of waiting for the gas to clear out." I shrugged, sucking the spongy remains of the cupcake's shell from my fingers. "Sometimes you've got to eat and you've got nothing in your credit bank but starving moths and wishes. Shotgun shells are easy enough to pack. A couple of drops in the bucket when there's a lake you can drink from if you only spill it."

"And Dempsey knew you did this?" He blindly took the napkin I offered him for his wet fingers and tucked the grape into its folds. "I mean, he knew you were… stealing? And he let you?"

"Who the hell do you think put me up to it?" I bit into the last of the nearly stale chocolate cake, sucking on the distinct chemical taste of the cream hiding in it. "Either finish the grapes or toss them, lordling. We've got a long ways to go, and you've got to get that off your hands before you get into my car. There's some water bottles in the back. Wash up and let's get going."

I learned paranoia early on in my Stalker career. It saved my ass more than a few times over the years, and right now, I was paranoid as hell about the heavy rains and the heavy rocks stuck precariously into a dirt mountain soaked through to the bones.

So when I heard something odd coming up from the gulch behind us, my hackles didn't have to go very far to be on alert.

I couldn't identify the sounds—a faint scrabbling growing progressively louder and then the telltale crackle of something, or many somethings, working through the damp but unforgiving brush. Wiping my hands on my jeans, I jerked my head toward the Mustang, then growled at Ryder as I reached in through the open passenger-side window for the shotgun strapped into a sling behind the front seats.

"Get in. Now. Something's—" The noise grew louder, a rushing scrabble up the gulch, and the brush growing up around the guardrail behind the automat erupted with movement. A grinding engine sound joined in—a whining, choking broken melody at odds with the snap and crackle from the brush. "Ryder! Get in!"

The gulch vomited up its chaos onto the bend, branches and weeds snapping as what looked like thousands of jackalopes crested over the rise. With cat-sized bodies heavy with muscle and plump with a growing winter pelt, they were a furry wave, cheeping and chittering in high distress, their antlers clacking together as they fled. Tiny claws scraped and tore at the ground in a mad rush to break away from whatever followed, and we were surrounded by the furry tide before I could bring the shotgun around. I fought to stay upright, nearly knocked over when one after another struck my legs. A few antler points dug into my jeans, but my boots kept most of my flesh safe from being torn open. One caught on a seam and its head nearly turned around, but it shook loose quickly, disengaging with a twist of its body.

"Here!" Ryder tossed me the leather belt Dempsey had modified for me to hold shotgun shells. "I'll grab the Glock you gave me."

"You'll shoot your damned fool head off," I retorted, but there didn't seem to be anything I could do to stop him. "Stupid stubborn lordling."

Leaning against the Mustang to support myself against the barrage of small bodies striking me, I fastened the belt quickly, letting it ride low on my hips, then braced to face whatever else was going to come up over the ridge. The spurt of a struggling motor grew louder, and the jackalopes didn't seem to be thinning out. I was about to dismiss the whole thing as the wild-eyed mutant rabbits being chased by a bike or perhaps an anemic dune vehicle, but then came a roar, a sickly, blood-curdling scream filled with a rage and hunger I knew deep down into my bones, and my guts twisted in on themselves, caught on the seam of my life just as the jackalope had been trapped on my jeans.

An ainmhi dubh.

Both the bane of my existence and the source of a lot of my income, the damned black dogs seemed to be everywhere lately, and it was harder and harder to discredit Dempsey's warning that they were hunting for me. Still, they'd hunted in packs or as loners long before I took up Stalking and had been the stuff of unleashed Unsidhe nightmares for an eternity, so I took Dempsey's sharp words with more than a grain of salt—more like a whole deer lick with a Dead Sea chaser.

And there was now one coming our way, chasing a sea of jackalopes and some idiot trying to outrun it on something that didn't sound up to the job.

"Hear that?" Ryder asked. "Can we get into the car and outpace it?"

"We can, but there's someone in front of it." The whining grew louder, choking and throttling on either the steep incline or a failing engine. "Get on the other side of the car. Shoot over the hood when the dog comes over the rise. And whatever you do, do *not* scratch the paint. Just got the damned thing back."

"Well then you shouldn't have brought it on the run," he snapped back, but my glare hit the back of his head as he ran around the front of the Mustang to put a bit of cover between him and the ainmhi dubh. "Don't get killed."

"You'll be fine. Keys are in the car. I go down, you get out of here."

There wasn't time to say anything more. Not when, still knee-deep in furiously scampering horned rabbits, a beat-up dirt bike broke over the lip of the gorge, its back wheel kicking up spurts of gravel and soil, then slammed into the thick metal guardrail running behind the automat's pullover pad. The motorbike came to a shuddering, complete stop.

Its rider, however, did not.

He was all fractured limbs and keening, tumbling in the air toward the Mustang. The angle of his arc was high, a wide bit of air any snowboarder or skate kid would admire if only he had a board beneath him. And wasn't screaming in terror. He smelled of blood and fear, curling up over my head, and I let him go, focused on the gulch and what he'd brought to our feet. I heard him land a bit behind me, an impressive feat considering I was yards away from the guardrail, but other than wincing at the sound of his body hitting the gravel-and-tar-patched asphalt, I didn't give him another thought.

"Kai?" Ryder shouted over the screams of whatever was coming up the cliff behind the unfortunate biker. "What do I do?"

"Stay there and shoot at whatever pokes its head up!" I yelled back. "He's not our problem right now."

The bike rider had on a helmet, and from the corner of my eye I could see him moving, slowly and painfully but still at least writhing enough to assure me he was alive. Honestly, he was the least of my worries. We had to survive whatever he'd brought with him, and as the jackalope wave diminished, we were going to be the creature's nearest source of food. I wasn't going to pick the guy up and toss him at the monster he'd woken up, but neither was I going to bend over and kiss his boo-boos, leaving my ass open to get munched on.

He was either going to die or live long enough for us to take him to a medical center. Either way, I couldn't spare him the time. I was too busy trying not to get us all killed.

I felt the ainmhi dubh before I saw it. Normally a black dog's stench permeated the air before it made its appearance, but this one was different. Or least different from the ones I'd hunted down for bounties, turning their pelts in to the Post for cash. I intimately knew its malevolent aura, tasting it in the marrow of my bones and at the back of my throat. When its magic-shaped bulk finally clawed its way up the side of the gulch, I was ready for it.

Because while an ainmhi dubh was a perversion of nature, the thing coming toward us was nothing more than a pure abomination brought to life by Valin cuid Anbhás, my father's disgraced apprentice and my older brother.

Ainmhi dubh were hungry—*always* hungry. Forged from magic and bits of flesh, they were the stuff of nightmares and the Unsidhe's greatest weapon. Their powerful bodies were usually reptilian, patched with bits of fur and scale, with horns and wings, but most of all, armed with evil natures and mouths bristling with sharp teeth. Their insatiable hunger drove them to hunt, and only their creators' will kept them in check. The more powerful the mage, the more powerful the ainmhi dubh, but there was a fine balance between pouring a lot of magic into a nearly uncontrollable simulacrum and being able to control it. The ainmhi dubh—the black dogs of the Unsidhe—fought against the restraints, eager to consume anything in their path, and all too often, they broke away from their creators, given too much power and not bound as tightly as they should be.

There were a lot of black dogs roaming the Western regions, their original hunts breaking free from their creators either from lack of control or because their master was killed during a conflict. They bred indiscriminately until the magic firing their blood died out, the litters getting weaker and weaker the further they got from the original creation.

What was stalking toward us was definitely not from a litter. I could see Valin's hand in its creation, feel his warped intelligence and twisted magic holding it together. I'd faced one of his ainmhi dubh before, standing shoulder to shoulder with an Unsidhe Lord, and while it seemed as if Valin was getting better at cobbling together his monsters, it didn't appear as if he had gained any control over holding them.

He must've been using whatever creatures' flesh he could find down by the border between SoCal and Mexico. The ainmhi dubh was mostly feline, or at least at one time had been perhaps a mountain lion, but its grace and elegance were long gone, burned away by the disjointed lengthening of its legs and the armor plating covering the joints. Its head was elongated, almost equine except for the curled-up and acid-dripping smile wrinkling its flaccid ash-gray flesh. Speckled with black patches, its body absorbed the uneven sunlight breaking through the thickening clouds, but the array of eyes scattered across its forehead gleamed red when it spotted me, and it took a step toward me, chuckling with low coughs, the turnoff's asphalt smoking where its spit hit the ground.

"Shoot?" Ryder yelled, catching the ainmhi dubh's attention. Its head drifted to a spot over my left shoulder, long enough for it to assess Ryder. Then its gaze came back to me, its eyes burning brilliantly in its misshapen head.

I didn't answer Ryder. There really wasn't much of a reason to, because no sooner had the word left his lips than the black dog attacked.

It was on me in a few leaps, but it was a long enough time to get a shot off. I was counting on Valin being a shitty mage, and for once, my gut feeling about my half brother's skills was on point. He either didn't listen to our father when Tanic was droning on about how to fortify a black dog's defenses or he just didn't care. Either way, I got a tickle of glee in my belly when my first shotgun blast hit its shoulder and punched through the joint, sending steaming, glistening dark blood gushing from its torn-up flesh.

The ainmhi dubh twisted from the momentum of the shot, tumbling to the side and landing hard. Scrabbling at the gravel, it righted itself, favoring its shot-through shoulder, and it screamed at me, a wave of fetid and rotting flesh. The magics holding it together seemed to be unraveling, or at least that's what it felt like. The wrongness of its creation hung heavy in my gut, curdling in my stomach. It simply *felt* wrong. Patchworked together with an inelegant hand and little care taken in its creation, it quivered in place, trying to get its feet underneath it. Baring its long teeth, it dug in its powerful back legs, then coughed out a warning, eyes narrowed.

A bullet came whirring over my left shoulder, too close to my head for comfort, and I risked a withering glance at Ryder to warn him off, pulling my shotgun up for another blast. I caught half of an apologetic look and a grimace on his too-pretty face as the cat circled, lowering its shoulders to take another leap.

The bike rider squirmed a few feet away from my left foot, the front shield on his helmet cracked either from landing on his head or possibly poor maintenance before he decided to become black dog bait. I couldn't see his face, but his panic was evident. His bare hands were bloodied from scraping on the bend's hard ground, and from what I could make out, he was pleading not to be eaten.

"Yeah, you and me both, idiot," I grumbled, stepping between him and the ainmhi dubh, tossing a prayer to Pele in the hopes Ryder wouldn't accidentally shoot me in the back. "Come here, you asshole dog, so I can get a good shot in."

The ainmhi dubh struck clumsily, its front paws flailing about and its maw snapping out of time with its leap. I let loose every bit of shot I had, and when it staggered from the hits, I twisted the shotgun about and slammed the stock into its wide head, hoping the crack I heard was its skull and not my weapon. Up close, its stench was even worse, and my eyes watered with it being near, stung by its acidic blood leaking fumes and its rotten-fish-and-moldy-tofu breath. It snapped at my leg but missed by a mile. Instead, its snout dug down into a bit of gravel, and I quickly pulled the shotgun back and loaded in another round, not caring if the thing chewed on the bike rider while I lined up my next shot.

The storm was finally over the mountain, crackling lightning and rolling thunder over us when I let loose both barrels into the ainmhi dubh's head, breaking apart its forehead and dimming its red eyes. A splatter of its brains and blood erupted from behind its low-sweeping ears, a pair of horn buds carried off on a bit of ragged flesh from the blast, landing near its twitching back legs.

I wasn't quite sure it was dead yet. Or at least what was left of its magic in its body wasn't ready to surrender. Its systems were slow to shut down, and its maw continued to snap and grind rocks between its teeth. The ainmhi dubh was done, and I wasn't about to waste any shot on killing it more.

I simply stepped back and let it unravel, its limbs and spine knotting and twisting about, searching for any bit of the intense hunger driving its malformed body.

A bullet buried itself inches away from the toe of my left boot, and I turned around to glare at Ryder. Tossing my shotgun up over my shoulder, I yelled, "What the hell?"

"Wasn't me." He held up his hands, dangling the Glock from his loose fingers. "It was him."

Sure enough, the damned bike rider was lying on his side, facing the dying ainmhi dubh and holding what looked like a pistol left over from SoCal's Wild West days. It was pitted and somewhat rusty, trembling in the guy's shaking hand. Pissed off, I took my eyes off the ainmhi dubh long enough to kick the gun out of the bike rider's hand and spit at the smoking spot on the ground.

The ainmhi dubh was groaning its final moments, and the battered, long-legged asshole we had just saved sat up gingerly, tearing off his helmet with a stream of grumbling complaints. He was skinny and pale, more of a scarecrow than a man, and his beak of a nose was bloodied, probably broken from being bashed into the front of the helmet. His hair was longer than when I'd last seen him but still a tangle of fine brown strands. One of his eyes was nearly swollen shut, but I recognized him as soon as he got himself free from the scraped-up helmet that probably saved his brain from leaking out one of the many holes in his head.

All things considered, I was seriously contemplating giving him another one and leaving him to the vultures to be picked over.

"Well shit," I snarled. "If it isn't little Robbie Malone."

"It's Crickets. I keep telling you, they call me Crickets." He peered up at me as best he could, his face smeared with blood and bruised to hell and back. "And I know you told me you'd shoot me if you saw me again, but I was kind of hoping you'd take me to a hospital instead."

Eight

"I HEARD about Dempsey," Malone muttered through the gauze Ryder slapped on his cheek to staunch some bleeding. "I'm sorry—"

"Don't even talk." I briefly met his eyes in the rearview mirror, scowling. "I promised you the next time I saw you I'd put a bullet in your brain pan. That offer's still on the table."

I was pushing the Mustang hard to outrun the storm, but it chewed and spat in our wake. It was a losing battle. I couldn't outrun the wind no matter how hard I tried, and having Malone in the back seat made my skin crawl. Ryder gave me a lifted eyebrow when I moved all of the weapons from the back, either stowing them away in the trunk or putting them next to him on the passenger side, but I wasn't going to take any chances. The last time Robbie Malone allegedly had my back, he'd driven a knife through my spine and tried to sell me off to a crazed Unsidhe woman with delusions of godhood.

The small oval black-pearl dragon scale embedded deep under the skin of my throat itched at the thought of it, a souvenir of the run and a frequent reminder not to turn my back on strangers, no matter how closely related they were to people I knew.

Of course the same could be said about Ryder. I liked his cousin Alexa before I liked him, and look what it got me—stuck on a drowned-out road in a muscle car trying to outrace the sky's fury with a backstabbing bastard sitting in the rear seat.

The road behind us was a swamp, obscured by sheets of water and fog, and the thread of asphalt in front of us wasn't going any better. I'd have pulled over somewhere, but I felt the weight of every drop of blood Malone shed and the twinge in every one of his moans. He'd hit the ground hard and moved like molasses when we tried to get him into the Mustang. Then again, he could have been lying and performing the hell out of fake injuries.

I just didn't trust the ass.

Above us, the clouds were streaked with long black tendrils, smoke-wisp eels riding on the rich electrical charges coursing through the storm.

73

They dipped and wove, and I'm sure if the windows were rolled down, we might have been able to hear them scream, but the rain pounded down on us, drowning them out. They were lower than I'd ever seen them, stringing themselves between the mountain peaks. We were about to hit the flatlands, and I needed to push for higher ground as fast as possible. Desert flash floods were nothing to laugh about, and while Oketsu could take a lot of hits, the Mustang couldn't fight a tsunami packed with debris and boulders from the nearby hills.

"I just wanted to say I'm sorry about Dempsey," Malone grunted. "He was practically my uncle. Or he would have been if he married Aunt Sarah. She just didn't want to... you know, I mean she didn't *know* you. It wasn't anything personal."

It was a good thing he stopped talking or I'd have pulled over and shot him right there.

"You checked him for weapons, right?" I glanced over to Ryder. "'Cause if he's got something that can go through my seat, you're screwed unless you can grab the wheel before the car goes off the road."

"I dropped my gun back there," Malone piped up. "Guess I forgot to pick it up before you shoved me into the car."

"*Iesu.* See? That's why something's going to eat you someday. Never choose flight over fight and never ever drop your gun," I scolded, giving him the barest of sneers in the mirror. "What were you going to do when it caught you? Gnaw on it? Ask it to let you go because you weren't ready?"

"You'd be a good mentor," Ryder interjected, "assuming we survive your driving. How are you even seeing the road?"

"Oketsu's easy to drive, and the road's darker than the sides. Not that hard." It was an easy straight shot, the bends slow and smooth, banking gently into the curves. "Border station's coming up in a bit. There's a medic center there Malone can be seen at. Give him a full workup."

Malone's not-so-soft groan when the Mustang hit a dip in the road whispered a thread of torturous pain through the slushing pound of rain. Since the suspension cost me a pretty piece of change to keep the ride as smooth as possible, the bumps and jostles were barely noticeable. I tilted my head, listening to his breathing, but it was steady—no sign of whistling or air sucking through his lungs. Still, it was obvious the tumble through the air then the sudden introduction of his body to the hard-packed ground hadn't done Malone any favors.

"You named your car?" Malone croaked out, his voice breaking at the edges despite his attempts at keeping it light. "Kind of... retro, isn't it?"

There wasn't a lot of muscle on him, and unless he was especially bendy, the hit he'd taken had rattled his joints and spine, maybe even broken him in a few places, but there would be no way of really knowing until someone zapped him. He'd tried to sell me back to the Unsidhe, cutting a deal to hand me back into my father's not-so-loving care, so I should have enjoyed every whimper and tamped-down moan he made.

I mean, I wasn't dripping with remorse, but I did feel kind of bad for the kid.

"Some Stalkers name their guns." I shrugged. "I name my cars. They last longer than the guns."

"Still stupid," Malone muttered under his breath, sounding as if he were talking between clenched teeth. "Guns... shit, this hurts."

"Can he have more of the pills?" Ryder turned halfway around. "Or do you plan on killing him slowly?"

"I'm fine," Malone grumbled from behind me.

"See? He's fine, but he can probably have a couple more." The storm was thickening, which I didn't think was even possible, so I slowed the Mustang down, throttling back the power surging out of the cell packs mounted into the engine. "We've got about half an hour to go. Border's not far. He's just got to hold on until then. And whatever you do, Robbie, if you hork in my back seat, I've still got a bullet or two I can use on you."

"Don't be silly, Kai," Ryder said, shaking out a couple of the painkillers from the first aid kit I kept in the glove compartment. "We both know you won't shoot him."

I gave Ryder what I hoped was my filthiest look. "You think I wouldn't kill him for throwing up in my car? The giving-birth thing was a fluke. Can't shoot a pregnant woman, but gotta say, I was thinking of shooting *you* back then."

"I *know* you wouldn't shoot him." He handed the pills over the back seat along with a bottle of water, Malone's pale, thin hand creeping up over my right shoulder to take them. "Because you'd much rather use your knives."

I WAS holding the Mustang down to nearly crawling speed by the time the Border Patrol beacon lit up my dashboard. Its signal punched through the white noise crackling across my screen, giving me some guidance into the compound. A few fraught, nerve-wracking miles down the now practically invisible road and the main drive's slope came into view, lit up by eye-watering spotlights.

Soupy fog kept us at a slow pace, and despite the sleek curve of a well-maintained road, Malone epped and sucked on his teeth at every slide from the Mustang's tires on the wet asphalt. I didn't remember the station being so far away from the road, because it seemed to take forever before we crested the final ridge and the mesa stretched out in front of the Mustang's headlights. Or at least as much of the mesa as we could see through the furiously working wipers.

Dots of lights punched out through the rain, nearly hidden by the clotting mist. Edging the Mustang closer, a pair of spotlights struck its metallic bloodred paint, flaring up sparks of pearly silver under the rivulets pouring off the hood. The headlights picked out a few slats of the rolling metal doors in front of us, and Ryder bent his head forward, probably trying to get a good look at the place through the deluge.

"Where's... it's just a solid wall of rock." He craned his neck, peering out.

"It's a mesa. The station's built into it." A few more inches brought us up to the keypad fixed into a square column of granite on the side of the drive. I punched in my license number and waited impatiently as the middle door fought the buffeting wind.

The storm's fury rocked the Mustang, pulling it up a few inches before letting it go, its suspension absorbing the rocking blow. Its struts laughed the storm off, but another few miles and it would have been a different story. Behind me, Malone was beginning to moan loudly, the smell of sick beginning to leak out of his sweat. Something in him was broken, and if he was lucky, the medics on call could do something for him. If not, I'd be making a phone call to Sarah about what to do with his body. Internal injuries sometimes hid for a while, even though he'd come back relatively okay. But it was better to be safe than sorry. He was getting feverish, and even as he protested about being fine, those mewlings were getting weaker and weaker with each mile.

The interior of the parking bay went deep into the mesa, running nearly the full length of the station. The buff-hued rock appeared to be a neutral wash from far away, but up close, especially under the parking bay's floodlights, its striations were vivid slashes of plum, tangerine, and lemon cutting through thicker layers of silver-flecked suede. Mechanic bays were carved out of the space on the right of the rolling doors and polished off with steel plating, their car lifts lowered and locked down. A pair of frosted-glass sliding panels were to the left, leading to the main part of the station, with its well-stocked medic bay and common rooms set aside for overnight personnel. As a Stalker, I had a right to one of those beds, and unless they were hosting a busload of weeping orphans, it's where I planned on parking myself and Ryder until the storm passed.

Malone was going to be passed over like a cold burrito, and after that, he wasn't my problem anymore.

"They built the station into the…." Ryder trailed off, his green eyes lit with curiosity. "I didn't know humans did that."

"They've been doing it for a long time. Remind me to take you over to Mesa Verde sometime." Pulling into the station was a relief, if only to be out of the storm. The parking area was mostly empty except for patrol vehicles. From the look of things, there didn't appear to be any other Stalkers on-site, but that didn't mean the station was empty. I drove the Mustang in, its engine's deep growl reverberating off the walls, parked as close to the entrance doors as I could, then cut the engine. "Malone, medics here are good. They'll patch you up, and after that, you're on your own."

"I'm fine." His protest was as watery as the storm outside, although with the steel door closing behind us, the downpour dulled to a whimper. "I can help you out with whatever run you're on. Let me fix things between us. I mean I—"

"Not going to happen, Malone. Only reason I didn't leave you to the jackalopes was because of your aunt Sarah." I undid my seat belt, then turned to Ryder. "Look, I want you to tone down as much of the lordling thing as you can. Most of the people out here in the desert aren't exactly on good terms with humans, much less any elfin. There could be some of those sand rats squatting here to ride out the storm. If someone gives you shit, keep your mouth shut, and come grab me if they start to look all stabby with a knife."

"Sounds like every bar I've ever gone into with you," Ryder muttered as the double doors slid open and a brawny Hispanic man in a telltale Border Patrol tan uniform swaggered out, his thumbs hooked into the black gun belt hanging at his hips. "Is this one of the people I should keep my mouth shut around?"

"I'd say yes, but knowing Isaac like I do, he'll just get you drunk to get you talking." I got out, then held my hand out to the chief, grinning at the gold star pinned to his broad chest. "Can't believe they let you keep that thing. I thought for sure you were going to get kicked to the curb as soon as they found someone with half a brain."

The bear hug he pulled me into crushed all of the air out of my chest, and I choked a bit on my tongue, catching an edge of it in my throat. I think I heard one of my ribs crack, and I definitely felt my boots leave the poured-concrete floor for a second before Isaac Hernandez set me back down with a hard thump. Whatever footing I'd gotten from having my feet on the floor was lost when he slapped a massive hand across my shoulder, sending me staggering back an inch or two.

"Good to see you, Gracen." He frowned, peering over my shoulder. "And that looks like… you've got an elfin apprentice now? Wow. Thought you'd be the only one SoCalGov would be stupid enough to let wear a badge."

"Long story, but first, I need to get someone to the medics." I pulled the driver's seat forward, folding it over to get at Malone. "I'll pony up the costs to slap a couple of Band-Aids on him. Took a header over a guardrail going about thirty or so on a motorbike."

"While being chased by an ainmhi dubh," Ryder interjected, giving Isaac one of his winning smiles. "Hello. Since Kai seems to have left his manners back in San Diego, I am Ryder, Clan Sebac, Third in the House of Devon, High Lord of the Southern Rise Court. Our injured companion is Crickets Malone in the back seat."

"He is *not* our companion. And his name isn't Crickets. You don't just get to make up your own nickname," I muttered, crouching over to see if Malone was awake. He blinked at me furiously, rubbing at his eyes. "Can you make it out or do you need me to help you?"

"I'm fine," he grumbled back, his frizz of hair sticking up in all directions around his gaunt, freckled face. "I just…."

He'd gotten one leg out when the rest of him slid onto the floor in a rattle of bones and cries.

I caught Malone before he tumbled down, his elbows and knees locking into knots while he tried to right himself. He smelled of fear-infused sweat and too many days away from a good bath. I'd smelled worse off of other things and people. Hell, I'd probably smelled worse myself, but on Malone, it seemed as wrong as the ainmhi dubh I'd killed back by the automat. Up close, he was even frailer and younger-looking, barely old enough to have earned the sparse hairs prickling his chin, and his freckles stood out against his pale cheeks, his skin drawn taut over his sharp features.

"I can walk just…," he slurred, pupils blown out to dark round dots, eating away the color of his eyes. "Just give me a minute."

"Yeah, I don't have time for you to get your sea legs under you, Bugs." Batting away his flailing hands, I scooped Malone up off the floor. He weighed nothing. I'd carried heavier bags of rice, but Malone insisted on helping, his legs scissoring about. "Stay still or I'm going to have Ryder knock you out. Can you get the door for me, Hernandez? He isn't much, but it's like holding a drunk *wana*."

"What should I do about the car?" Ryder called out when I fell in step behind Hernandez. "Should I lock it up?"

"Just close the doors, Lord of… whatever it is you're in charge of," Hernandez drawled. "No one in their right mind would steal from Gracen here. Not unless they want to spend the rest of their days running for their lives."

EVEN WITHOUT the storm, it was always hard to tell what time it was deep inside of the station. Where the perimeter rooms ran heavy with thick panes overlooking the slopes and road, the station's inner hall walls were solid rock, duct work and pipes run through dugout trenches and fastened to the stone with metal anchors. The station's many rooms and cubbies were finished off with drywall and frosted-glass doors, metal department signs fixed to the right of the entrances to help anyone lost in the rocky maze, but after we dumped Malone off with the medics in an already-busy infirmary, Hernandez edged Ryder and me toward the cafeteria instead of down to the sleeping docks.

"How about if we sit down and get some coffee while I get Bradley to shuffle some people around to give you a space to crash? We're pretty full up, but there's a couple of open rooms. Most of the sand rats we've got are in the common space." Hernandez waved Ryder to the right, herding him along the way. "Flooding's pretty bad in the lower valley, so we pulled up everyone who'd come, and most of them brought their dogs and some livestock with them. It's like a damned ark down there. Woke up this morning to help break up a camel fight. This is a crazy job. No one at the Academy ever told me I'd be working in a damned looney bin."

"Better in here than out there," I said, falling into step next to him. "Coffee's not a bad idea. Neither's food if you can spare some."

"Mostly beans, rice, and tortillas. Went for staples and canned goods once the radar went red with rain. Didn't have a lot of time to stock up, but if you're lucky, I can probably scrape up some cheese." He gave Ryder a quick glance. "His kind eats that kind of stuff, right?"

"His kind is my kind, Hernandez. Have you known me to turn away food?" I reminded him, smirking when Ryder broke into a wide grin. "Don't get any ideas there, lordling. Just pointing out the obvious."

"Sends a thrill of delight through my heart to hear it," Ryder commented behind me. "And yes, Chief Hernandez, all of that sounds lovely. Traveling with Kai usually means lots of noodles floating in hot water flavored with salt packets. Or dried meats of dubious origin."

"He's still traumatized by the cuttlefish," I muttered at Hernandez. "I mean shit, feed the guy a handful of suckers on a stick once and he complains about it for the rest of his life."

"Well, good to know there's something we've got in common with the elfin," Hernandez spat back. "Feed me anything with suckers and I'd hold it against you too. Here we go. And don't pay any mind to the staring. Most of these people haven't seen any Sidhe up close before, so chances are, you're going to catch everyone's attention."

"Even Kai?" Ryder picked up his pace, leaving off his study of the station's architecture.

"Hell, especially Gracen. Far as most of them are concerned, he's like Dracula and the boogey monster rolled up into one. They know he's on their side, but now that Dempsey's gone, he's off his leash and they don't know what he's going to do." Hernandez stopped in front of a pair of double doors much like the ones in the staff parking area. My hackles were ruffled from his words, but I knew the truth when it was shoved up against my teeth. "You know how some people are, Gracen. No matter how often you pull them out of the hole they've dug for themselves, they're still going to fear your shadow falling across theirs."

He wasn't wrong. Or at least not about all eyes being on us when the doors slid open to let us into the cafeteria. The room was larger than the parking level, set up with round tables and folding chairs to absorb the station's increased population, and while not packed, it was still busier than I'd ever seen it, filled with everything from sunbaked families to grimy old loner sand rats huddled over metal plates of food. A long counter on the long side of the room was lined with chafing dishes heaped with beans, seasoned rice, and warmed-up canned mixed vegetables. Clusters of hot sauce, shoyu, and chili-pepper water sat on each table, their squat bottles surrounding tall plastic tumblers stuffed with utensils and folded napkins.

The cafeteria smelled of cheap, stomach-filling food and human sweat, and once the doors were fully open, any chatter and clanking metal stopped, leaving behind a stillness so weighted I could hear the old woman sitting nearest the entrance breathing through her flared nostrils.

"Coffee's not much, but it's hot and strong." Hernandez's rolling, deep voice boomed through the quiet, startling a few people enough they jerked in their seats. "Let's grab one of the staff tables and I'll get someone in the kitchen to bring us some plates."

I was used to being stared at. Every time I rolled into a station, there were always one or two people who found themselves either on the wrong side of the law or in desperate need of help, so I ignored the whispering that kicked up in our wake. Ryder, however, stiffened up and stood there, not hearing me when I muttered his name under my breath.

"Don't stare back. You'll make them uncomfortable." Tugging on his shirt, I got his attention with a sharp jerk. "Told you this would happen. Just let them get used to you being here. Get some food in you and we'll crash here for the night. No sense going back out into the storm. If the road's flooding out, we'll be found in a ditch somewhere under a pile of rocks. If we're lucky."

"They're... scared of us," he whispered back. "Or at least the adults are."

"Yeah, well, wars and shit kind of make that happen. Give the kids a few minutes. They'll come wandering by." I jerked my chin toward an empty table in a blue-walled niche. "Just sit on the outside. You're pretty. They'll come. Probably want to stroke your hair. It's all gold and sparkly. Kids like sparkly."

"You're a pain in the ass, you know that?" Ryder walked toward the table. His jeans were too new, too perfect-looking despite the muddy ground we'd rolled around in during the black dog's attack, but I watched him stride off and caught a woman eyeing his ass as he went by. Sniffing, he said, "I have candy in my pockets. If any come near me, I'll bribe them."

"Yeah, that's going to go over well," I snorted. "Big pointy-eared cat bastard luring kiddies in with candy. Their parents are going to *love* you."

"Works with you," he shot back, settling down on the chair closest to the cafeteria buffet.

I eased around him, taking the seat facing the door. The nook in the wall brought us out of eyeshot of most of the people in the area, but enough could see us to make my skin itch. The glances were quick, flashing over me and lingering on Ryder. I recognized a few, mostly the older ones with folds of dry skin crisscrossed with deep wrinkles hanging off their skinny faces. Beards were longer and grayer than I remembered, but the suspicious glares were the same.

"Ah, just like coming home." Sighing contentedly, I leaned back in the hard metal chair. "Give it five minutes and someone will come by to spit on us. Bonus points if it's one of the kids."

"They're not that bad," Hernandez chided, coming around the corner. Setting down the steaming coffee mugs he'd carried over, he grimaced. "Crap, there's something I forgot to tell you."

"Let me guess," I drawled, hooking my arm over the back of my chair, slouching toward Ryder. "Jerem Samms is here."

"Shit." His grimace deepened, etching long brackets on either side of his thin mouth. "How'd you know? Grapevine whisper into your ear?"

"Nope," I replied, nodding toward the cafeteria door filled with a broad-shouldered man with his long brown hair pulled back from his craggy face. "The son of a bitch just walked in."

Nine

IT'D BEEN a hell of a long time since I'd last seen Jerem Samms. He recognized me, dusky sloe eyes widening when he spotted me sitting next to Hernandez, and a quirk of a cocky smile dug into his left cheek, pulling up a familiar dimple. The swagger was still there too, his shoulders rolling slightly in time with the long strides he took. Armed with a sawed-off shotgun tucked into a back holster, he was given a bit of room by an old man scuttling out of the door, the wild-haired hermit shuffling quickly out of Samms's reach.

Dressed in pretty much standard Stalker gear—jeans, boots, and a heavy leather jacket—Samms wore his passing years well. There was more silver than brown in his hair now. I could see it more clearly as he got closer, and a few flecks glistened in the several-days-old beard on his more weathered face. He'd lost the cowboy hat at some point, or maybe he'd left it in his ride, its dragon-scale-studded band something he'd been very proud of, having come away from a sand lizard fight with a handful of silver dots and a thin scar running down to the right of his eye and over his cheek, a souvenir from one of the dragon's dew claws.

Samms was definitely more seasoned, experience adding to his confidence, and the slight imperfections of his face, like the white scar line on his cheek and his twice-or-more-struck Roman nose, only added to the man's allure. He drew the eye in a different way than Ryder, but unlike the lordling sitting next to me, Samms liked the attention he drew, even tinted with caution and nervousness. The man I'd known enjoyed living on the edge, and he carried that razor sharpness with him, promising trouble even before he opened his mouth to speak.

"Damn, you have not aged one bit, have you, Gracen." Samms smelled of the desert, leather, and gun oil, as familiar to me as the bite of electricity in the air from a coming storm. There were crow's-feet at the edges of his dark eyes, but his gaze was still sharp, slicing over to rest on Ryder for a brief moment, then over to Hernandez when Samms gave the man a quick nod. "Didn't get the ping on my link that another Stalker was in, Chief."

"Must have forgotten to send it, considering they were hauling in someone from a black dog attack." Hernandez slowly stood up, snagging his coffee from the table. "Didn't seem as important as getting the kid to the medics, but I'll make sure that's taken care of right now. Gracen, stop by the duty desk to get the key to your bunk. And good to meet you, sir. The food here is probably more plain than you're used to, but it will stick to your ribs. Just avoid the lettuce. Not too sure where they get it from, but it always gives me a stomachache."

Samms didn't step aside for Hernandez, forcing the border officer to brush past him to get out. It was the kind of dick thing he'd do to people in a pub and something I'd have thought he'd outgrow at some point, but I guess I was wrong. He waited until Hernandez walked out of the cafeteria before sliding into his abandoned chair, giving me another slow smile and leaning on the table with his elbows.

"Taking on apprentices now, Gracen? Decided you got sick of humans and got one of your own?" The edge on his voice felt easy, as if I'd been the one who'd put distance between us. Or maybe I had, but I had quite a few damned good reasons for it. Samms held out his hand to Ryder, his arm stretched in front of me. "Stalker Jerem Samms. Who are you?"

"Ryder." The lordling took Samms's hand firmly. I waited for the litany of titles and bloodlines the Sidhe habitually used to introduce themselves, but it didn't come. Instead, Ryder said, "And I'm not Kai's apprentice. I'm…." He flicked a glance toward me, measuring his words. "His friend."

"Friend?" Samms snorted, releasing Ryder's hand. "Gracen doesn't have friends. He has ex-lovers, soon-to-be ex-lovers, and the four or five people he trusts to have a gun behind him. But none of them are friends."

"Then I am sorry you do not truly know Kai, because he has many friends," Ryder replied smoothly, the expression on his face as diplomatically placid as I'd ever seen it, but his smile was carved straight out of his grandmother's haughty arsenal. "And I am glad to be counted among them."

I was caught between them, both smooth liars when they wanted to be, and I never thought I'd be in a position where an elfin sitting at the table was the more trustworthy, but the man to the right of me was definitely the one I'd prefer to have behind me holding a gun. I might question his aim but never his intent. I couldn't say the same for Samms. Sure as hell not after what he tried to do to me.

"How long has it been since we sat down together, Gracen?" Samms smiled at the harried young server who came by to refill our coffees, asking her to bring him a cup when she had time. He was charming, giving her his best charismatic façade, and she blushed and hurried away with a promise to come back. Waiting until she was out of earshot, he turned back to me. "Twenty years? Twenty-five?"

"About that." I did a quick mental accounting. "Seen you afterwards, of course, but didn't give enough of a shit to stop and talk."

"You always did hold a grudge." Chuckling, he took the coffee cup from the server as she passed by, thanking her with a flash of white teeth. "Gracen tell you about me, Ryder?"

"He's never even mentioned you," Ryder remarked softly, adding sugar to his refilled cup. "And we've had plenty of time to talk."

"We should check on Malone." I drained my coffee cup, swallowing the hot brew quickly. "Then get the room before they give it away to someone else. A Stalker's badge means shit if there's a cute, wide-eyed kid with a sob story for the guys sitting at the desk. Grab what food we can carry with us and leave the rest."

"You never said what you're doing up here," Samms said, reaching forward to touch my arm. His hand hovered, nearly brushing the back of mine before I pulled away. "Things so calm down in SoCal you've come into Nevada to do some hunting?"

It wouldn't do any harm to tell him, and considering I was in his backyard, Samms would be a good source for info. He liked to share, sometimes too much, and even though I couldn't trust him to have my back, he was always honest about being in it for himself. In a lot of ways, he was a hell of a lot more trustworthy than the Sebac.

"Not on a run. Dempsey died last week." I stopped, trying to count the days when the lump in my throat lodged itself in so tight I couldn't swallow without choking on my own spit. Samms looked like he was going to say something, but I stopped him with a shake of my head. "Old man's gone. Nothing more to talk about except heading up to New Vegas to give some of his ashes to his brother, Kenny. We were on our way when we stopped for some automat food and Sarah's nephew, Robbie, came up over the ridge with a black dog hot on his ass. He took some hits, so we pulled in here to get out of the storm and to dump him on the medics. Once it's clear, we'll be heading up, then back down."

"Ken Dempsey?" Samms frowned mockingly, pursing his lips. "Short dude. Potbelly. Looks like someone built your fake dad using the really shitty, saggy bits? That one?"

"Yeah, unless he's changed much." I stood up, hoping Ryder would catch the hint that we were leaving. The lordling was busy stacking paper dishes together, holding them tight enough to bend their lips, making sure there definitely wasn't any room for anything to leak out. "Haven't seen him in a while, but Dempsey kept up with him. Told me where to find him."

"Here's the thing, Gracen. Kenny Boy's on the run. There's a wet contract out on him by some of the fine people up in New Vegas with a couple of casinos and a bad temper." Samms leaned back in his chair, then ran his fingertips over his scruff, lifting his chin up to get a spot above his Adam's apple. "Picked up the specs a couple of days ago. Seems like your boy's making a run for it down to San Diego, so either he hasn't heard his big brother's checked out or he's coming to you to look for some saving. So if you know where he is or where he's headed, you'd best get there before I do, because the price on him is pretty damned high and they don't care if he's brought in with all of his pieces still attached."

MALONE WAS drugged up to the gills when we stopped by the medics' bay, and the desk officer barely looked up when he slid the keycard across the counter at us, motioning toward the hallway where the bunk rooms were located. Ryder was quiet throughout our walk, smiling at the people we passed, although he did murmur hello a few times to anyone staring at him long enough to notice.

Okay, so he talked a lot, just not to me. People stared, and he went about his business, making the Sidhe look like the bright, beautiful, and peaceful creatures the telenovelas sold them as. I knew different. I'd gotten drunk more than a few times with quite a number of them now, and they were as gassy as hell after a few beers and mouthfuls of cheesy burrito. Not to mention, Ryder snored sometimes. Especially after a long day of travel or fighting off something trying to eat us.

The room was miniscule, barely large enough to hold a cot and a duffel. Still, it smelled clean and the linens were recently washed, no sign of someone else having slept on them. Like the cafeteria, the walls were drywall and insulation screwed into steel girders and runners bolted directly into the surrounding rock. Ducts kept the air circulated but a bit chilly, enough for Dempsey to complain about the cold getting into his joints whenever we stayed there.

I'd slept on the floor the last time we came through, using the sleeping bags from Dempsey's truck as a bed. He'd gotten up in the middle of the night, a drunken stumble to the shared bathrooms at the end of the sleeping hall, kicking me in the ribs, then falling over my feet. It was one of the last runs we made up to New Vegas, a long-ago memory of a time when his knees were getting worse, and as much as he wanted to ignore the pain, his body couldn't carry him any longer through rough road and hard kills.

"You take the bunk." I nodded to the cot fixed to the floor. "I'm going to crash in the Mustang. It'll be more comfortable. Eat some food and then crash. I need you to lock the door behind me, though, and hold on to the key. Don't let anyone but me in. This isn't the safest place to be an elfin, and I don't want to have to explain to Alexa about why I'm returning you without a nose or toes."

I couldn't sleep there. In that room. Even Ryder's presence couldn't wash away the filthy debris of my memories flooding through my mind. I dug the card out of my pocket with every intention to hand it over, when he sat down on the cot and studied me with those soul-piercing green eyes, digging into me and ferreting out my discomfort.

"Can I tell you something?" Ryder's whisper dripped with concern, and he leaned back, resting his shoulders against the wall. "Well, more to talk to you. About... this is hard for me. Probably not as hard for you because I feel like this place holds ghosts for you and that's why you're running away from me."

"Truth?" I sat down next to him, echoing his pose against the white-painted wall. I picked a fried potato off of one of the plates, but I wasn't very hungry. I nibbled at its edge, then chewed it down quickly, swallowing at the tasteless ash it left on my tongue. "Not really running away from you, just... I can't be here right now. Too soon. Too raw. Dempsey's the first one... I've lost others before. Hell, Stalkers don't live long lives. Remember me telling you that? He died in his sleep, which is a good death for one of us. It's just... hard to be here without him. We made a lot of runs down this corridor."

I opened, then dug through the duffel I'd slung onto the cot, coming up with a small silver flask of whiskey. I'd bought the bottle because it shared the same name as the magic type Cari practiced, mostly for a chuckle, but it turned out to be surprisingly good, becoming one of my favorites. After undoing the cap, I laid it down, then took a swig and passed the flask over to Ryder.

"Am I just supposed to take a gulp?" He took it with a bit of trepidation. "Sometimes I think you give me stuff brewed in someone's sock just to see me choke on it."

"Sip on this one and don't waste any," I warned. "And whatever you do, never wipe at the rim. Especially in front of someone who's just given you a nip. It's an insult."

"I'd never do that to you. Sometimes this is the only way I can get a kiss from you, sharing something we drink together." He grinned foolishly at my scoffing snort. His sip was small, but a flush soon warmed his cheeks. "Oh, that's good. I've had this before."

"That you have," I reassured him, taking the flask back after he had another drag. "I'll be more comfortable in the Mustang. Seats are better than the floor, but I'm serious about locking the door behind me. There's a lot of dangerous people holed up in tight on top of one another. I don't want any of them coming to look for you for a bit of fun."

Again he regarded me, tearing me apart bit by bit. I was lulled by the whiskey, but there were landmines set between us, and I wasn't sure what he was going to step on. Sleep tugged at me, seeping through my marrow, and suddenly sleeping in the cold garage, slung into the passenger seat of my Mustang didn't seem like such a good idea.

"Who was that Stalker to you?" he finally asked. "A hunting companion? A brother? It seems like you knew each other well but it ended badly."

"Badly isn't a strong enough word for how it ended." Exhaling hard, I debated what to tell Ryder… or rather how much. "Samms and I were lovers for about four years. Nothing formal like a house with a picket fence but more than casual. Why?"

"That's what I thought. You see, today as we sat in the cafeteria, I realized I've never actually seen you… outside of who I had built you up as in my mind." He inched closer, our shoulders touching, and the warmth of his body against mine was as tongue-numbing as the whiskey in my belly. "Today, I think I got my first glimpse of you as other people see you."

"I'm not any different around people." I shrugged. "I am who I am. I don't pretend to be more."

"No, that's… I've always thought of you as very young." He shook his head at my quick glance at him. "To me, you're barely into adulthood. And everyone around you, from Dempsey to Jonas and even Cari, knows you as a son or a brother or something like that. It's shaped my idea of you. In a Sidhe household, you would still be living at home, continuing your studies and just learning to make connections with the adults around you. The idea of you having sex, having relationships with others when you were younger is… incredible to me."

"You thought I was a virgin, maybe?" The whiskey still burned my belly, but its heat was spreading. "Dude, that cookie crumbled back when I was with Tanic."

"That doesn't count," he retorted. "You didn't have a choice—"

"People keep saying that, but the truth of it is, it happens. Happened. Doesn't change if you want it or not. Your body's not the same. Doesn't mean that asshole or whoever did it to you owns you, and you don't have to like it, but nothing's the same," I refuted softly. "Duffy just taught me how to like it and it didn't have to hurt. I own myself and took back a bit of what Tanic carved out of me, but I'm not going to shove it all under some rock and pretend it didn't happen."

"Okay, I can understand that," he conceded. "I wish it weren't true."

"If wishes were bottles of rum, Pele would be drunk all the time," I tossed back. "But yeah, I've had sex, Ryder. Lots of it. Mostly with people who I didn't see again. Other times, with people I saw a lot. I've killed more people than I've ever wanted to, and chances are, I'll kill some more. I've lost count of how many black dogs I've brought in, but I've kept count of the dragons I've brought down. I'm a Stalker, lordling. I've been one for almost thirty-five years now—first as an apprentice, then as a full-fledged, badge-carrying bounty hunter. I might be young for an elfin, but for a human, I've got a lot under my belt."

"That's what I realized today. That's what I'm telling you." The flask made another trip across the cot, coming back to me only slightly lighter. "Today I saw a side of you I forget exists. You talk about dangerous people being out there, but I'm probably with the most dangerous person in this station right now. I watched Samms give you a wide berth, and for all his posturing and jabbing at you, he kept his distance. Hernandez treated you with a respect earned by actions, not just because of your status as a Stalker. And Malone, he worships you. Even as you threaten to kill him, he hangs on your every word.

"I saw you today. Really saw you as others see you. As the humans see you." His voice took on a huskiness I wasn't sure I could ignore. It rolled over me, rubbing against me like velvet. "You've endured things I can't even imagine and then shaped a place for yourself in a society that hates our kind. I've known that. But it was knowledge I didn't truly understand until today."

"Does it change how you think about me?" My whisper was soft, forced out around the now-growing lump in my throat. It was already there from Dempsey and from my struggles with the others. I didn't think about how taking Ryder on this run would introduce him to what I was. I thought he already knew I was trash—something dark and fanged the humans kept in the shadows to hunt their monsters and make the world safer for their own sake. Something in me was threatening to break, and I wasn't even aware I had anything left inside of me that was still whole. "Because I've got to tell you, driving you back—"

"It doesn't change how I think about you. Not that way." His hand found mine, squeezing my fingers. The rough Army-issue wool blanket we sat on scratched at my palm, but I didn't mind. "It's changed me. Made me realize you've done so many things, been so many things to so many people. You warn me about things, and I don't—and I know this—don't take you seriously enough sometimes. I trust you. I trust your judgment. I need to remember that you might be young in my world, but in yours, you've lived through—survived—so much and thrived. I have to respect that. If anything, I think I cherish you more, finally understanding this."

"And it took meeting one of my ex-lovers to realize this?" I tipped the flask back again, taking a final sip before pulling my hand out of Ryder's grasp so I could fasten its cap back on. "Hell, remind me to dig up a few more. Maybe that'll help you learn how to aim better when I tell you to shoot something."

"If they are all like Samms, then I will question my sanity in wanting to be with you," Ryder said, making a face. "What did you see in him?"

"Someone like me. Someone who hunted. A guy who didn't fit into the world as much as I didn't. Being a Stalker keeps you on the fringes. Not like I'm going to live in a split-level ranch and come home every day to pick the kids up from school." I chuckled, trying to imagine myself driving a wood-paneled station wagon. "It was good until it wasn't. And that was okay."

"Well, if you're going to shoot someone, make it him and not Malone." Ryder nudged me with his shoulder. "I wouldn't mind using him as target practice. What drove you apart? The distance, or did he cheat on you?"

"Can't cheat on someone if you're not actually with them on a permanent basis," I pointed out. "But no, bastard tried to cut off my ears so… on that note, I'm going to go crash in the Mustang. Because right now, you might trust me more, lordling, but I just don't trust myself."

Ten

"ODIN'S TEATS, it's freaking cold out here." My breath turned the windshield into a frosted pane, but the tiny cell heater I'd stashed in the driver's-side space finally kicked in, letting out a whisper of warmth. It wasn't much, but it was safe to run inside of a closed vehicle. I was counting on the sleeping bags and the survival blankets I'd liberated from the station's stores to keep me from losing any toes. "Okay. Warmer now. Or frostbite's just kicking in."

It probably was a mistake sleeping out in the Mustang, but I felt raw inside and needed a little bit of distance from Ryder, if only to keep my brain from spinning into places I didn't need to be.

Sleep wasn't coming easily. The parking shelter's lights were dimmed, doused down to a dark blue wash over the pale stone with runner LEDs along the ground, leading to the frosted doors. One of the best upgrades I'd done to Oketsu was installing smart shield glass in its windshields and windows. I'd dialed it over to black frost, deepening the shadows of the interior, but even the dousing of the lights down to pinpricks didn't help. I was restless, my skin too tight and my head too busy with fleeting, buzzing thoughts.

There was also something inside of the damned car with me.

It was something small. That much I was sure of. It scrambled about in the back seat, giving off a tiny squeak when it hit something solid. I wasn't going to turn on the light, but damned if I was going to try to sleep in the Mustang while something was tap-dancing across the back seat. Opening the passenger-side door, I switched the overhead light on to low, guessing whatever'd gotten in would be startled by the light.

I was right.

Sitting on the stock of my sawed-off shotgun was a small trembling horned jerboa, its fluorescent rainbow mane glittering and mantling over its head and down its back. The puff at the end of its tail was nearly round, warning me off in a fierce display of courage, or as much fearlessness as a three-inch furball could muster up. Standing up on its kangaroo-like back legs, it extended its height to its fullest, weaving its head back and forth so its tiny stubby horns glistened in the Mustang's soft interior light. Chirruping, it squeaked a battle cry, baring its short front teeth at me, but I could see it glancing at the open door, its tiny brain calculating if it could make its escape before I could grab it.

There were over one hundred and twenty types of jerboa in the desert and mountains between California and its surrounding states. None were venomous, and all were driven by two things—sex and hunger. Placid to a fault, most jerboa only mantled when threatened, although I'd seen one launch itself at a hawk hunting her young, piercing its skull with her sharp teeth as it swooped down close enough to grab one. This one was cute but not something I wanted pooping all night in the back of my car.

"Hold on," I told it, unraveling myself from my covers and biting down a hiss when the cold air grabbed me. "Let me get you something nice."

Dragging a dried pineapple slice from the bag Ryder got from the automat was easy enough, especially since he'd left it tucked in one of the cupholders in the aftermarket middle console I'd put in. Either the rattling of the bag or the scent of the fruit caught the jerboa's interest, because its tail deflated a bit and it stretched toward me again, sniffing at the air.

Waving the ring in front of its twitching black nose, I made sure I had its full attention, then tossed it out of the open passenger door, grinning when the jerboa took off after it like it'd been shot out of a cannon. The pineapple possibly grazed the floor, but I doubted it. The desert rat snatched it up in a move that would have any raptor envious, ducking back under the Mustang to scuttle off with its prize and then darting beneath one of the station's heavily armored trucks.

Watching the jerboa speed hop across the parking floor must have been guidance from Pele, because I caught the station doors sliding open, illuminating a long rectangle in Oketsu's darkened glass. I'd parked nose in, so reaching for the shotgun probably would be hard, but after closing the passenger door just enough to turn off the interior light, I gave it my best effort. I'd mounted the holster to make it easy for me to reach while driving, and I was pleasantly surprised to feel it draw out smoothly, its shortened barrel clearing the gap between the seats without a hitch.

Even behind the shadowed glass, I could make out the silhouette of a man walking deliberately toward the Mustang, striding as close to the columns as he could to give himself some cover. Too broad for Ryder. And too short. He also moved human—more of a stomp than an elfin glide—and there was no reason for any human I knew in the station to be heading toward my car.

Especially since only Ryder knew I'd come out here.

While there were cameras, a quick flash of credits and a favor or two could turn them off. Hernandez wasn't manning the desk, and he was the only one on staff I'd trust not to take a bribe. I was going to assume whoever was darting from shadow to shadow meant either me or the Mustang harm. Either way, he wasn't going to like what he found.

A flash of light on steel and a crouch near my passenger back tire was all I needed to know, and I came up out of the partially open door, shotgun barking off a warning blast over the guy's shoulders. The heat of the blast coiled over him, and he fell back, knife clenched tight in his hand and his face set into a wary stubbornness I remembered so very well, despite the years we'd spent apart.

"Hello, Jerem." Stepping carefully all the way out of the car, I kept my aim steadied on his chest and shoulders. "Didn't think I could lose any more respect for you, but screwing with a man's car, that's low. Even for you."

To his credit, he dropped the knife.

The storm raged outside, battering at the bay doors, bringing a roll of thunder into the bay from the rattling steel. As chilled as I was, the cold on my skin was nothing compared to the chunk of ice in my belly. Samms had fallen a lot further in my mind, willing to strand me at the station for reasons I couldn't imagine.

But I intended to find out.

"Slashing tires?" I asked, taking a step forward to kick the knife out of his reach. "Were you going to stop there or try for the brake lines?"

"Mind if I stand up?" He gestured elegantly with a callused hand, trying a sweet smile on to soften my stance. "Concrete's cold as hell."

"Mind if I blow a hole through you?" I drawled, moving back against the car, bumping the door shut with my hip. "Floor's a good place for you right now, especially for a snake like you."

"Just one tire. Maybe two. Enough to slow you down. That's all," Samms said, shifting forward to fold his legs under him. "I would never do anything to harm you."

"You tried to cut off my ears," I reminded him.

"They would have grown back."

Snorting, I countered, "You don't know that."

"Your thumb did," he replied, nodding toward my left hand. "You probably would have grown two good ears. Would have gotten rid of that notch you've got in that one."

I considered his reasoning for about half a second, enough time to spit in his eye if I'd wanted to. It was still flawed, especially considering I'd have been earless for who knew how long, and that was if they grew back. There was a good chance they would have, but the notch was permanent, a clipped-out piece Tanic took great delight in snipping out, then rubbing iron dust into the edges every day until the flesh refused to fuse back together.

It was my punishment for catching and eating one of the salamanders he'd been using as an experiment. I had no regrets then. Just as I had none now for keeping Samms sitting on his butt on the cold cement floor.

"Don't think so." I resisted the temptation to rub at the triangular notch, a habit Dempsey tried very hard to break me of, but it never really took. "How big is this contract on Kenny that you're willing to screw with my car to get to him before I can find him? Because that's what this is about, right?"

"Truthfully?" He shifted, the cold probably eating away at any heat in his legs.

"Samms, you lie so much you actually change the meaning of the words coming out of your mouth whenever you use them," I retorted. "You probably think you're sitting on the sky right now."

His mouth twisted into a grimace. "Okay, I probably deserved that."

"You deserve getting shot for what you were going to do to my car." It was a time-honored punishment for poachers, rustlers, and anyone stranding someone in the no-man's-lands between cities. The West was wilder than it'd ever been, but its vigilante laws seemed to hold up. Even standing in a border station with more than two dozen officers nearby, I could have blown a hole through Samms's head and his death would have been written off as justified. "I report this and your license will get stripped. You know that. The contract on Kenny so high you're willing to risk that?"

"You tell me," Samms said through chattering teeth. He named a number so high it stole the breath from my lungs. Chuckling at my shock, he rubbed his hands together, blowing on them to get warm. "Yeah, that's what I said too. And I'll trade you a piece of information for not reporting this. Something bigger than what they're offering for Kenny. Something that will really make your head spin. Just let me get off this damned floor. I can't feel my toes anymore."

"Info first." I gestured with the shotgun in case he'd forgotten about it. "I still haven't decided whether or not I'm going to let you walk out of here without an extra hole in your head."

He stared up at me, a mournful expression on his face. "You're a lot harder than you used to be."

"Yeah, well, considering you're one of the people who made me that way," I said with a shrug, "I suppose you can't complain. Talk. What do you have to trade for your license?"

I didn't have any intention of blacklisting his license. Catching him in the act was good enough, but I'd drop a word into Hernandez's ear, just in case the cameras had been turned off with a bit of slick passing over someone's hand. Either way, he'd be holed up tight into a pocket he couldn't get out of, and Hernandez would know to watch out for Samms in the future.

"You already told me there's a contract on Kenny and he's run down to San Diego. What else you've got?" I prompted him. "And it better be big."

"Thing about you, Gracen, is that sure, you're a damned good Stalker. Better than Dempsey even, but you always walk on the right side of the line. You'd be a hell of a lot more well-off if you dipped into the shadow market once in a while. Since you don't, a lot of Stalkers feel like you think you're too good for everyone else. That pisses people off," Samms started, getting up on his knees but keeping his hands where I could see them. "Kenny's contract is to bring him in, but not to any casino. It's a private debt. Sealed but on the books. But there's another one out there. Bigger money, and a lot of people perked up when it dropped a week ago. Made a few people sit up straight and begin to wonder how damned good you really are."

"What the hell are you talking about, Samms?" It was getting a bit too chilly for me, but I needed him to finish talking. "There's another contract on Kenny? What the hell's he done that's so shitty people are putting call outs on him?"

"See, your brain. It goes to all the good places and none of the dark." Samms was uncomfortable. "It's a shadow market. Open to any and all with enough guts to do the job."

He fidgeted and squirmed, but the cold wasn't as strong as his need to draw things out, to stroke his own ego and force me to wait. Typical Samms. It hadn't bothered me when I was younger, but a few decades under my belt and I just wanted to crawl back under the blankets and get warm. Maybe even get some sleep. Or it could have been I'd finally taken on some of Dempsey's more impatient, antisocial traits. Either way, my patience with him was at an end.

I knew about the shadow-market contracts. I even knew how to find them, but I'd not only inherited Dempsey's distaste for mollusks, I also had his healthy dislike for under-the-table bounties. *I'd* been the last shadow-market contract he'd entertained, and I hadn't even known he'd done them until he lay dying in a hospital bed.

"Look, Samms. I know you love to hear the sound of your own voice, but could you hurry this up?" I let the shotgun drop, pointing the barrel at the ground. "Seriously, we're both freezing our asses off here, and you're not getting any younger. I mean, I could stand here all century and be okay, but you—"

"Screw you, Gracen." He placed his hands on the ground, using them to balance while getting up. Grunting, he slowly stretched out, his knees popping and crackling when he shook out his legs. "You used to be a hell of a lot nicer."

"Yeah, well you were prettier then, and I was stupider," I replied. "Just spit it out and we can all just go about our business, providing you mind your own and don't cross mine again. What about this contract? The second one?"

"It's not on Kenny, you idiot. It's on you." This time his smirk had no charm to it. Nearly serpentine and glittering, it curled up over his cheeks, bringing out that damned dimple of his. There was no doubt in my mind he was enjoying this. Samms always did like to play with his food, and right then, I was his prey, despite being the one holding the shotgun. "Someone put out a shadow-market bounty on you. A hell of a lot of coin. Quarter if you're not breathing, but it still would be a huge chunk of change. Got the boards buzzing because—"

"They've posted a hit on a Stalker." The thought boggled my mind. A lot of Stalkers lurked on the shadow-market boards to plump up lean times, but no matter how deep one fell into the dark side of things, no one would target someone with a badge. "Who the hell would target a Stalker?"

"Contractor's masked. They usually are, but the money's there. Released on delivery. Arrangements to be made once the bounty's been confirmed," he rattled off. "Board went nuts. Most Stalkers are calling for a ban on the contractor, but a few of the good ones are staying silent, either minding their own business or—"

"Thinking about adding to their bank account," I finished for him. "You know what this means, right? It's open season on any Stalker. Not just me. Hell, on anyone with a star. And you weren't going to say shit to me about this?"

"Actually, I was going to leave you a note on your windshield. Got the envelope in my pocket." Samms shrugged. "Right after I slashed your tires. I just want Kenny. Bringing you down would set me up for life, but let's face it, you hold a grudge, and despite everything, I kinda like you. Besides, if I take a shot and miss, you'd hunt me until my bones were worn down to nubs. No one in their right mind would come after you, but there's a lot of crazy people out there, Gracen. Someone's going to look at all of the zeros behind that first number and start thinking about where they could buy their own island. I'd tell you to get some people to watch your back, but you're not the kind of guy who actually has people around him long enough to do that."

"That's where you're wrong, Samms," Ryder said, stepping out from behind the column nearest the Mustang's front end. "Kai's got a lot of people who have his back, myself included. He's a member of my Court, a very important member, and he's got his family. So it wouldn't just be him you'd be running from if you tried to take a shot at him."

He held the Beretta I'd given him, properly squaring off and steadying his stance, centered on Samms's chest. I nearly brought up the shotgun, stopping the rise of its muzzle before it swung away from Samms. He'd come up silently enough for us not to notice, and I wasn't sure if I was more ashamed for not hearing him or proud as hell he'd pulled it off.

"You okay, Kai?" Ryder asked softly, not taking his eyes off Samms.

"Yeah, I'm fine. And you can lower the gun. He's already taken his best shot at Oketsu and got caught." I stepped away from the Mustang to give Samms some room. "So now I've got to watch my six for Stalkers?"

"I'd say no. Not anyone worth their salt. Everyone wearing a star's got the same idea as you. They might be jealous of you or wish they were better than you, but when it's all said and done, you're a Stalker. You'd come armed to the teeth if a call came out that one of them needed help," Samms replied, brushing his hands on his jeans. Tugging an envelope out of his pocket, he grunted when it finally came loose. "See? Note. Even if you wouldn't let me cut off your ears, I wouldn't have jacked you over like that. I was going to tell you. Because if we let someone hunt you, then we're letting anyone hunt any of us.

"Thing is, there's going to be people out there who are going to look at you like a pot of gold at the end of the rainbow, and some of them are people you might even call friends," he pointed out. "Everyone knows you, Jonas, and Sparky had a blowout at the Post. Money's tight for some people, and if things are broken between the people you hunt with, who's to say you aren't now just another black-dog pelt to them?"

"Get out," Ryder barked before I could respond. My stomach was someplace down around my knees, and any breath I had coming out of my lungs couldn't get past my closed throat. "Leave the knife and go."

The chipping away at the wall around me was constant, doubts and thoughts working like ivy through the cracks I'd made in my confidence, in my faith in the people I'd drawn near me. I wanted to shove everyone away, keep myself safe by distancing myself from anyone who could get ahold of me, but isolation had its own dangers. I'd seen that in Dempsey. He'd become an island of bitterness in a cold, hard desert, waiting for me to swing by with carcasses to peel skin off, all the while hammering at me to be better, to do better as a Stalker—anything to take his mind off of how far he'd let himself fall.

I didn't mind carrying him. He'd carried me far enough, but neither was I going to bend myself over to hoist his burdens. Trusting people—elfin or human—was a leap of faith I needed to take, especially if I'd ended up on someone's hit list.

And that trust was going to start with Ryder.

"Jerem, just go." I jerked my head toward the door. "If I get to Kenny before you, I'll let you know, but I'm taking him off the table. He's got something of mine, something Dempsey left him. If you get him before I do, I'll match the contract for him. Whatever it takes. We'll work it out."

"Deal," Samms said with a nod. He took a step toward the front of the car but then changed his mind, shifting directions to walk past me and go around the back. He didn't need to brush against my hand, but he did, sliding the envelope between my fingers before pulling away. "That's a copy of the posting. I wasn't going to screw you up, Kai. I might be an asshole but not that kind of asshole. It was just going to be one tire. Enough to slow you down but not take you out."

"Get. And keep your word about Kenny." I clutched the corner of the envelope, bending the paper between my pinched fingers. "I'll see you around."

Ryder and I both watched him leave. Then I walked over to pick the knife up off the floor. It was a good blade, heavy steel with a sharp edge. It would fit in several sheaths I had on me, and I liked its matte black steel, less likely to catch any light while on a nighttime run. Turning around, I found Ryder staring at me, a bemused look on his face. He was wearing sleep clothes, a pair of loose cotton pants and a T-shirt that looked gray under the garage lights. But their illumination was suspect, also turning the Mustang a dull dark shade of maroon. For all I knew, he was wearing something bright neon yellow and left everyone he'd passed by in the hall bleeding from their tortured eyes.

"What?" I teased. "Not like this is the first wet contract taken out on me. I got Dempsey out on the last one. And before I forget to tell you this, good job on coming up on us. Gun and everything. How'd you know he was out here?"

"I didn't." A sheepish look slipped over Ryder's features. "I... um... had to go to the bathroom and—"

"You went to the bathroom with a gun?" I arched an eyebrow, glancing at the Beretta in his hand.

"Seemed prudent. You kept going on about how dangerous it was for me to walk around. I thought having a gun on me was a good idea."

"And you came out here to check up on me?" I crossed my arms, rested them on the Mustang's roof, and leaned against the car, getting a kick out of Ryder's odd, sudden bashfulness.

"Well, more like I had to come find you," he muttered, an actual flush of pink creeping over his high cheekbones. "See, while I remembered the gun, I forgot my shoes and the keycard. So I'm not only locked out of the room, I also might have stepped in something while in the bathroom, and I've tracked it all over the station's hallways coming to get you."

Eleven

THE MUSTANG took the curves of the Post's steep hills with ease, rumbling in a deep throaty growl as if warning other predators away. While I was grateful for Cari's family letting me borrow the Nova, I was glad I had Oketsu back on the road. It'd been too long since I'd been cradled in his black leather seats, letting the wheels eat up the miles on a distant run. The trip back had been shorter than going up, but that always seemed to be the case. Finding out Kenny Dempsey had bolted toward San Diego cut the trip short, but it'd been a good one.

Except for one thing, and that was sitting in my back seat, complaining about how his rib cage hurt and about the bellyache he got from taking the antibiotics the station medics pushed on him.

"If there was anything that really convinced me I didn't want kids, it was this trip back down." Muttering at Ryder didn't help, because he barely glanced at me. "The twins don't cry this much, and they barely have teeth."

He probably was used to hearing people complain. More than likely it was the first bullet point on his Grand Poohbah job description. A Sidhe probably didn't even get their lordship title until they sat through at least six ten-day sessions of people whining about how their skin hurt or that they didn't get guacamole on their carne asada burrito. Either way, he seemed to be immune to every single one of Malone's whine fests.

"Bugs, can you maybe hold your breath for five minutes? If you can, Uncle Kai will give you a nice shiny silver coin." I gritted my teeth, ignoring Ryder's nearly imperceptible chuckle. "Don't laugh at me. It's still not too late to shoot him."

"You promised his aunt you would bring him to her at the Post," the lordling reminded me in a smug tone that made my hand itch to curl into a fist and punch his perfect nose. "It's only a minute or two more."

"Less if I gun it." Oketsu leaped forward when I pressed down on the gas, jerking everyone else back into their seats. "Sooner we dump Malone into Sarah's lap, the sooner I can get down to business."

At least Ryder took the acceleration easily. From the sounds of things, Malone might have tumbled around a bit, but at least he stopped talking. The switchbacks were tight, throwbacks to the days when engines were horses and the Merge pushed the hillside out and up, creating a towering mesa point. We came up onto the parking lot fast, hitting the last curve with a dip of the car's suspension to hug the angle in the road.

We'd made good time coming down from the border, stopping at the automat again to grab some food and a little bit of sleep. Scavengers—the human kind—had already made off with the black dog's corpse and the mangled motorbike, leaving behind only a greasy smear, a crimp in the guardrail, and the acid-etched pits in the ground where the monster's blood and spit scored the asphalt. Dawn was just a thin slice of orange along the edge of the mountains when we hit the county line.

The sun chased us into the city, edging up over Julian, and its rays stroked the length of the 8 as we approached the turnoff for the Presidio, an historic park whose buildings now served as the central hub for the SoCalGov's State Offices. Situated in a former museum-slash-chapel, the Post was where most Stalkers did their business, measuring black-dog pelts for bounties or turning in evidence of larger kills. It was also where a licensed Stalker could pick up a contract or arrange for payment.

It was where I was finally going to be able to dump Robbie Malone out of my car and into the questionably maternal arms of his aunt Sarah, one of the Post's directors.

The parking lot was mostly empty, with a few cars in the employee spaces at the edge of the drive. Circling up to the main lot, I spied Jonas's beat-up truck angled under a weeping pepper tree, and gave Ryder a dirty look. He returned my glare with one of his smug expressions, looking much like the entitled lordling I'd opened my door to months ago.

"I think I'm going to be sick," Malone groaned from the back seat.

"Swallow it," I growled. "You call him?"

"Yes." Ryder's chin lifted, his nose a long stretch of arrogance I could have easily wiped off his face with my knuckles. "Because… with what you're going to be dealing with, you should have your family around you. I'll take care of Malone. You go talk to your… uncle. Make things right, Kai."

Pulling into the space next to Jonas's truck, I let the Mustang idle, its engine purring softly. I couldn't hear Malone horking behind me, so he was safe for the moment, but there was always a chance he'd let loose something over my upholstery and carpet. Still, I weighed my options, torn between ripping into Ryder for making decisions for me and the rightness of what he did. I knew my faults. I was stubborn and prideful more often than not, choosing to shoot first and ask questions later. Suspicious and paranoid— those traits kept me alive, my senses on high alert for anything odd or out of place. Trust was something I was always reluctant to give, and I'd handed it over to Jonas before I ever learned humans were as wicked and cruel as any elfin. He'd been a constant in my life, a rock I could lean on when the raging waters battered against me, and to find out he'd been willing to pass me over a line for a handful of silver... *hurt.*

The pain was raw, abraded wounds from losing Dempsey roughened by the sharp scrape of rejections I hadn't known existed. Ryder was asking a lot of me, more than what I ever asked of myself. Betray me once and I walked away. Even taking Malone up to the station with us was an aberration. Although, as tempted as I was to leave his bruised and dinged body where we found him, it felt right to pour him into the Mustang.

I still regretted letting Ryder talk me into bringing him down with us, but I was a sucker for Ryder's green eyes and soft pleas. In a few years, I imagined our nieces would be able to wrap me around their little fingers and I'd be bringing home baby nightmares for them to use as ponies because they'd asked for one.

Sure, there was that tug between me and Ryder, the curling tickle of want and lust driven down into my guts by some genetic pull and, oddly enough, my growing fondness for him. I liked the way the sun hit his hair, picking out the metallic gold strands from the sunrise blond, and while he wasn't strikingly handsome compared to other Sidhe, he was still breathtaking. More because he was honest with me, something he'd learned along the way. He was willing to stop pushing at me and listen, hearing me when I explained why there needed to be a trade in dragon bones and other artifacts to keep food on people's plates. And he always pulled the trigger whenever I needed him, despite sometimes disagreeing with my methods and reasoning.

He trusted me. Fully and unconditionally.

It was about time I did the same for him.

"Okay. Grab the shotguns and any other weapons we've got up front. Post rules—no firearms." I put the Mustang into Park, then turned off the engine. Ryder said nothing, but I caught the wisp of a smile as he undid his seat belt. "And don't gloat or I'm going to jiggle Malone until he pukes all over you. It'll be like a fire hose of egg salad sandwiches and sweet tea."

"I didn't say a thing," Ryder murmured, stepping out of the car.

"You didn't have to," I shot back, reaching for my weapons from where I'd stashed them out of Malone's reach. "I can hear you breathing smugly."

I FOUND Jonas sitting in the open walkway at the top of the parking lot, a ways away from the Post's main doors. The wide cement walk curved and dipped through the Presidio's green spaces, a slatted wooden cover following its path, its posts scavenged from the old Gaslight district. The verdigris metal stands were wired for light. Perhaps they always had been, but I'd rarely seen them on. The Post wasn't someplace I hung out after dark, although I know quite a few of the old-timers spent evenings at the Stalkers' Wall, drinking heavily and telling stories about the dead.

It was ironic to find Jonas sitting on a bench at the fork in the walk, one branch leading down to the Post where Stalkers came and went, burdened with money or contracts, while another path led to the dead, the silenced hunters whose ashes were pressed into hard bricks with only a brass plaque to remember them.

Stands of weeping pepper trees grew behind the walk, their ash-green leaves brushing the posts when the wind picked up. Brilliant golden-throated hummingbirds whipped through the trees' bristling frond branches, stopping long enough to dip their sharp beaks into the nectar-rich flowers growing in planters every few feet, the enormous barrels still bearing the stamp of the North County winemakers who'd donated them to beautify the city's parks. I'd wondered why no one ever thought to paint the damned things until it dawned on me no one would see the names of the donors otherwise. Like all things, even charity came with a price—favors traded or promises made.

Of course, the same could be said about practically everything else in life.

Somewhere close by, a pair of peacocks screamed out challenges, the birds a remnant of some rich guy's need to have a pair of arrogant pheasants with butts full of cat toys wandering around his property. I caught sight of one farther up in the gardens, a place meant for picnics and family gatherings for anyone visiting the Presidio, but no one took into account most Stalkers didn't have family. Jonas was an exception to the rule, building up a clan around a four-way marriage and a pack of children raised wild and free. I walked up the slight incline toward him, stopping a few planters away, unsure of what I wanted to say or even what to do. My anger whimpered under my need to connect with someone I'd admired and even loved, both sides of my mind whipping into a frenzied argument about betrayal, blood, and family.

"Jonas, I'm… I screwed up." Admitting my anger and hurt was hard, the words scraping out of my throat like I'd chewed sandpaper and was spitting it back up. "I was just… so damned mad. Still am mad. Dempsey—"

Jonas took care of my indecision, standing up, then closing the distance between us with a few long strides, his powerful legs quick and sure. He was in front of me before I could say anything, a towering hard-hewn black man with broad shoulders, a bit of gray in his neatly shorn hair and smelling of the earth and peppermint. As tall as I was—especially compared to most humans—Jonas dwarfed me. He was a giant of a man with a reach long enough to snatch the biscuit off of my plate from across a wide dining table if he wanted it.

Those arms were around me, pulling me into his chest, smashing my nose into the rough scrubby denim of his overalls, digging a metal button into my cheek and nearly lifting me off my feet. Breathing became difficult, and I tried fighting him, pushing at the mountain of muscle holding me, but it would have been easier to eat the Mustang with a blunt spoon. Jonas wasn't letting go.

So I hugged him back, hoping he'd feel it before my body went numb and I slipped off into unconsciousness.

"Jonas," I tried to say, though it came out garbled and all I could taste was dust and denim on my tongue instead of air. Pretty sure Jonas heard nothing but me mumbling. Possibly felt me squirming, but it was hard to tell because I couldn't see or hear anything other than faded white denim and his heart pounding behind his rib cage. "Dude, let go. People… watching. I'm a Stalker, for fuck's sake."

"Just… let people hug you sometimes, boy," Jonas murmured into the top of my head. I was surprised I could hear him, but my ears seemed to be open. If only I could breathe through them. "Nothing shameful in being hugged. And I know you're feral and probably going to bite me to blood once I let go, but I… just let me hug you. No one's going to think you're weak for letting me hold you. You're my boy. My son. Just as much as you were Dempsey's and—"

A flash of metal caught in a bit of sun was the only warning I had and one I couldn't even act against. The knife came down quick, slashing into Jonas's arm and straight for my face. Twisting about, I fought free, pulling myself out of Jonas's slackening hug as a rush of steaming hot blood splashed over my jaw. Cursing, Jonas yanked himself back, stumbling over the curb. His legs kicked out, trying to find some purchase, but he was too off-balance, too much in shock from the deep gash in his upper arm. His overalls' thick fabric possibly blunted the attack, but his arm had little protection, clothed only in the thin T-shirt he wore underneath.

With Jonas fallen back, the man who attacked us leaped at me, his fleshy face twisted into a hungry expression bordering on lust. I knew him, knew him to be a Stalker, but the only thing I had eyes for was the large blade he held out in front of him, ready to skewer me with its glistening tip, Jonas's blood sliding down its length and onto the man's fat fingers.

My knives were out before I took another breath. Kept in oiled sheaths at my back, they were an easy enough draw, and while I mourned the empty holsters on my thighs, the blades were going to work fine. I spared a quick glance at Jonas, just enough to make sure he wasn't bleeding out, and a giant of a man lunged at me, taking advantage of my shifting gaze.

Broad and lumbering, our attacker either just came off a run or wasn't too in touch with his hygienic side. Like Jonas, he was wearing a pair of worn-down overalls, but they were filthy, pitted with acid burns from skinning ainmhi dubh, and the henley he had under them wasn't in much better shape. Up close, he smelled of caked-on sloughed-off skin and unfiltered cigarettes, his hands stained a dark brown from nicotine and Iesu knew what else. As slovenly as he was, he knew enough to keep his knives sharp, because the edges were scraped tight from a good stone with no burrs along the hone.

Circling around, I placed myself between him and Jonas. He followed, keeping his knife low, its wicked hooked tip canted up. I would have to be careful of how he struck. The tip would be all he needed to sink into me, digging down past my skin and sliding up or down through whatever meat he wanted to carve out of me. I'd used those kinds of knives before, liked them for monsters, but on people? Never. Too much damage. Too much to go wrong with guts and all the squishy stuff held in by skin and firmed up by bones. Him using a hooked-tip knife told me a lot about the man and what he intended.

The son of a bitch came to kill me, because once I put myself in front of Jonas, I was all he saw.

"Clyde." His name came to me, striking the front of my brain like I'd smacked into a low-hanging beam. "Fat Clyde Gibbons."

He wasn't going for small talk. Instead his dark eyes narrowed, his heavy brow dipping down low in a frown, and he shuffled forward quickly, far faster than I'd have given odds on for a man whose belly strained to burst through his overalls. His heavy boots scraped on the asphalt, kicking up small gravel bits into the curb. Caught between the walk and the parking lot, I was at more of a disadvantage than I liked, not knowing how far the walk was behind me or how far up it was. One wrong step and I'd be on my ass and Gibbons would be on me, carving under my skin with his blade until my intestines spilled free.

A lot of people think fights last forever. They just feel that way. Anything longer than fifteen seconds and the adrenaline wears off—if the fighter is sober—and fatigue sets in. The knife gets heavy in the hand, and if there's blood, it slickens the hilt, making it hard to hold on to. I'd seen bar fights where two guys went at it for a full minute and the one everyone placed bets on winning faltered in the end, his body drained of strength, and I've also been there for those times when a well-aimed kick-and-slash puts someone on the floor in seconds. There are only two ways to win a fight— fast and quick or simply to outlast the other guy.

In Gibbons's case, it was going to have to be quick, because he moved, conserving his energy until he needed to strike, making him a dangerous fighter. And since it didn't look like anyone from the Post was coming up the hill to rescue me or shoot his head off, I was on my own.

Fast and hard it was going to be.

Or at least I hoped so, because damned if the asshole pulled the one thing I didn't expect him to but it was my own freaking fault I let him get that close.

Jonas's loud moan took my attention off of Gibbons. I was more worried about his dying on me than losing the fight, and in that moment, Gibbons made his move. He jumped in close, too close for a punch, then grabbed me around the chest, pinning my arms down and lifting me off the ground.

And here Jonas said hugs weren't dangerous.

There were bands of steel built into Gibbons's flabby body, hidden pockets of strength most people wouldn't have given him credit for. But this was a man who made his living hunting and hefting ainmhi dubh—solid blocks of mass with heavy bones and acidic blood. It made for powerful thighs and rock-hard arms, both thick enough to crush a man—or an elfin chimera—if he had enough motivation.

Considering the price Samms told me was on my head, there was more than enough motivation for Gibbons to squeeze me hard enough to pop my eyes out of my skull.

"Son... of... a...." I grunted, flailing to get a good kick in, but Gibbons's stranglehold on my torso was tight and there wasn't any wiggle room. I was losing feeling in my hands. Then my fingers went numb, my knives dropping to the ground. I gave myself a few more seconds before I blacked out, and then I'd be meat under Gibbons's blade and there'd be nothing Jonas could do to stop him. "Shit... Jonas."

"Bleeding out and gone." Gibbons's sour breath choked out what little air I could get into me. "He ain't coming to save you."

Something in me cracked. I felt it ping, the crunch of bone following the telltale aching sting of resonating pain. As tortures went, this was small potatoes compared to what my father could do, but Gibbons was probably hoping to crush me into unconsciousness and either slit my throat or toss my limp body into the trunk of his car. Either way, if I didn't do something quickly, I was going on a one-way ride to somewhere I wouldn't like.

"Come on, you bastard, go down," he growled, probably disliking the fact I could actually get by on a lot less oxygen than the humans he'd more than likely pulled this on before. Another squeeze and another crunch, this time one farther up across my chest. The damned asshole was powerful, I had to give him that. "More money for you if you're alive, but if I've got to take you in dead, I'm good with that. Won't be the first time I've gotten a bounty on a pair of pointed ears."

Jonas was still moving. I spotted his foot jerking up and a brush of his knee at the corner of my eye. Still, Gibbons would take him out if he could, eliminating any witnesses. It didn't matter that I was elfin. I was still a Stalker and an official law enforcement officer for SoCalGov. The cops might hate Stalkers, and not many people love my species, but I still carried a badge. That had to count for something, and Gibbons's endgame was to get me down and taken out before anyone could see him. It was a good plan.

One I had no intention of letting him execute.

"Die, you damned son of a bitch," Gibbons practically shouted in my notched ear, his teeth too close to my lobe for my liking. "What's it going to take to kill you?"

"Hell of a lot more than what you've got," I muttered between my teeth, unable to force more than a whisper out of my lungs. Red splashed across my vision, anger and frustration seeping over any rational thought I had left. I'd survived a hell of a lot and didn't plan on dying in a parking lot, being squeezed to death by some overgrown bald yeti with bad teeth. "Ain't dying today."

Pressed up against Gibbons, I went with the weapons I'd come into the world with.

My teeth.

I sank my fangs into his face, digging down into the meat of his cheek, and latched on tight. His blood was hot and bitter, pumping out onto my tongue and down my neck. A bit dribbled down my throat, and I fought not to gag on its metallic taste. Rage and pain shifted the odor of his skin from an unwashed, embedded grime to something sour and ripe. Clamping down harder, I felt my teeth meet, and I jerked my head quickly, rending off a bit of flesh, and with a hard yank, I ripped his cheek clean off the bone.

Gibbons dropped me, howling and clutching at his torn-open face. Landing on my feet, I spat out the foul mouthful on my tongue, grabbed my knives, and went in for the kill.

Okay, sometimes there were more than two ways to win a knife fight, but it always comes back to the blade. Even with my face painted red with Gibbons's gore and my teeth filled with the shreds of his flesh, I was going to peel him apart and crack his bones open so Odin's ravens could suck out his marrow and shit out his fingernails like discarded shrimp shells.

"Kai, no!" Ryder yelled at me from somewhere past the murderous fog I'd pulled around me. I had Gibbons on his back, shoulders pressed into the asphalt, blood running in rivers down his increasingly ashy skin, and there was Ryder, begging me to be... merciful.

I was in no mood for mercy.

I wanted Gibbons dead. I wanted him to be splayed out on the ground, spatchcocked and bled white with only the thinnest flaps of skin holding his meat together. There were other voices, shocked murmurs and rumbles, warning someone else to stand back while another deeper voice—a woman's voice, *Sarah's* voice—urged people to let her through.

My knives were against Gibbons's throat, their edges dipped down into his skin, and I dragged them down toward his Adam's apple, peeling back a layer until a bit of pinkish serum dripped down the curve of his wattle. My knees were pressed down into his belly and crotch, pinning him. He could have tossed me if he wanted to risk slicing his own throat open, and I half wished he would try. Any shift of his limbs would be enough of an incentive for me to carve him open, and I wasn't even sure I would wait for that.

"Kai," Ryder murmured this time, his hand on my shoulder to pull me back. Gibbons groaned, the changing angle of my body digging into his crotch, and he pounded at the ground with his fists, barking his knuckles raw. "Come on. Get up. Jonas is fine. You're fine."

"Bastard tried to kill Jonas." I debated driving one blade through his hand, twisting it around until the bones broke and he'd never be able to hold another weapon again, but I had a feeling in my gut his license was already in ashes, and the sirens on the wind meant Gibbons would be spending a lot of time staring at blank walls. "Tried to kill me. Give me one good reason I should let him walk."

"Because you're not a killer," Ryder said, and from behind him, the small group of Stalkers who'd pounded up the walk to stop Gibbons snorted in a wave of varying disagreement. He gave them a lordly, dismissive stare, which they ignored.

It was always a good day when the Sidhe lordling got a good kick in his ego to remind him he was just another piece of meat like the rest of us.

"Boy, I'm okay," Jonas said, shakily on his feet with Sarah propping him up. "Let the guys in blue handle him. You've got enough on your plate. You don't need to be worrying about where you're going to hide three hundred pounds of rotting flesh, especially since you live in a damned warehouse with no backyard. And you sure as hell aren't putting that in my ground. Dogs will dig him up and play fetch with his skull before all the meat's worn off."

I got up off of Gibbons, moving gingerly when my ribs protested my straightening up, and he gave out another tortured groan when I gave him a final dig with my right knee. A police cruiser screamed up the curved drive, followed by two more, and an ambulance from Medical rode their tails. Sarah lodged Jonas onto the bench, ordering a couple of the Post's security guards to keep Gibbons busy while she got the cops straightened out.

Ryder wiped at my face with a cloth and shook his head. "I can't even leave you to patch things up with Jonas without you drawing blood. What happened to just talking?"

"I *was* talking." I fought the swiping for a bit, then finally let him get it out of his system. My ribs were throbbing but seemed to be doing fine otherwise. Breathing in deeply didn't make me wince, so as far as I could tell, my lungs weren't pierced through. "Stop that. And if you put spit on that cloth and wipe my face, I'll do to you what I wanted to do to Gibbons, but with my fingernails."

Rubbing at my side, I spat again, trying to get the taste of human blood off my tongue. Then I spotted Martins, one of the guys I'd done runs with when Dempsey first brought us down to San Diego. Nodding at me, he smiled and held out his hand to another Stalker, a gaunt scrawny man barely old enough to grow a whisker on his chin but already with the cold, hard gaze of a seasoned hunter. The young man sighed and dug into his pocket, then handed Martins a wad of cash. Frowning, I cocked my head at Martins, wondering if I was going to have to worry about him next, when he cracked a grin at me.

"Told him you bit, but he didn't believe me," Martins called out, turning to head back down to the Post now there was nothing else to watch. "Drinks on me next time, Gracen. I owe you a beer."

Twelve

NEWT WAS there to greet me by the time I dragged myself up to the top level of the tower the Court built for me. I'd left Oketsu in the courtyard below, eyeing the long garage still growing up out of the cobblestones near my tower's front entrance. I didn't trust the place enough to park my Mustang in something still struggling to grow walls, and if the damned tower took offense by that, there'd be nothing I could do. I still patted the wall and thanked it for thinking of me.

I didn't trust it, but I wasn't an asshole, not that anyone would think that if they listened to Newt.

Pushing Newt out of the way with my foot so I could get to his food, I scolded, "Stop screaming your fool head off. I'm going as fast as I can."

I'd showered before feeding him, earning me a black mark on his shit list, but I smelled too bad and needed hot water on my bruises. Enduring his claws digging into my back when I crouched down to open a new box of cat food, I regretted deciding that cotton pants and a tank top would be good to sleep in. He hooked into my skin through the fabric, making me wish I'd pulled on full riot gear. Then he seemed to double down in the spots where Gibbons did the most damage along my sides.

"Newt, stop," I hissed, trying to dislodge him, but he was determined to make his ascent. Standing up with a packet of food, I tried to reach for him, but the twisting about only made my ribs hurt more, and the scars along my back tightened up in response to the waves of pain. "Just... give me a minute, you damned cat."

Reaching my shoulder, he stood triumphant, all four and a half pounds of mottled fur and scraggly ears, and screamed in my ear, defiantly ordering me to stand and deliver his food lest the devil take me.

"Shit, what is this?" I stared at the can and then down at the box on the floor. "This isn't tuna. Tuna and egg? Why is it the same color as the normal tuna ones? Crap, this isn't your food. I mean, it's cat food, but it's not—"

Newt's eardrum-curdling aria told me exactly what I could do with the can in my hand once I emptied its contents into his dish.

"Listen to me, you furry idiot." I shook the can under his nose. "This is tuna and egg. You've not eaten this before. You might not like it. Just hold on."

I opened the can and gritted my teeth when Newt objected to the wait once again. Dipping my finger into the meaty churn, I took a bit out and sniffed at it. It smelled mostly of fish, but there were definitely small yellow chunks in it. Ignoring Newt's protests, I licked the concoction off my finger and tasted it, trying to compare the memory of Newt's normal food to what I had in my mouth.

"Did you just eat the cat's food?" Ryder stood in the doorway, his face twisted into an expression I usually only saw when I offered Newt a piece of broccoli.

"You think I'm going to feed him something I haven't tasted?" Sniffing once more at the can, I held it up for Newt to inspect, since he was already perched on my shoulder. "It tastes the same to me, asshole. You good with it, or are you going to do what you did last time and try to starve yourself to death?"

I took Newt leaving long furrows of bloodied scrapes on my skin after jumping off my shoulder and landing with a ferocious scream at his empty food bowl for him to be okay with the tuna and egg.

Leaving the cat to his dinner, I grabbed one of the cloths I'd left on the kitchenette counter to dab at my shoulder. It stung enough to be noticeable, but getting to the spot proved to be more painful than it was worth. My ribs were definitely not knitting well, or at least not fast enough, and every time I lifted my elbow up, the bruises marbling my sides ached more. Hissing, I padded over to the low-slung couches, dabbing as I went until the slow burn faded, only to find Ryder frowning at me.

"Now what?" I frowned back, balling the cloth up in my hand to toss it toward the small sink on the other side of the room.

"Nothing," he replied, shaking his head. "It's always just when I think I've figured you out, you do something that makes me...." Ryder paused, framed against a sunbeam and I caught a delicious aroma coming from the tray of covered food he carried in with him. I narrowed my eyes and he said with a smile, "Readjust my understanding of you. It's not a bad thing, that."

The rag bounced off the counter, then slid into the sink, but the pain kicked up again along my ribs, stealing my breath. Hissing, I rubbed at the spots I could reach and gingerly sat down on the couch opposite of the one Ryder took. "This can heal at any time. Who the hell knew Gibbons was so damned strong? Medical said he cracked five ribs. Feels like he tore down my spine."

"You could let one of the healers see to you," Ryder muttered at me, lifting the lids on the dishes. "Unlike the human staff at the Medical Center, they know elfin anatomy."

"The last time one of them put their hands on me—Celia, I think, the tiny one with the pink hair—she puked up through her nose," I reminded him, carefully leaning forward to see what he'd brought. "Every single one of them hugs the walls when I go by. I'm a golem, lordling. Tanic shaped my flesh and pulled me into existence. I'm everything wrong about their kind of magic, and touching me is their worst nightmare. Leave it alone and don't ask them. They'd do it but end up hating me because of it."

He looked like he was going to argue with me, something I'd come to expect, but instead, Ryder closed his mouth and passed me a pair of chopsticks. "Here. Eat something. You look like you're about to fall over."

There were slices of rare beef over a bed of butter noodles and seared sugar peas for me to pick through—enough meat to fill my empty belly and fuel my healing. My hunger stomped down my stubbornness at being told what to do, and I once again reminded my recalcitrant brain that sometimes agreeing wasn't a bad thing. I took the dish and chopsticks, plucked a sliver of nearly raw meat from the mound, and tucked it into my mouth, chewing while I stared out into the city lights fighting off the darkness with their sparkling web.

Newt came by with fish-and-egg breath to shove his face into my dish, hoping for a handout. I picked out a small piece, holding it pinched between my fingers until he sank his front teeth into the morsel, letting go when he tugged on it. A bit of movement over Ryder's shoulder caught my attention, but the flash of yellow and blue turned out to be a flock of macaws coming in to settle for the night. All around us, the Sidhe stronghold and its lands were quiet, steeped in shadow, with only a few lights at the edges of the territory to mark its boundaries and walls. The silence was a bit disconcerting, especially with the cityscape clearly laid out to the south of the tower, but I'd grown used to it. The rest of the Court lay behind me, the buildings growing toward the north and west, leaving my view open. I liked the feeling of isolation, especially with the empty courtyard below. I'd have to go home at some point, return to the warehouse with the sometimes noisy clatter of the harbor drifting up and the pounding of the sea on the shore during a storm, but for now, the stillness was what I needed.

Especially since I had some planning to do.

"There room on the couch for me?" Cari knocked on the open door, hefting three bottles of dark-chocolate milk tea up as some sort of offering. "I bring Abuelita and some dried fish snacks for the monster."

"Which monster?" I asked, putting my dish down. "Me or the cat?"

"Don't—" Ryder cut himself off, sliding down to make room for Cari. "You are not a monster, Kai."

"Been called one by enough people," I replied, taking one of the bottles from Cari. "And it's a joke, Ryder. Sometimes the best way to deal with crappy stuff is to make fun of it. You made good time. I just messaged you ten minutes ago."

"I was downstairs with Alexa." She shrugged at me when I looked up. "I probably spend more time here than you do. It's nice talking to elfin that don't growl at you when you take more bacon. Now, tell me what you've got planned, and was Jonas still awake when you left the hospital?"

"Out like a light." I gave Cari a quick rundown of Jonas's injuries and how he fought to get released. "Spouses weren't having it. He's an asshole when he's sick. They probably want the nurses to deal with him until he feels better. The Post's picking up his medical bills, so that's one less worry. They'll probably give him stop-gap payments, because he won't be able to do runs until that's all checked out."

"Oh, he's going to be pleasant. You know how he gets." Cari set one of the bottles down in front of Ryder, then picked at my leftovers, finding a pea I'd left behind. "So you two are all good?"

"We'll talk more when he's out," I said, taking the bottle from Ryder after watching him struggle to open it. I popped off the cap and handed it back. "There wasn't a lot of time in between Jonas trying to squeeze the air out of me with a hug and Gibbons trying to kill us. What about you and me? We good?"

"We're always good." Cari gave me a brilliant smile. "Especially since, with Jonas off the board, you're stuck with me as your backup. What's the plan? We going after whoever put the blacklist contract on you?"

"Sort of." Sliding my plate over to Cari, I continued, "We're going to go find Dempsey's brother. He's got an actual bounty on him, and Samms on his tail. I've just got to get to Kenny first. He's got some stuff Dempsey gave him—things related to the original hit put on me—so I want to get that from him. Chances are, whoever put that first one up is the same someone who's tagged me for this new one. I mean, I've pissed a lot of people off, but not the kind of people who can put up that much money to take me out."

"Yeah, a contract on you doesn't make sense. You're not the kind of person someone would kill for a handful of coins," Cari said with a chuckle. "Love you, but the contract doesn't make sense. You're a Stalker, for Bast's sake, not some politician who steals candy from little kids."

"Hey, if it's the right candy." I found another snow pea and slid it over to Ryder's bowl, ignoring Cari's playful warning hiss. "Tonight I'm going to go to sleep with a full belly, and first thing in the morning, begin rattling the trees for info on Kenny. He's down here for something, and it sure as hell isn't me. Someone's got to be offering him someplace to squat until he can shake off the bounty on him. Either that or he's got something worth selling. Either way, he's going to be leaving a trace. We just need to find it."

"What will you do with him when we find him?" Ryder asked, and Cari's chopsticks stopped moving, a few grains of rice trembling on their tips.

"There's no *we* in this, lordling," I replied. "You're not coming with us on this. We'll be heading deep down into the understreets, and that's not someplace for the likes of you."

If the room had a nip in it before, it was positively frigid when Ryder's gaze hardened and settled on me. I met his stare, waiting it out until Cari finally cleared her throat and began to stack the dishes together. Plucking the utensils out of Ryder's fingers, she stood up and stretched. Newt mewed an objection to something or other from his place on the bed, probably annoyed the lights were still on, but he was going to have to take a number to rip skin off my back. Ryder's shoulders were stiff, and he had on his politician face—the smooth façade of someone choosing his words more carefully than a mushroom picker selected from the fungi sprouting across a field of cow shit.

"Well, since it looks like you two are going to fight, I'm just going to take these down to the kitchen so you can get to it," she remarked lightly, nudging Ryder's leg until he moved out of her way. "Kai, drop me a line when you're ready to go. I'm staying down at Alexa's. Just give me enough notice so I can make sure I've got enough ammo. Ryder, do us both a favor and don't forget about that purple salve the healers put in the bathroom. He's less crotchety when he's not as banged up."

Cari gave me a wink as she went by, a saucy smirk more to remind me to play nice than to chew Ryder apart. I was tired, and now that I'd eaten, there were stretches of my skin and bones throbbing beneath the tank top I'd pulled on after my shower. She wasn't wrong. I was getting grumpier by the minute, and as the night wore down, there was nothing more I wanted than to crawl under clean sheets and fall asleep while listening to the rain slap at the tower's enormous glass panes. I didn't have the energy to fight with Ryder. Hell, I didn't even have the energy to argue with him when he came back from the bathroom with a small jar of glowing purplish sparkly goo and motioned for me to make my way over to the bed.

"Come here and take your shirt off. Cari's right. The least I can do is try to soothe the bruising, but the healers and I are going to have a talk after this." Ryder's frown deepened when I let out a small audible groan as I stood up. "They're... *healers*."

"Yeah, well, technically so is my father," I pointed out, padding over slowly. It was hard to get my arms back up, and I felt every twinge while trying to get my shirt off. Taking a deep breath was a mistake. It only hurt worse, and despite the satisfying warmth in my belly, my dinner threatened to come back up. "I don't need you to—"

"Just... once... let someone take care of you," Ryder growled at me. He sat in the middle of the bed, his bare feet tucked under his crossed legs. "Lie down and let me do this for you."

"You just want me on my back so I can't argue with you," I muttered, swallowing the press of my stomach against my throat as I crawled onto the wide mattress. "Pele's teeth, it feels like Gibbons cracked my spine."

No matter how much I grumbled about the Sidhe and their spoiled ways, the damned Court sure as hell knew how to make a bed. The mattress cradled me, the linens I'd left rumpled slithering softly against my tortured skin, and it wasn't a hardship to lift my head up to let Ryder put a pillow beneath me. Newt rumbled a soft mewl, jostled by my stretching out, but he quickly curled up over my bare ankle, resting his sharp fangs against one of my toes.

Ryder was too close, too warm and present for me to be comfortable, so I closed my eyes and let the sound of the rain drift over me. The shushing roll was quiet, a gentle patter compared to the storms we'd fled under during our desert run, and the scent of the water was different—greener and lush—and carried with it the sweet perfume of the maile vines growing along the balustrade. My shoulders began hurting again, forcing me to stop and think about why. I was tensed up, knotted in on myself, and I nearly jumped out of my skin when Ryder's fingertips skimmed over my right side.

"Do you want to fight now or later?" he asked softly, his voice as deceptively sweet as the maile in the air. "Because I have a few good arguments about why I should accompany you. Or is this going to be another one of your... 'my run, my rules'?"

"Partially," I conceded, opening my eyes only to discover Ryder leaning over me. If my belly wasn't already twisted up from the ache along my muscles, it churned in double-time with the sight of his dark emerald eyes swallowing up all the light around us. I couldn't see anything past his handsome face and its golden fall of hair, the glittering metallic strands curving into a curtain around us. It wouldn't take much to tangle my fingers through it, wrapping bits of starlight and sunshine around my own flesh, but that was a whole lot of trouble I wasn't prepared to deal with. "I think we're coming to a point, lordling, where you've got to decide what exactly is it you want from me and who the hell you think I really am. Because so far, we've danced around a lot of things, including each other, but the hard reality of life is... I'm a Stalker and you're the Lord of a Court. My life is full of blood and monsters, and that's not where you spend most of your day."

"I know who you are, Chimera," Ryder whispered. "I've never forgotten."

"No, I don't think you really understand." I sat up, holding my left side until it stopped screaming in agony. Ryder's chin came up, and he threw his shoulders back, giving me room. "You're ruffled because I'm going to go digging around under the city for a fugitive and not taking you with me. Here's the thing. You'll be a distraction. You can't shoot for shit, and there's no way in any hell that you'll be able to blend in with the crowd. You simply are not someone I'd take for that run. I can't babysit. I can't trust your instincts to tell you when someone's dangerous, and I sure as hell don't want to spend my time keeping one eye on you while on the lookout for someone who would sooner stick a knife between my ribs for a bit of spare change than to look at me."

If I thought he was stiff before, he was practically a redwood by the time I got done speaking.

"This is how I live, Ryder," I continued as gently as I could. "This, all of this around us, that's how you live. And neither way is bad or better. Okay, so maybe you've got better food and beds, but we each have our places. And it's been cute flirting with the idea of something… more than what we are, but I'm going to ask you something—what the hell do you think I'm going to do here in your Court? I bring nothing to this place. And before you start talking about destinies and towers with a hard-on for me being here, I want you to really fucking think about what it is you believe I can do here. Because I'm going to be honest and say I have no idea. Living here in a tower like this would kill me. I'm a hunter of monsters, Ryder. I go out and I kill things so other people can live their lives, and they might hate me because I've got pointed ears and fangs, but their money spends the same whether they love me or spit when I walk by."

There was so much more to him now than the lordling who'd pounded his fist against my front door, demanding I dance to his tune. I wanted him. All of the gods knew I did, but I wasn't going to bend down and show my throat to whatever tickle our blood shared.

"There's something between us. I know it. I can feel it. And I'm not denying it's there," I said, moving Newt onto one of the pillows. "But I'm not going to let that tangle dictate to me how to live. I'm not going to be your puppet, Ryder, any more than you're going to be someone I drag along on runs for shits and giggles."

"I never once thought of you as… a puppet." His whisper loosened as he continued, but the tension in his throat kept his muscles tight. "I want you with me. Not just because you make my bones sing, but because I can… count on you. You're not just someone I reach for because you're there. You're a friend, and sometimes the only one who tells me what I really don't want to hear. I depend on that. I *need* that. Do I want you in my bed? Morrigan, there are days where it hurts so much with the want of you, but I know you're not… you're not one to be bound. I know that. I might not like it, but I know it. I don't know what your place is here except… that I want you with me. So whatever that looks like, that's what I need. And if that means there are times when I have to watch you ride off toward a killing field, then I'll have to deal with it. Just… stay here with me. In some way, Kai. That's all I ask. Because that's all I need."

Thirteen

"YOU'RE STUPID for going, boy."

I had to look up to make sure it was Jonas talking and not Dempsey because, except for the difference in their grumbling voices, those were Dempsey's words coming out of Jonas's mouth. The man looked like shit, his skin stretched tight over his strong bones, and he looked half warmed up from dead, his mouth and eyes tight slits in his ashen face. Leaning against the old International Scout he'd somehow driven from the ranch to the courtyard I'd claimed as my own, Jonas looked like he was ready to do battle despite his shaky stance. A few feet away, his son Razor met my curious glance with the universal expression of a son backing off arguing with his old man—a widening of his eyes, a shake of his head, and his hands held up in a quick surrender.

Najiri's son was no fool, and other than an apologetic grimace, he used the long legs he'd gotten from his father to quickly take himself back to the battered Chevy truck he'd bought off Dempsey months before. I had fond memories of that truck and was mostly responsible for the Bondo-repaired shotgun holes along its front quarter panel and hood, but Razor'd done his own mark or two on the vehicle, having played apprentice to more than a few runs in his youth. Now a fully licensed Stalker himself, he'd taken up residence at Dempsey's old place in exchange for keeping the place up, and despite the slight distance between him and his family—or perhaps because of it—he seemed to be getting along fine.

Right up until the moment his father decided he was going to drag himself out of his doctor-enforced rest and Razor volunteered to keep Jonas company. Or at least that's how I imagined things going, and then I heard Jonas's link chirrup angrily and caught a bit of his own grimace when he glanced at the message.

It was early afternoon, and the sun was making the same soft whispering promises a fickle lover made about loving forever, but in a half-drunk slur no one with any sense believed. Around us the Court was going about its day, and I'd spent most of the morning on my link or scanning vid feeds, looking for any sign of Dempsey's younger brother. I started to get hits at noon—small trickles of information leading to a few possible sightings—and then word began to solidify, mostly because of the famous Dempsey lack of charm leaving a distinct impression on people as Kenny fucked them over. The disgruntled murmurs left in Kenny's wake pretty much reassured me he hadn't grown any more pleasant, and I couldn't imagine having a price on his head improved his mood any.

The rain backed off before I had my first cup of coffee and a handful of painkillers, and from the growling sounds Newt made over his dish, I assumed breakfast was suitable enough to fill his belly. Other than a few tender spots and a spread of inkblot bruises along my right side, I seemed to have survived Gibbons's attack. Still, I was surprised as hell when Jonas showed up, arm in a sling and with Razor in tow, slowly maneuvering through the Court's maze of roads to get to my tower. His spouses were going to kill him for sneaking out, was my first thought when I saw him nearly tumble out of the old battle tank of a Scout he'd brought for Cari and me to use on our bounty hunt. The second worry came hot on its tail, a deep fear Najiri and the others would think I'd convinced him to bring the Scout himself.

Behind us, the Court went about doing whatever it was that occupied a nest of elfin in the middle of an enormous overgrown park. Ryder was up before me, leaving the bed we shared before I'd been forced out from under the bedsheets by my ravenous cat. The sheets still smelled of him, and I'd taken a long moment inhaling his scent on my pillows before creakily stumbling toward the bathroom. There was a part of me aching to crawl back into that bed and bury myself back into its soft caress, but Kenny had a piece of my past I wanted and I had a piece of his I needed to give to him. The wafer of Dempsey's ashes was beginning to weigh on me, a negligible white disk shaped out of the remains of the man who'd fed me, taught me how to shoot, and in his own way, called me son.

And now I was going to hunt down his brother, force him to hand over whatever it was Dempsey gave him to hold on to, and possibly drag him back to the Post to cash in on the bounty on *his* head while trying to avoid getting killed by anyone coming after me like Gibbons did.

Or, a typical Gracen Tuesday.

"That Mom?" Razor's voice cracked, at odds with the growing redwood height he'd also gotten from his father. His face was all Najiri—

elegant lines stamped with a regal beauty—but the rest of him was pure Jonas, including the healthy respect he had for the woman who'd brought him into this world. "Because if you don't answer, she's going to ping me next, and there's nothing you can promise me that'll make me not answer."

"Hold on. Just...." Jonas gritted his teeth, huddling over his link. "Give me a minute. She doesn't know I came with you."

"Well, that takes the teeth out of the dog's bite," Cari drawled, swinging a duffel into the Scout's open back hatch. "And it's not like you're going to be alone. I'm coming with you."

"Don't get me started on you going with him," Jonas hissed under his breath, one hand covering his link. "Because—"

"Hi, Najiri," I said loudly toward Jonas's wrist as I walked by with the bag I'd packed up. He gave me a panicked look, and I heard Najiri's querulous prod at her husband, asking him where he was. "Thanks for dropping the truck off, Jonas. I should let Razor take you back home."

"Oh, that's just cold," Razor called out from the Chevy's open window. "Dragging me into this. Dad, get into the truck!"

"I'll be fine, Jonas." I dumped my bag into the Scout, then ambled back over to where he stood, still trying to dampen down Najiri's rising voice. Patting him on his uninjured shoulder, I murmured, "Thank you for letting me borrow the Scout. If it gets blown up, I'll buy you a new one."

"Do not—Najiri, let me call you back. I need to talk some sense into this boy," Jonas muttered. "No, the pointy-eared one. The one you and I made is hiding in the truck trying to pretend he didn't just yell at me to move my ass."

Razor rolled up the window and began to studiously ignore all of us, burying his nose into a battered paperback I'd read more than a few times myself, its pages rolled and stained from living in the Chevy's glove compartment.

"There's going to be hell to pay when I get home, but I couldn't in good conscience let you go wandering off to get killed without at least trying to talk some sense into you." Jonas lurched his way around to the back of the Scout, his mouth set into a thin, painful line. Medical probably argued like hell to keep him in, but knowing Jonas, he'd bullied his way out, promising to do everything his spouses told him to do in order to get better... then promptly broke every single one of those promises before Medical was even a dot in the car's rearview mirror. Still, I appreciated his stubbornness, even if I thought it was misplaced. "Did you pack enough sterile shot packs? Different sizes? You'd be surprised at how many of those thin ones you go through. Seems like I'm constantly replacing them."

"I wasn't planning on getting shot that much," I drawled. "It's a simple recon. Go down, ferret him out, and drag his sorry ass back up to the surface. He shouldn't be that hard to find. I've already got a lead on where he's holed up. I just need to pin him down. The med kit is set up, and if push comes to shove, we just blitz out of there."

"I just think it's a mistake. And yeah, I know you can handle yourself. Christ knows I've watched you get out of some tight scrapes, but this time it feels different. I don't like someone putting a target between your shoulder blades." Jonas wiped at his face, but the fatigue graying his skin didn't magically disappear. He looked beyond tired, edging close into old, but I wasn't sure how much of that was his needing to step back from Stalking or the stress of Gibbons's attempt on his life. "How far in are you going to be going? Past the river?"

"Yeah, past the river." I mapped out in my head where one of my contacts said Kenny was spotted. "Not past the tik-tik lines but close. I'm guessing he's trying to avoid any LEOs. Farther in you go, the less badges you run into, but people are going to know he's got a bounty on him. He's got to stay hidden, but why come down here? At least up in Vegas, he'd have his own contacts. He's spinning in the wind here."

"Unless he's burned all his bridges there and someone down here owes him a solid. Kenny's worse of an asshole than Dempsey ever was." Jonas grunted, and he shifted, easing his shoulder. "He's down here for something or someone. Think he's going to pull you into something?"

"Hasn't tagged me, so I don't think so, but Kenny's never met a knife he didn't love to stick into someone's back." I shook my head. "I don't know why Dempsey gave him the contract stuff to hold on to, but he said it seemed like the last place in the world anyone would think he'd stash it."

"This stuff's that important?" Jonas eyed me. "What do you think it's going to tell you? You know where you come from. I mean, you said you're wearing your daddy's face. What more do you need?"

"I don't know," I admitted, scratching at the black-pearl dragon scale beneath my skin. "It's stupid, and it's not like it's going to change who I am, but I feel like I've got to at least know who is out there putting targets on me. Tanic *made* me. I don't even know the Sidhe he used to get that half, but I can't imagine their family being too thrilled about it, if they even knew. There's just too many pieces floating around out there, and I've got to put a face on whoever knows I exist and wants to make sure I stop existing."

"And we're sure it's not the Wild Hunt Master? Wouldn't put it past him to want someone else to do his dirty work. He's sent others before. Maybe he figures sending a human this time will do the job."

"Now, maybe? Back then, no. It was someone else. Dempsey was paid to pull me out of there and hand me over, dead or alive," I reminded him. "So that's one unknown. The contract on me now could still be that person or Tanic. Whatever Kenny's got will give me some idea on where to start on the past, and push comes to shove, I'll start digging into the now if he doesn't get me any answers."

"So you're figuring either way, you've got to know who besides Tanic knew you were alive then." He chewed on his upper lip, staring out into the forest beyond the Court's gardens and roads. "Makes sense. I guess I keep... forgetting there was someone who hired Dempsey to pull you out of there."

"Pull me out or kill me. They didn't care which." I shrugged. "So I'm going to find Kenny, dig that out of him, and then decide what to do with him. No matter what, I need to find him before anyone else does, no matter *why* he's down here."

"Just try to keep an eye out." He grimaced when his link beeped again. "Tag me if you need help. I might not be able to get loose from the wives and husband, but I might be able to find you someone to help in a pinch."

"Maybe. Maybe not. Going to be hard to tag anyone for help down that deep. Signal repeaters are still screwed to hell," I reminded him. "City didn't want to fix the routing system. Took a lot of arm-twisting just to keep the transit running. You think they care if there's free links up? I'll be lucky if my satlink can punch through the streets down there. It's far in."

"That is not what I want to hear," Ryder said, strolling out of the walkway, a plastic grocery bag folded up and tucked under his arm. "Hello, Jonas."

"Goodbye, Jonas," Cari shot back, closing the Scout's tailgate. "Let me help you up into the truck and you can head home so Najiri can skin you. Hey, Ryder. Nice shirt. Stole it from Kai?"

"Seemed prudent. It's one of his favorites. If I keep it and his cat, I figured it would give him incentive to come home." He mocked my frown, getting out of Cari's way as she steered a still-grumbling Jonas toward the truck. Peering into the back of the Scout, he held the grocery bag out for me to take. "Here. Because you'll forget to eat."

"I'll be with Cari. We'll be eating on the hour every hour. She's like a pika. Have you forgotten that?" I peeked into the bag anyway, delighted to see packages of my beloved coconut-marshmallow-covered cupcakes. "Okay, these are awesome. Thanks."

He stepped toward me, pinning me to the Scout's side. His fingers were warm on my belly, tucking up under the hem of my T-shirt—my second-favorite T-shirt, since apparently he'd taken a liking to the one I'd gotten from a San Francisco ink shop. His mouth sang against mine, sending a fire through my blood, and I nibbled on his lower lip, reminding Ryder he couldn't always just take what he wanted, even if it was me.

"Hey, lordling," I cautioned. "Getting kinda ballsy here. I mean, I just let you sleep in my bed. Haven't done anything to bring on a big dramatic goodbye kiss in front of the kids. It's not one of those old black-and-white movies you like. I'm not a soldier going off to war, and you're not my husband wishing I were already home before I've even left."

"I do want you to come home. I wish I were going with you. And yes, damn it, I wish I'd done more with you than simply sleeping in your bed, but that doesn't mean I can't wish for you to come home safe. Just...." Ryder leaned his forehead against mine, inhaling my breath when I exhaled. "And it's not because I don't think you're capable. Gods know, you are fierce and feral and so much more of a survivor than I can ever be, but I just... don't want to let you go. Even as I know I have to."

"I'll be back." I groaned when his fingers dipped down against the button of my jeans. "Stop that. Seriously, you're going to lose your napping-with-me-and-the-cat privileges. I'm literally not leaving the city. I've been on worse. This is a simple bounty hunt... with the slight complication of other Stalkers who might or might not want to take me down too. Not much different than a Pendle Run. Just with less dragons."

"Just be careful, and don't get shot." He gave my waistband another tug, his gaze firm on my face. "Besides, you definitely have to come back, because I might love you, but I am not going to taste your cat's food for him. There's only so much you can ask a man to do, and that's too far, even for me."

SAN DIEGO'S tiered structure was a common one, folds and pockets of neighborhoods tucked into crevices opened up by the Merge. San Francisco did it the best, using the long stretches beneath old districts as a mirror to what one could find aboveground. But New York suffered from the expansion, its skyscrapers unable to withstand the shifting ground. Tokyo didn't even blink, and Singapore celebrated the increased space, quickly filling in the vacant areas with housing and gardens, thankful for any extra square inch they got. San Diego ended up as it always did, creating a mishmash of neighborhoods where a bit of extra income meant a larger footprint to live in, and the closer to the ocean someplace was, the more expensive it was to live.

Kenny was *nowhere* near the coastline.

Instead he was buried as deep into the understreets as he could go without actually ending up in the series of catacombs and caverns leading in stringers out to the California desert far outside of San Diego proper. I had a decent mapping system of those caves and corridors, but the last thing I wanted was to chase Kenny Dempsey through what would be another circle of Hell Dante thought up in his spare time.

"How well do you know this guy?" Cari slouched against the passenger-side window, working at a gris-gris bag she'd promised Alexa. "I mean, he's your uncle. Kind of."

We weren't that far into the understreets, close enough to one of the level's entrances that there was still sunlight flashing on the buildings behind us, but in a few minutes, we'd be over a ridge and dropping down into the murky almost-twilight beyond. There wasn't ever a direct route to where you needed to go below. The streets were in a grid pattern, but only enough to frustrate when a building sprouted up in the middle of a thoroughfare and traffic was forced to go around to get to the other side.

It was midafternoon, but traffic was already skimming at a high pace. All around us bright blue tik-tiks dipped down to nab fares, then skipped back up the line to do battle with the trolleys overhead. A few rogue tik-tiks dove into the fray, their harried drivers skimming into the crowds of office workers disembarking from the escalators connecting the undercity to the bustling metropolis overhead. Spotting a black bubble of an illegal tik-tik careening down to slide into a space behind a licensed blue cab, I swerved to the left, gladly avoiding the ensuing snarl. Like clockwork, the blue-cab driver was out of his vehicle, abandoning his place in line and stomping over to the black skipper behind him. Horns bellowed, and a stream of profanity ladled hard with anger erupted. Then it was in our rearview mirror, swallowed up by more traffic and a few right turns.

"I don't really know him. He's an asshole. More than Dempsey ever was. I actually never knew anyone who liked him." I shrugged, recalling very little about the man who Dempsey called the most miserable bastard he'd ever known. Considering how many miserable bastards Dempsey had in his life, I took that as a fair warning. "He was always hitting Dempsey up for money for one thing or another. Worked hard not to work, that's what Dempsey would say. There was always this scheme that would hit it big, pay out millions, and Dempsey would tell him to fuck off."

"Well yeah, Dempsey had a retirement plan." She snorted, poking me in the ribs and of course finding one of the still-tender spots. "I'm sitting right next to it."

"I never begrudged the old man one cent." I slowed down for a stoplight, rubbing at the spot she'd stabbed at. "Even after... all of this... all of these secrets... he did right by me. Hell, even righter than I thought. He had something on whoever hired him to get me back then. That's the only thing that makes sense to me—that he was given something or he found something that held their hand—because now he's gone, it's all creeping back out. Kenny's got that something, and we need to get our hands on it."

"And him," she murmured, putting the gris-gris aside and picking up her tablet. "Took a look at your uncle's contract. It's like he went out of his way to cheat every single hard-core criminal in New Vegas he could find. I mean, they're pissed off. There's a bonus if he comes in with broken fingers and a hint that you'll get a free townhouse if he's turned over to the Post without his jewels. Like, a strong hint. Place looks nice. It's got a pool."

"Not one for swimming," I reminded her. "Elfin don't seem to like the water that much, but then again, considering what they brought over with them and dumped into the oceans, it's hard to love splashing around in places where even dragons are afraid to go. I've seen some of those fish they've pulled in up in Alaska—teeth the size of Great Danes and eyeballs bigger than this Scout."

The gloaming hit over the next rise, and any true sunlight was lost to us. Around us, the streets turned milky and blue, punctuated by splashes of neon and strips of white spots running along the high-pitched overhangs built to hold the upper city in place. Buildings shifted, getting lower and turning residential. Many were painted a vibrant white at some point, a bit of effort put in to push back the shadows, but grime and soot eventually crept in, turning the landscape a nearly uniform gray.

There were still spots of color, flashing signs, and rolling screens advertising everything from supermarkets to face masks with a bit of litigation thrown in for good measure. The tik-tiks were plentiful here, cramming in and out to drop off passengers, then making their way back to the front lines, eager for fares. On the ground, buses took up most of the lanes, hissing and spitting steam as they settled down at each stop. Marquees rolled around the segmented transports, announcing route numbers and destinations in a spidery crawl below their tint-darkened windows. Graffiti added a bit of flavor to the walls, but the storefronts on the busy street seemed to be losing their battle with the taggers, some of their glass fronts nearly covered with indecipherable scrawls. A few clusters of townhomes made some attempt at gentrification but, like the stores, were victims of the eternal twilight and visual noise that came with the understreets.

No one wanted to live in perpetual darkness, and as soon as they could, many fled for the outer rings of the undercity, with a few exceptions of those too poor to gain any foothold against their circumstances and the roaches passing for human in the tangled streets beyond the light.

I was counting on those roaches to help me ferret Kenny out, and I knew exactly what rock I needed to turn over first to begin my hunt.

"Got your badge?" I asked, glancing over at Cari. "You're going to need it."

"Hell, somewhere." She frowned, reaching for a backpack by her feet. "Why?"

"Because running down a bounty's different than hunting monsters. Law says we've got to be badged up clear as day," I told her, winding the Scout around to avoid a slow-moving transport truck. "Open carry's allowed, but badges have to be in sight. Besides, where we're going, a bit of metal goes a long way in either shaking people out of the trees or telling you who you've got to shake harder."

"Where exactly are you taking me, Gracen?" Cari came up from her digging, triumphantly holding up her Stalker badge, its plastic wrap still taped down around its curve. "I thought you knew where this guy was?"

"Not so much, but I've got a good lead on who's got eyes on him. Which is a damned good place to start." I wrestled the Scout into a holding zone, flipping on the SoCalGov permit light band attached to its windshield.

People on the street edged away from the old battle tank, eyeing its flashing LEO warning. The spot was perfect, not more than a few feet away from the alley I'd been looking for, and judging by the streams of people flowing in and out of the tight opening between the buildings, our showing up would disrupt a bit of business and everyone we would speak to would want us out of their hair as soon as they could.

"Slap the gold on, and make sure you've got your weapon tied down. We're going into the Market to see a woman about some curry," I said, stepping out of the Scout and fixing my badge to my belt. "And maybe shake her down for illegal possession at the same time, but mostly I just want some curry."

Fourteen

THERE ARE always places in a city where anything could be had for the right price. In Los Angeles, Santee Alley was where you stopped for anything from elote to prom dresses, and St. John's Park in San Francisco had things in its stalls guaranteed to boggle the mind, but in San Diego, the Market on Adams was where someone could find narwhal ivory carved into a snow leopard scene and pick up a few street tacos while debating what kind of Sig Sauer would fit neatly under a leather jacket.

For the most part, law enforcement left the place alone. For one, it was pretty much a sprawl of courtyards and alleys connecting around and through slender old buildings stacked on top of each other where people lived packed in like sardines for a few dollars a week. Navigating the Market was tricky and the stalls shifted over time, sometimes opening up a path one day and becoming impassable the next. The big players remained entrenched in their customary spots, but the fly-by-night sellers, with temporary goods liberated off the backs of trucks or suddenly found in empty lots, slid and slipped into the cracks between the old-timers, making it hard to find someone twice. The buildings crammed up tight against the Market's kiosks gave the whole place a prison feel, and the rows of uniform thin windows gave anyone a clear shot down into the crowds.

While everything could be found, it also meant nothing was off-limits, and there'd been more than a few reports of bodies being dragged out of the Market and dumped into the street, naked and bloodied from a knife wound or gunshot. There was no honor among thieves or gentlemen's agreement down here. If you went into the Market looking for trouble, it would find you soon enough. And if you were simply there to buy whatever cheap produce or groceries you could find among the stalls, you did so as quickly as possible, clutching your bags tightly to you and your wallet even tighter.

If we got eyed on the street, it was only a preview of the shunning we got once we ducked into the alley. Badges blazing, we were pariahs, lepers wearing gold plague masks on our waists, and in some ways, the space around us was a sense of false security. Or at least for Cari.

"Kind of nice," she murmured, looking around. "This place is insane, and we've got room to move. I should wear my badge more often."

"Yeah, just remember, now there's space for someone to pick us off with a quick shot from one of those windows," I said, nodding to the row of arrow slits running along the buildings tightly packed around the Market. "Better chance of a clean hit, so keep your head down, and the sooner we get into the stalls, the better."

To call the Market chaos was to say there were a lot of stars in the sky in the middle of a deep desert. There's a certain point when the visual noise simply takes over everything around it and nothing can puncture through the sea of colors and textures your brain struggles to take in.

I liked grabbing things from the Market when I had time, so I was familiar with the legacy stalls, but the pop-ups were always interesting, offering everything from cheaply made ammo to ostrich eggs. We were closer to the food stalls, where whiffs of fish-scented ice carried through the densely packed crowd, then disappeared under the weight of piles of fresh mushrooms and truffles nearly spilling over stacked baskets at a corner stall. I was tempted to grab a bag of peeled lychee, but the last thing I wanted was sticky fingers in case I had to draw a weapon, but Cari wasn't going to go by the kiosk without stopping.

"Starfruit, Kai. They have sliced starfruit with tamarind powder." She dug into her pockets, looking for change. "Do you want me to grab some lychee for you?"

"On the way out. If we're still alive." I scanned the walls above us, looking for movement. I'd activated the patches on my leather jacket, lighting up my badge sigils on my shoulders, and Cari's jacket sleeves proclaimed she was SoCalGov law enforcement, the tiny lights a soft glow under the blaze from the bands of lights strung overhead. "Don't grab too much. Where we're going might not have bathrooms, and you know what happens when you eat too much lychee."

"Worth it." She held her hand out to me. "Give me some money. I'm short."

"In more ways than one," I grumbled, digging into my pockets. Coming up with a handful of credits, I handed them over to her. "Grab napkins. Lots of them. And some wipes too."

She strolled next to me, happily stabbing pieces of chili-tamarind-mottled starfruit out of a cup with a tiny skewer the *fruteria* man gave her.

The bag of lychee was stashed somewhere in one of the thousand pockets her jacket had sewn into its lining. If there was one thing I could count on with Cari, it's that she was stocked up with everything she needed to toss out a spell or two should we need one. A good *hibiki* came prepared, her mother used to lecture her, and prepared sometimes meant having everything from packets of salt to single shots of tequila squirreled away in your jacket.

It also made for passing the time on stakeouts a lot easier, because most of the time, a good dose of tequila, some *li hing mui,* and salt made getting through a long cold night a piece of cake.

"Here. This way." I nudged her to the right, toward the inner part of the maze. "We're looking for Spicy Kat."

"Hey! Gracen! Come here!" The Cantonese man calling out to me from a corner stall waved one hand up over the crowd, jumping to catch my attention. He'd moved his stall closer to the food kiosks, mainly to take advantage of the thicker crowds, and I'd *known* that. Known it coming in, but it was still a shock to see his slender hand waving a paper-wrapped rectangular package high over his head. "Last one! You come get it!"

"Looks like that guy wants to talk to you," Cari murmured, nudging the small of my back. "That does not look like anyone named Spicy Kat."

"No, it's not. Just… hold up," I answered. "Be right back."

"You just told me to watch my back," she reminded me, keeping in step behind me. "You think I'm going to let you wander off? Keep walking, Gracen. I'm right here on your ass."

I got up close to the booth, careful not to jostle the glass bowls and spirals stacked on risers on a table running across the front of the space. The more expensive merchandise was behind Henry, with a bit of contraband tucked away in various spots beneath the tables. But that was an open secret. Most of the stalls in the Market did a shadow-market business of one kind or another, and Henry was the man you came to when you wanted something exotic to inhale or smoke.

Much like the packet of thick, cheap, disgusting, hand-rolled, Philadelphia-made cigars Henry was holding in his hands.

I was glad for the table, leaning against it for a bit of support. I shouldn't have lost my words, but they were gone, my attention focused on that stupid paper-wrapped box Henry waved about as if he were surrendering to an invading army. My knees were shaky, nearly cut out from under me, but I took the box when he held it out to me, my fingers slightly numb from the unexpected shock of Dempsey's loss hitting me once again out of the blue.

Just like him. Take your eyes off him when he was trying to teach you something and he'd smack you like you had a squadron of mosquitos on the side of your head. That's what it felt like to hold the pungent box of cigars and know Dempsey would never have another one again.

"This is the last one I can get for you. Maybe it's time for him to quit. The company is folding. Family sold it to some guy in Jersey, and I don't think he's going to continue doing this cheap crap. There's tobacco farms down on the coast that's supposed to be as good as Cuban, so they're putting all their money into that." Henry nodded at Cari, as if I always had a sloe-eyed hibiki-Stalker shadowing me. "This stuff's bad for him. It'll kill him. Bad for anyone. Even you. Hold on, I'll throw in some *kreteks* for you. Good faith so you come back and get yours from me. If he wants to change, I can find him something, but maybe better for him to quit."

"Yeah, I'll tell him. Last package," I replied, finally holding my wrist out for Henry to scan my link. "I'll come back to you for my kreteks. Thanks for doing this for him. I appreciate it."

Cari said nothing to me and fell in beside me as I turned away. We were shoulder to shoulder for a few strides. Then she tossed the rest of her fruit into a bin, shoving her hands in her pockets once she wiped them off on her jeans. The silence lasted another few steps. Then she cleared her throat.

"You didn't tell him Dempsey died," she said, pulling in close against me.

"He'd blame himself. Been telling the old man he had to stop smoking those things for years." The weight of the cigars dragged down my pocket a hell of a lot more than any of my weapons, and for a brief moment, I debated tossing them into the next bin we saw, but something held my hand back. I carried a lot of Dempsey on me—his ashes, his cigars, and probably more than a little bit of his attitude. I couldn't keep shedding parts of him hoping I'd feel better about him being gone. "Better to let Henry think he did Dempsey one last favor with these. Maybe I'll give them to Jonas. He liked to puff on one every once in a while."

"Only if you want Najiri and Angus to kill you," Cari snorted, pulling a face at me. "Those damned things stink."

I was going to leave Dempsey behind. At least for now. I couldn't carry the weight of him and hunt down his brother at the same time. Once I pinned Kenny down, I'd deal with everything else—providing no one killed me first.

"Come on. Sooner we find that asshole, the sooner we can go home." I wove through the crowd, half of my attention on any movement above us.

"Funny you should say home," Cari teased, a sly smirk curling over her impish features. "Where exactly is that now? The warehouse or... the Court."

"Wherever my cat's at, brat," I snarked back. "Keep up, will you. That's Spicy Kat right over there."

Working past the outer fringes of the Market brought us to the serious core of the place, where shouting and dealing happened at a furiously fast pace and where anything could be had for a bit of coin and some favors. We were shoulder to shoulder with chefs looking to bring something unique back to their restaurants, jostled about as they went from stall to stall, pinching bits of powder between their fingers and sniffing at the aromatics much like a Regency aristocrat pulled a bit of snuff from the mons of their hand.

The scents were nearly as overpowering as the wash of colors, assailing us in waves from curries to teas with a bit of pungent unknowns folded in between. The worst part was keeping Cari focused on moving forward. As much as she loved to delve into the exotic spices from far-off cultures, the hibiki in her blood drew her to the mounds of vibrant powders and leaves, entranced by the potential power trapped within. Avarice gleamed in the depths of her dark, hooded eyes, and I could practically see her mouth watering at a stall specializing in different types of garlic.

"Keep your head on you, Cari," I scolded, hooking my hand under her elbow. "You can come back and play witch later. For right now, I need info."

Spicy Kat saw me before I could get Cari moving, and she glanced about, gauging the crowd. Round-faced and freckled, Kat was typical of the understreet dwellers—mixed race with pulls of Japanese and a few other things tossed in for good measure. A bit taller than the gaggle of Korean women gathered around her stall, she was able to get a clear line of sight on me, her chin raised up when I began to work around people. The swing of her leather jacket was heavy, a clear sign it was armored, but she'd left it open, displaying a worn gray T-shirt printed with the oak tree logo of her spice stall. A slash of pink lipstick was her only concession to makeup, but she'd already chewed off a bit of it, probably digging her teeth in when she bargained someone up from a low price. Every bargain with Kat was like pulling teeth, and she took pride in making each coin scream before she handed it over.

"You wait until I'm done here," Kat grumbled at me, measuring out a bit of saffron from a basket. "And don't touch anything. I don't want to have to watch your thieving fingers."

"I have never stolen anything from you in my entire life," I scoffed. "Your spices are stale and weak. I'd be better off scraping up sawdust from the chair-carver in the third quarter."

"Pele's fire, and you're wearing a badge. Why not just bring a health inspector with you." Her eyes narrowed even further, and she glanced quickly at the women clustered around a bin of orange-rind tea. "Do not lose this sale for me, Gracen."

"Then don't accuse me of stealing," I shot back, keeping my hand on Cari's elbow, trying to make sure she stayed out of the way. "If you're nice to me, I'll let this one go, and she will shop until her fingers are bloody from testing things out. Probably pay your month's stall rent."

"Stop that," Cari hissed. "Let go. I'm going to go look. You can go do whatever it is you need to, but I've got my eye on those lime leaves."

I waited as Kat dickered and dealt. There were eyes on us, or at least me, but none of the people staring looked like they were either curious about an elfin in their midst or concerned about the badge markers plastered on my jacket and at my waist. The weight of my guns was a reassuring press against my back and hips. I was uneasy—more so after Gibbons—but it seemed like a typical day at the Market, people more concerned with getting in and out before the evening rolled in and things got dangerous than some Stalker slowing business down for a spice seller.

"Lara, come ring these up," Kat called out to her assistant, a pale wraith of a woman hovering near Cari. "Then sell that one everything under the sun. Don't let her bargain you down."

"Good luck with that." I nodded toward Cari. "She came out of her mother haggling for a deal."

"Come over here." Kat motioned me to the back of the stall. "Let's go talk in the bay."

As a generational-legacy stall owner, Kat's family secured a spot up against one of the buildings and used a docking bay as a lock-down area for her stall and inventory when the Market closed at night. The rectangular bay was empty, except for a few barrels of supplies and a pair of folding chairs set around an empty wire spool Kat and probably her mother before her used as a table. It was gouged out with pencil and pen marks with a few scorches of cigarette burns here and there. Kat sat, flopping down into one of the chairs with a heaving sigh, staring up at me as she rubbed her belly.

"You going to sit?" she asked, nodding toward the other chair. "Or are you going to make my neck hurt looking up at you?"

"Sitting doesn't seem prudent. Someone's got a price on my head." I debated the chair, then decided leaning against the wall was the most relaxed I was going to go. "Maybe you've heard about that."

Kat crossed her arms over her chest and stared out into the Market. She chewed her lip for a moment, taking off more of the pink lipstick, then finally nodded. "Heard about it. Lot of people have. They don't like it. But they're also kind of wondering why you're going after Kenny Dempsey when you don't do bounties. That changed?"

"Just for Kenny," I replied, my attention drifting out toward the Market as well, wondering what Kat was looking at. "I just buried his brother… my mentor—"

"Man was your father. Everyone knows that. Call it what it is," Kat laid into me. "So you're hunting his brother?"

"Kenny's got a bounty on him. I take him in, he'll make it to jail. Someone else does? Who's to say?" If Kat knew about the price on me, she probably knew the details on Kenny. I wasn't going to show my hand on anything about Dempsey's original contract, but she was right; I wasn't known for bounties. "I owe him a fair shake. At least for Dempsey's sake."

"Dempsey hated the bastard," Kat spat. "But this is the kind of stupid thing you'd do. Sort of like biting off a guy's face."

"He was trying to kill me," I pointed out. "Almost killed Jonas. What did you expect me to do? Just let him?"

"Nah, you don't go after Stalkers, especially not ones as pretty and stupid as you are. You're an easy touch. Hardly any of those around. Don't got enough money to get rid of that banshee pack in your lake? Shoot Gracen a message and he'll go out there and take care of it for a bag of peanut-butter-and-jelly sandwiches."

"I'm not that bad," I refuted. "Okay, if it's guava jam, maybe. How about if we just cut to the quick of this so I can get out of your hair and you can go back to dealing reefer plugs tucked into your bay leaves."

"You going to bust me?" She gave me a hairy eyeball. "Because that's just not cool."

"I just want info on where I can find Kenny. I'm not the only one out there looking for him, but I'm the only one who'll guarantee he'll still be breathing once I hand him over. Samms is on his trail." I grinned at her derisive snort. "He's probably got a fifty-fifty chance with Samms. Can't say the same for anyone else. I read the docket. Kenny pissed off some pretty powerful people. You don't go taking money from criminals, even if they're legitimate businessmen."

"Those are sharks, that's what those are." She glanced up at me, then back out into the crowd. "Your girl is fleecing mine. I'll be lucky to have the canvas roof left by the time she's done."

"Warned you," I reminded her. "Come on, Kat. I don't have all day. Hell, Kenny doesn't have all day. Where is he? Sooner I can put my hands on him, the better it is for him. How much do you want?"

"Let me see." Kat tapped at the spool, pretending she was doing some mental calculations, but it was a lie. There's no way she hadn't already figured out exactly how much Kenny would be worth to me. The price she named was ludicrous, but I wasn't going to argue over it. I had the money. Hell, it wasn't even close to the bounty on Kenny's head, and information was as good as coin and sometimes even better.

"That's doable," I conceded. "Half now, the other half when I find him. Assuming he doesn't see me coming and bolt."

"Funny you should say that," she snorted, pushing herself up out of the chair. "He's holed up in the Diamond Kitty. Seems that's something he and Dempsey have in common. Both of them have a thing for pointy-eared bastards. There's no way he's going to see you with all the skin jobs walking around in that place. Not unless someone tells him."

Fifteen

"SO THIS place gives you the creeps?" Cari asked, shifting in her seat and ducking her head down to look up at the sunlight bulbs flickering above us. "The Diamond Kitty."

"You've got a bunch of human kids—mostly kids—who spend money to sculpt their faces and... everything... to look elfin," I replied, cursing the drips splattering the Scout's windshield when we got caught under a faulty rain line. "Imagine going into the Court and seeing a bunch of them with cutoff ear tips and squared-off jaws. It's... weird. Just saying, it's not my kink."

"Still getting used to seeing an elfin in the mirror?" She tilted her head to look at me, digging down into one of my troubles.

"Yeah, sometimes," I admitted. "I'm not saying they're the problem. Because people need to shape themselves sometimes. I get that. Maybe it's because I look at them and I see... me. It bugs me, and I'm not good about dealing with it. There's been other shit on my plate to eat."

We were deep into the understreets at this point, not to the depths but close enough to be skirting its edges. Above us the lights should have dimmed down to twilight, but only about half of them worked, and the ones that did seemed to be set either to full-summer blast or midmorning fog. The flashes of daylight over the Scout were disconcerting, and my eyes fought to maintain some kind of control over the wavering darkness as I drove. The tik-tiks here were a fast and furious dive in and out, tiny blue spiders skimming down across the waters to pluck up their prey or drop off corpses. The last time I'd been down to the Diamond Kitty, there'd been a scatter of industrial places around its old warehouse shell, but the neighborhood had changed, with small pop-up trailer homes and cargo-shipment containers turned into dwellings sprouting up where junkyards and mechanical yards used to be.

With the influx of residential dwellings came other business, flocking to pick off the bones of people barely scraping by. Bodegas sat on every other corner, gouging and scalping people too tired and poor to head out to other districts to gather groceries, and tattoo studios shoved for space next to paycheck-advance kiosks, their doors shadowed by large, muscular men with mean eyes and a nose for trouble. The junkyards and repair places were still there, mostly doing their best to hold up the edges of the district, but it wouldn't be long before they were pushed out. All it took was one lot being sold and cheap housing to go up for a district to shift for the better or worse, and easy maintenance of a property was a hell of a lot more profitable than working a trade and paying employees.

The food truck parked at a curb between two lackluster clubs was doing a brisk business, and my stomach growled when the smell of grilling carne asada snuck into the Scout. It'd been a long time since breakfast, and the quick chew of a granola bar a few hours ago hadn't quieted my belly. And even though Cari had been eating all day, I figured I'd give it about five minutes before she complained she was starving.

Instead, she dug down again into my nerves.

"So," she murmured, not trying to hide the sly grin on her face. "You and Ryder? Actually doing the thing?"

"What the hell?" I slammed on the brakes to avoid hitting a tiny beep-beep car abruptly deciding a yellow light meant stopping instead of gunning it through the intersection. "Why… shit, I don't even know what to say to you. Who the hell raised you?"

"Well, technically, you had a hand in that," Cari shot back. "Come on, it's not like I haven't known other people you sleep with, and everyone's kind of noticed him coming out of your room in the morning, and his bed's not slept in. We can do the math. It's not that hard."

There were times when it was difficult to remember Cari was a full-fledged adult. Usually it wasn't. Of course, normally we were standing shoulder to shoulder in situations where there was gunfire and lots of shit happening around us, so not exactly a place I'd think of her as a kid, but there was always this niggle in the back of my head—that scatter of memories of a tiny larva of a girl with big brown eyes and a toothless, drooling mouth holding my finger while trying to learn how to smile.

This was definitely one of those times.

I pulled over, taking the Scout out of the thin traffic before I got both of us killed, and let the engine idle, trying to wrap my head around talking to Cari about sex and Ryder.

"Look, who else are you going to talk to? Jonas?" she pressed on. "I'm literally your best friend. Probably after that damned cat, but still, your best damned friend. I mean, hell, I'm practically your sister. Who else are you going to talk about this with?"

"No one," I growled, still staring out the windshield, looking anywhere but at Cari's face. It wasn't like I was known for long-term relationships. I avoided them like they were diseased, hungry dragons, but I didn't drag any of the people I slept with through my life. They were as disposable as the paper wrappers from the taco truck, balled up and tossed when we were done. "Look, Ryder and I—"

"They've got bets going on in the Court about the two of you," she interjected. "About if you're moving in. What you two are doing. When you're finally going to be together. They're very long-sighted, those people. Like, they think fifteen years is a short dating span. I told Alexa it'll be faster than that. Ryder's fallen hard for you, and, well, you think like you're human. I need an inside track. You could seriously score me enough money to buy me something solid from Sparky."

I gave her what I hoped was my hardest look, and she shrugged at me.

"Look," she said. "At least I'm honest. And it's not like I don't care about you. If anyone needs someone in their life, it sure as hell is you. It'll be nice to see you happy for once. Or even just less growly."

"I am not… growly," I muttered, pulling the Scout slowly back into traffic. "I haven't… shit… why do you care?"

"Because I love you," she replied, her voice turning deep and soft. "And I want to see you happy. You deserve to be happy, Kai. Even if you don't think you do."

I chewed on what she said. My life had a big hole in it where Dempsey once stood. While we didn't talk about intimate things, he'd always been the one to tell me I didn't have to settle for anyone who'd just have me. To take my time, and if I didn't want anyone, it was okay—this coming from a man who married a harridan who took off when she found out she wasn't getting anything when he died. But I figured he'd had his reasons for marrying her. He made bad choices in his life, and I counted myself as one of them. Cari wasn't wrong. She was the closest thing to a sister I had, and despite the fact I sometimes had a hard time remembering she wasn't a little girl anymore, she could hold her own. I knew that. I'd helped teach her to be that strong woman, and I was proud of her.

Talking to her about sex was… definitely going to be a challenge.

Thank Gods the traffic was a still life or I'd get us both killed. Without anyone shooting at us.

"Look, this thing with Ryder is complicated. There's this pull we have, like this gut punch of a want, and it's not something emotional or mental.

It's something the elfin have, some reaction or crap like that," I started. "It's strong and it's always there. Like my blood telling me that's who I have to have in my life. And it's the same for him."

"Yeah, I can't see that going over well with you," she said. "Alexa told me about that. She says she feels a bit of it with you."

"A little bit. Not like with Ryder," I continued. "And not like it was with the Unsidhe Lord we saw down in Mexico. It was a bit there with her too. But Ryder, it's… a hum. Always there. Singing through me. And yeah, I'm not… good with any kind of blood stuff. It's too much like being forced into something. I don't want to be led into anything. I'm not anyone's property and no one's mine. So right now, no. We're not… together. He sleeps with me. We talk. We sleep. But it's got to be more than just this blood-want thing. There's a lot of stuff between us, like the Court and me being a Stalker. It's complicated, Cari. And I'm not sure how to uncomplicate it."

"Does it have to be?" She cocked her head and pursed her mouth. "Complicated, I mean? Can't you just be with him and see where it goes?"

"I'm not good with relationships. Last one I had… the last real one didn't end so well." I thought back to all the fights and shoving, the strain being away from each other had on both of us, and then the wondering if it was all worth it. "He comes with a lot of entanglements, and, well, I come with a lot of baggage. Thing is, Ryder isn't someone you can try stuff out with. I step into that pond, it's deep, and it's either going to be I drown or swim. There's no climbing out."

"And you hate water." She sniffed. "Should have used a different example."

"Only one I could come up with. And I don't really hate water. I just don't like swimming in *deep* water. Never know what's going to come up and eat you," I countered. "I've just got to figure out if I want to, and, well, Ryder's got to figure out if I'm worth it."

"I think he already has." Cari's attention went back to the street, watching a thin stream of people crossing it. "Ryder's just waiting for you. And yeah, he's Sidhe, probably going to wait forever. But you're not. You're not elfin. Not in your head. You're as human as I am, and that part of you needs someone, Kai. Someone who knows who you are and accepts that. And I'm telling you, that guy is Ryder."

"Yeah, but how do you know?" I said, glancing at her. "Because I sure as hell don't."

"You told him he couldn't come with us because he isn't good enough with a weapon." Cari dug back down into her backpack, pulling out a handful of dried tangerine slices, offering me one, then shrugging when I shook my head. "Does it feel like time's too slow when he's not around? Do you *miss* him?"

I didn't have to think about it. More than a few times in the Market I'd almost turned around to tell Ryder to look at one thing or another, but he hadn't been there. The space at my side was empty, and I felt the loss—not heartbreaking but definitely *looking* for Ryder.

"Yeah, I miss him, but he's where I know he'll be okay. Down here, he won't be. Most people know me or at least give me a bit of room. He… glitters. Ryder can't help but be Ryder, Clan Sebac, Third in the House of Devon, High Lord of the Southern Rise Court, and that's not someone I can take down here." It was pointing out the obvious, but my words hurt, twisting about in my belly. "He's the Court's lord. He can't go traipsing off with me to kill monsters when he's got people he's got to feed down here. That's the reality of it."

"Then sometimes you're going to have to stay with him and make soup," she murmured. "And sometimes he'll go with you on things he can help with. It's about blending your lives, Kai, not shoving them apart. I think you're in love with him and it scares the hell out of you. And that's saying a hell of a lot, because knowing everything you've gone through, I never thought love would be the bullet that stopped you."

"Well, right now, I've got to stay focused on Kenny Dempsey, and that means going to deal with Orin Bennett. He's the guy who owns the place, and he's probably not going to be too happy to see me. And if he's the one I've got to shake Kenny's location out of, it's going to cost me something fierce." Someone honked, and I had to snag Cari's hand before she could lean out the window to flip off the car behind us. "Don't do that."

"Asshole deserves it. And why does Bennett not like you now? Last time he was practically preening to get to you. Elfin are his *thing*."

"Because I killed his brother, Oscar, remember?" I shook my head at Cari's quiet and thoughtful murmur. "Yeah, let's hope he wasn't that fond of Oscar or it's going to be a shitty time for us in the Diamond Kitty."

THE DISTRICT was going to seed and fast, every block we passed painted more and more with grime, graffiti, and neglect, the people on the street shifting from day workers coming home from the upper city to the type of characters one only finds on the edges of the understreets. Small pockets of men and women stood on the corners, smoking cigarettes and chatting. Some were obviously in the skin trade, calling out to anyone passing by, but most just seemed more interested in doing deals or simply hanging out.

A neon cat winked in the distance, her curves a bright purple splash of light strong enough to push back the clinging shadows. The sunlamps here rarely reached full brightness, leaving the district in a steamy dusk. I found a place to park the Scout about twenty feet away from the club, angling it to get a good view of the front entrance as well as the side door leading out to a wide alley. It was now early evening, not late enough for the true nightcrawlers to come and ply their trade, but there were a few of the elfin skin jobs already standing at the front of the Kitty, smoking herbals and letting its neon lights play over their altered features.

Some had more work done than others, but they seemed to be openly touching the pieces and parts they'd changed. One kid was fully immersed, his face and hair altered to be a glittering mimicry of the Sidhe living in the upper city. His hair was a blend of metallics, silver and gold strands flashing about his lupine face. Even from where we were parked, his eyes glittered like emeralds and a rain-drenched forest, not unlike Ryder's. Still, his movements were wrong, lacking the innate grace most elfin had, but that also could have been him. Some of the others moved with the fluidity of trained dancers, their hands dipping and gliding about as they spoke, pale sparrows dancing in the false full moonlight.

I'd seen their kind before—disaffected young men and women looking for a place they could fit into. Hell, every walk of life had them. Humans were driven to explore not only the world around them but themselves. That was the one truth I knew about the people who raised me. There was a constant, roaming quest to discover the depths or heights of humanity, and sometimes that journey took a hard left turn into a what-the-hell neighborhood.

Maybe it was because I was elfin. Hell, as a chimera, I was a blend of both Unsidhe and Sidhe, not exactly a poster child for the sane and normal, but watching the elfin-human hybrids laugh and chat under the lights of a place they gathered to be a part of a tribe, I wondered where the hell I would actually feel like I belonged.

I didn't know what went into altering someone's features, at least on the human side of things. Human healers like Cari's mom couldn't shape flesh like the elfin. I didn't know the mechanics of magic either, just the limitations, or mostly the accepted ones. Cari knew a hell of a lot more than I did and picked at the Court's Sidhe healers to glean whatever she could to strengthen her own magics.

I didn't think she would ever get to the point where she could take a human ear or face and sculpt its bone and flesh to look elfin.

But I could be wrong.

"They're not open yet, but soon. We'll go in and hit Bennett up when they do." I gestured toward the small groups framed in the Scout's windshield and unclicked my seat belt. "Surgery? Or do you know healers who can do that?"

Cari studied the group, then nodded at one with elongated ears poking out through her long pink hair. "Implants. Some healers will do that. It's just cutting stuff open and then stretching the skin out. Like gauging. Sort of. Same thing with the cheeks and chin. That one had her jaw shaved down. Not much different than getting a boob job."

"Yeah, I don't get that either." Shrugging, I leaned back against the vinyl seat, listening to it squeak against my leather jacket. "But I guess it's whatever makes you feel like you, right? That's all that matters."

"If someone could make you look human, would you do it?" She undid her seat belt, shifting until she faced me a little bit but keeping her eyes on the Kitty. "Take off your ears?"

I caught myself touching the notch in my ear, the triangular chunk taken out by a pair of iron-dust-laced snips Tanic liked to use on my flesh. Trying to imagine myself with round ears and a blunter face was hard, oddly enough, even though my elfin features still sometimes shocked me when I saw them in the mirror.

"Maybe before," I confessed with a nod. "Now, probably not. It's different now. Used to be even hearing Unsidhe made me sick to my stomach, but I broke that magic. And could be I'm just more accustomed to seeing people like me walking around. Makes me feel less... alone. Probably the same reason these kids get together. Here, they're normal. And that's something huge when you feel lost inside."

"That's all you can ask for, I guess," Cari murmured. "I've got some granola bars. Want one?"

"No. And what the hell? Did you bring the whole damned kitchen?" I peered over at her backpack. "Gonna pull out a ham next?"

"Like I'd share ham with you," she snorted. "We could be here a long time waiting for him to not show up. Hell, I don't even know what this guy looks like."

The side door opened, the heavy industrial lamp fixed above the frame turning on, dousing the alley with bright light. Someone stepped out, his body a stocky silhouette against the unpainted brick. The empty lot next to the Kitty was thick with weeds and surrounded by a chain-link fence that had seen better days or maybe was never new, because it sagged in places, swooping down and bulging out around the property. We could make out the guy standing under the light for a moment before he stepped out, taking himself out of the intense sheen, and the light finally hit his face when he turned to light a fat chewed-on cigar, cupping his face as if a wind were somehow going to flare up to douse the match he took to its end.

The match light brought the cigar to a bright red, and his blunt features were achingly familiar as he sucked on the cigar. He was shorter than Dempsey by a good five inches, his face a crude echo of the man who'd raised me, much like the half-done sculpting of the kids standing at the front of the building. Shaking the match out, he tossed its blackened corpse to the ground, pulling on the cigar to get a puff of smoke going. Bags tugged down on his flaccid, mottled skin, his hair a greasy curtain around his round face. He looked like hell and fidgeted, his eyes moving constantly, but the Scout seemed to be outside of his notice.

Or at least for now. I was about to take care of that for him.

"I'll be damned. The gods are smiling or laughing at us. One or the other." Undoing the holster straps on my Glocks, I nodded toward Kenny Dempsey and murmured to Cari, "Kenny looks exactly like that. In fact, we probably want to go shake him down for an ID and get him the hell out of here."

"Well, this is going to be a walk in the park, then," she said with a grin, pulling her jacket back and lighting up her badges. "We do this right, we might even be home in time for dinner."

"Don't count on it," I warned. "Because if there's one thing I've learned, it's never count your fire chicks before you can get them into the goddamned Nova."

Sixteen

THE SCOUT'S doors opening must have been enough movement to catch Kenny's attention, especially since he was probably as jumpy as a naked cat in a tattoo shop of drunk inkers. He tilted his head back, peering through the smoke first at Cari, then at me. Any hope I had of him thinking I was one of the Kitty's skin jobs coming in for a good time was gone, because he choked on a mouthful of smoke and bolted.

Damn if the asshole wasn't carrying a hell of a lot more weight than Dempsey did but still moved like the wind.

"Okay, not so easy," Cari grumbled, breaking into a run. "Shit."

I tapped on my badge, lighting it up, and drew my weapon before rounding the Scout. There was some commotion from the front—unclear shouting—but stopping wasn't in the plan. I didn't know the area, and chasing a runner through the understreets was a hazardous game. Out in the open with a creature was one thing. Animals, even black dogs, were wired to instinct, making them at least somewhat predictable. Humans, not so much. Especially this one.

"Cut him off?" Cari shouted, hitting the alley in full stride.

"No. Just... go." I passed her easily, my longer legs eating up the distance, my boots pounding on the alley's hard concrete.

Kenny dove to the left at the back of the building, and I turned the corner hard, keeping my weapon down and close. There was a small stretch of asphalt behind the Kitty, mostly parking for its employees, but a few kids were pulling themselves out of a tiny box of a car. Their shifting weight tilted the car up and down, its single middle-mounted front wheel dipping to one side then the next as the diminutive car vomited out its passengers. Even with only Kenny's back to me, I could almost hear him debating hijacking the car and half wished he would. Shooting him at this point wasn't off the table—just enough to slow him down—and it would be easier if he were in a piece-of-shit dot on three wheels whose top speed was probably barely above a drunk slug.

Sadly for me, he chose to lumber on.

The kids were ahead on my right, wide-eyed and pointy-eared, mouths open in surprise as they watched us approach. Kenny panted heavily, sucking in all the sour, foul air coming up from the sewers, and his slapping feet kicked up pieces of garbage with each step he took. Even from far away, I could see the kids were barely kissing the edge of adulthood, most of their modifications silicone constructs applied with a crude, uneven hand. Their clothes were outlandish, elaborate costuming with some of it half left in the car, obviously too big to wear and fit into the scrap metal that brought them there.

"Don't make me shoot you, Kenny!" I yelled at his back, gaining on him with each stride. "You know—gods damn you."

Bastard kept running.

Alleys and backdoor parking lots are never anyone's highlight, but the Kitty's back bins seemed particularly ripe. The stench alone was enough to bleach out someone's nostril hairs, and I nearly gagged from the miasma rising up from the scum-clogged grates set into the ground. I tried to avoid the slippery algae pools growing across the wet gully running down the length of the alley, but some places were too wide, even with my long legs. Kenny had no such qualms. He splashed through the soggy moss, splashing up waves of sour water with each pounding step.

If I was going to catch up with the son of a bitch, I was going to have to be less delicate.

"What the hell," I muttered, sidestepping another grate, careful to keep my feet clear of the mini swamps dotting the ground. "I'll just hose the Scout out when we get back."

Cari was somewhere behind me, shouting something I couldn't make out. If she was asking me to get out of the way so she could get in a clear shot, I wouldn't have blamed her. The farther we got down the walk, the thicker the smell, and I was surprised the kids hadn't passed out from the stench. Kenny lumbered past them, his arms churning up and down. A hard sprint toward him almost put me on my ass when I slid over a piece of something clinging to the incline, and I righted myself with a flail of my arms before I took a spill in front of the kids scrambling to get out of the car.

I was about to pick up my pace again when I heard the first gunshot and one of the kids' shoulders exploded in a gush of bone and blood.

Their screams were shrill, keening, and sharp, punctuated with panicked cries for their gods to help them. I wanted to keep after Kenny, but the splash of blood brought me to a stop. Metallic and cloying, the scent of fear and pain carried over me. A second boom hit, another tearing sound through the already high-pitched confusion, and a window shattered somewhere. Then came another shot, popping up bits of concrete and water. I shuffled to the side, pulling one of the kids behind the car and crouching down to drag the injured one out of the shooter's line of sight.

She fought me, eyes wild and white. My fingers dug into her jacket, an oddly constructed knockoff of a formal Sidhe robe. A piece of fastener tape ripped as I tugged, the front opening up to give me a peek of the white T-shirt now soaked with blood beneath the jacket's embroidered front. One of her ears flopped off, tangling in the pink-streaked metallic gold wig she'd tugged on while getting out of the car. The silicone swoop of fake cartilage tumbled out when I gave another yank, a pale floppy island poking up out of a sea of grit and muck.

"Come on, kid. Quit fighting me." Murmuring the same stupid things I said to gut-shot Stalkers dying on a job seemed silly, but the girl quieted down a bit, going slack instead of helping me, but I took what I could get. I'd hauled out bigger and heavier. Tracking and taking down ainmhi dubh often meant hiking miles with hundreds of pounds of acidic meat slung over my shoulders or dragging the load behind me on a soft sling. "Hang on. You're not that bad."

The boy I'd pulled in first shook and trembled, his cheek dotted with the girl's blood. I grabbed his wrist, pressing his hand on her wound, and he blinked at me, his own crudely elfin face bleached from fear. Staring down at his friend, he retched, gagging on his own terror.

"I can't… I'm only fifteen," the boy gulped, swallowing air he didn't need in his belly. "My mom doesn't even know I'm down here."

"Yeah, figure that out later. Press down. It'll help stop the bleeding." I did a quick head count. The girl was sliding in and out of consciousness, but her eyes were still tracking. Flicking on my link, I pinned down the location and sent out an EMT call, attaching my SoCalGov badge number to the request. I got back a quick confirmation, acknowledging the gunshot civilian I'd tagged the call with. "Where's your friends? Shit, you two! Come here."

"Got 'em!" Cari tumbled in, shoving at the remaining kids. The other two—another boy and girl—were older but with the same wide-eyed terror stealing the color from their faces. "Stay down. Kai, you're going to lose him."

"Girl. And she's fine. Clean through. Shoulder hit. Medics were tagged and are on their way." I glanced down the alley. "Crap, you mean Kenny. I can't dump you here. These kids—"

"Go! I'll take care of this." Cari ducked past me, shoving at the faux elfin boy next to me. Broken from his shock, he stumbled to hide behind the old van I'd gotten the others behind. "You guys stay behind the cars. Kai, go! I've got this. I'll find you. Don't lose that bastard. And don't get shot."

"Thanks." I almost kissed her forehead but figured she'd either punch me or it would discredit her Stalker status with the kids. "Wish me luck."

Kenny was a dot on the far end of the alley, hanging a sharp right with a skidding slide. He went down hard, slamming into a crumbling brick wall. While I was too far to hear what he said, I knew the look on his face. A Dempsey-like thundercloud rolled over it, flushing it redder than the flashing sign fixed to the building wall, an erratic lit-up shout to buy more cans of shaving cream. Kicking himself over, he struggled to get up, his hands sliding out from under him until he could get a good purchase on the ground, gravity and his plump belly giving me enough time to catch up. I was less than half a block away when he staggered to his feet and broke into a limping gallop, hurrying away from the alley as fast as he could.

"Kenny, just freaking stop!" I pulled up my Glock, then shook off the filmy trails of slime I'd somehow picked up when I slid down to avoid the gunfire. I sighted Kenny's shoulder, but a whining ping smacked the brick by my right ear, careening stone fragments into my face. "Damn it."

Someone was definitely aiming—however badly—to kill me or Kenny, but I wasn't sure which. I couldn't see where the shooter was and actually had hoped it'd been circumstantial gunfire, an unfortunate but way too frequent occurrence down in the back part of the understreets, but the wall hit next to my head put that theory to rest. Putting the building between me and the asshole lurking somewhere down the alley would do the trick, or so I thought, because as soon as I took the same sharp turn Kenny did, I found myself in a tight alley, staring at a nine-foot-tall wooden fence covered with warning signs that promised impending doom.

"No way in hell he went over that." The dumpster against the brick wall across of the shot-up building was open and had enough garbage in it to drown a cow. "And he sure as heck wouldn't fit in there. So…."

The brick building with the crumbling walls was an old throwback to a time when San Diego didn't have an underground—a pre-Merge dinosaur waiting to be crumbled to dust. Most of its upper windows were blown out, either removed for the glass or picked off by someone with a gun. Bits of pebbled glass littered the ground by my feet, crunching under my boots as I carefully picked my way across the front of the building.

It was a prime pick-off spot, much better than the alley, by my reckoning. Glass shards hung from off-kilter window frames, pieces of plywood hammered across some of the gaping holes in a halfhearted attempt to keep out looters or squatters. They needn't have bothered. There was nothing but the shaky brick walls to offer anyone more than a cairn to be buried under should a heavy truck decide to tap the alley-side face. The building was held together by a lick and a prayer, or at least that's what it looked like. But something or someone was moving inside, someone large enough to kick something metal, hard enough to make it sing a lolling sound and send a pair of rats scrambling for the partially unhinged steel-mesh door.

I kept my weapon up, wary of being ambushed. I didn't know if Kenny was armed, and with someone else taking potshots at me from their position above the alley, I couldn't be sure if I was walking into a trap or just after an incompetent scared man trying to outrun karma.

"Too many damned players on the board," I muttered under my breath, ducking beneath the pried-back mesh. My shoulders nearly brushed the rusted filthy orange metal, and its proximity sent shivers down my spine and bile running up my throat as if I'd spent five days drinking rotgut gin. A bit of peeling paint on the remains of a sign lying near the front door informed me that, at some point, a man named Mike Carillo ran an ironworks business in the now-abandoned building.

Iron.

"Might as well just drink a damned cup of belladonna and wait for the pink elephants to come dancing across my eyes." I sighed, moving as carefully as I could to avoid snagging any part of my skin on the flaking door. "Why iron, Mike? What was wrong with steel? Or even ceramics? Why the hell did you decide to dance with the elfin devil and make my life even shittier today?"

The interior of the building had no inner walls, or at least nothing whole enough to count. Girders and beams held up what was left of the second floor, but even that was more sieve than ceiling. The sunspot above the alley let in enough light through the broken exterior to give me some illumination to see into the space, and what I found was disheartening.

Because other than the few rodents scurrying about, there wasn't anyone in the damned place but me.

Then I looked up and was caught in the wonder of pixie fireflies swirling off the steel beams. Petite slashes of yellow and blue light danced about the air, their glow beginning to brighten as their internal clocks shook them from their slumber. Despite being buried underground, beneath a massive city, the sylphlike insects woke to the rise of the moons, their slender bodies rolling through different light patterns, signaling hunger, lust, and whatever else a bug needed to tell its swarm. With delicate rainbow-flecked wings, they swooped about, each nearly as long as one of my fingers, then dove down toward the middle of the building, dipping into a dark gash between two girders.

"Huh." I stepped carefully, feeling the scrape of airborne iron against my skin. Kenny either knew what he was doing or was just damned lucky. Since he was Dempsey's brother and an asshole at the best of times, I figured he knew exactly how the building's rusting artifacts would pull and tug at my elfin flesh. "Had to have planned this. Probably seeded the rumors. Got to hand it to you, Kenny. You always play every side you can."

The urge to scratch my exposed skin was strong, but my hands were busy, one holding a Glock while I had the other ready to pull a knife in case I needed to do some up-close work. There was no doubt in my mind that I was walking into a trap, but I couldn't figure out Kenny's angle.

"Unless he's got someone like Gibbons in his back pocket." Mulling over that possibility, I followed the fireflies' trail, carefully stepping around as much of the debris on the uneven floor as I could. I kept my attention on my surroundings, checking every shadow for a heavy-breathing man who probably smelled of canned sardines and cigarettes. "And that's definitely something ole Kenny would pull."

My suspicions about where the sparkling insects had gone proved to be right when I stepped around a leaning cubicle wall and stared down into a wide sinkhole filled on one side with a pile of fallen brick, moldy drywall, and boulders. The tumble of rocks formed a natural staircase down into one of the many caverns below the city, pockets of Earth trapped beneath understreets from the Merge.

The pixie fireflies' egress left a trail of faintly glowing dust scattered around the hole with a single trail of footsteps clearly stamped into the layers of fine powder. Judging by the smear of a handprint against the wall of the toppled cube, someone recently came around the stained fabric-upholstered partition and used it to balance himself for a moment while he stepped down into the hole. I'd gone down quite a few of the pre-Merge subterranean caverns, often chasing a creature down to its lair for a contract, and knew from experience they were problematic at best. There was never any rhyme or reason to their size, and the chunks of pre-Merge Earth moldering in those dark depths held surprises both good and bad. I'd found Oketsu in one while chasing a monster bent on chewing its way through a nursery school, but I'd also fallen into a pit of black-hooded scorpions that did their damnedest to puncture past the leathers I'd been wearing so they could dissolve my flesh and eat the liquefied goo.

A bit of the floor crumbled off and bounced down into the hole when I stepped closer. I didn't like the way the ground seemed stretched to nearly its breaking point at the edges, pulled too thin by either the worlds buckling and expanding to shape around each other or worse, some idiot decided on having an underground hidey-hole and dug the pit out before the Merge without thinking about the mass above it.

"Hole got here somehow," I reminded myself, taking a careful step down to the largest embedded rock I could see. Keeping one hand free to balance myself, I tightened my grip on my Glock. Going in blind wasn't smart, but the cavern probably connected to another one, or even to the nest of tunnels and crevices leading back up to the surface outside of San Diego proper. Snorting to myself, I took another step down. "Right, like Kenny's going to last that long of a trek without water or food. He'd get eaten by a muddle of guinea pigs before he got a mile in."

The pixies were still swirling about me when my foot touched the floor of the cavern, their minute sparks dimmed by the presence of luminescent ivy vines threading over the cavern's uneven walls and some of its rocky outcroppings. If anything, the cavern seemed to be brighter than the building above me, but I still had to move carefully, letting my vision adjust.

"Damned place looks like it took a shelling," I muttered to myself.

There were boulders and stalagmites everywhere, and the fireflies seemed to be interested in a constellation of algae-clogged puddles to the right of the rock pile I'd climbed down. The insects dipped and swirled, their long prawn-like bodies flashing gods-knew-what to the swarm, celebrating their water-drenched salad or perhaps adding me to the list of people they'd drawn down to their deaths. Kenny's path through their dusting faded off to the left, heading toward a thick copse of columns covered with more ivy, the spires stretching up to connect with the cavern's ceiling nearly twenty feet above. A trail of sparkling yellow footprints led off clearly at first, but then grew fainter as his shoes sloughed off the fireflies' powder.

"Hold up." I frowned, glancing at the ground, then at the fireflies. The glowing motes were everywhere, illuminated circles surrounding each puddle, with a fine layer of dust floating on the surface where the bugs dove down to snatch up whatever it was they found in the stagnant water. "What the hell am I stepping in? Is this bug shit? Is that what this is?"

I sniffed at the gold glitter stuck to my hands, prepared to recoil or gag at the smell.

Nothing.

Still didn't mean it wasn't shit, so I wiped my hands on the nearest rock before plunging deeper into the cavern, following the trail of unevenly paced footprints Kenny had left in his wake.

The bubble of space only extended a few feet behind the rock pile but stretched out into the shimmering depths past the columns. There were signs of pre-Merge Earth scattered about the ground below the hole in the building's floor, bits and pieces of a broken-apart restaurant dotting the rocks near the pools. A small fryer basket stuck out of a stalagmite near me, its mesh nearly rusted through and thick with pixie dung.

More evidence of forgotten Earth cropped up as I walked, the ivy wrapping around not only the rock but also half a car and what looked like a collection of dead-eyed dolls dressed in frilly age-filthy frocks made of lace and tulle. I kept my eye on the toys as I stalked by, braced for one of their cracked legs to move or for one to sit up and lunge for me to drink me dry of my blood.

Oddly enough, the remains of a tik-tik lying against an elephant-sized boulder gave me pause, the blue taxi's battered body covered with hangul and SoCal Mexican graffiti, with a pair of snapped rail cables draped over its corpse like a gift bow. Lying close to the part of the cavern where the walls tucked in closer, I only had myself to blame when an elfin male stepped out from behind the boulder, his hands stretched out in front of him, a crackling magic playing over his fingers with a delicate ease.

There was no sign of Kenny, but I knew the fat bastard had to be lurking around somewhere. The cavern closed in a hundred yards past where I stood, and there were enough large rock formations to hide him, a handful of walruses, and maybe even a bus or two.

The airborne iron dust didn't reach down into the cavern, but it felt as if its poison was still working through my lungs, making it difficult for me to breathe. He still wore my face, and the time since I'd last seen him hadn't been good to it. I imagined he looked more like me than ever before. The polished aristocratic smugness he'd always drawn about himself was gone, replaced by a grittier, more damaged appearance. His hair was longer, more the length of mine now, and streaked thick with purple and silver, muting the black around his lean face. I couldn't imagine what could have made the scar running from his right eyebrow down to the rise of his cheek, but it flashed white against his sun-kissed skin, going deep down into his flesh. He was lucky he hadn't lost the eye, but then again, I'd been surprised to find he'd survived the fall into the raging river to the east of the Southern Rise Court when his poorly crafted ainmhi dubh attacked me on my recent run down to the Mexican Unsidhe border.

"Ciméara cuid Anbhás." Valin's voice rolled around my name, its tones melodically accented with a thick Unsidhe purr and so hauntingly familiar my marrow quivered in response, anticipating the agonizing pain that normally followed those words. "It's so good to see you, brother. Especially since the time's come for me to even the score between us."

Seventeen

"LET ME guess, you're the one who put the contract out on me," I said, keeping an eye on my brother's hands while I circled him. Like our father, he was a flesh-shaper, and my body wore more than a few scars from their experiments on my flesh and bones.

"Seemed like the easiest way to get my hands on you," Valin replied with a smirk. "It's the only thing these animals really understand. Their one true god is Avarice. Why should I spend my life chasing after you when I can have one of them bring you to me? The irony of your savior's brother dragging you to my feet isn't lost on me. It has a delicious poetic justice to it."

I regretted not having an iron-tipped blade on me, but what was poison to my brother was doubly so to me. He wasn't walking around with shards of rusted rebar under his skin, its sour kiss leaching into my blood and guts. One of Ryder's healers speculated this made me more immune to the deadly human metal, but the others thought she was off her rocker. It didn't matter much what any of them thought, because none of them were willing to try to get the crap out of me and there wasn't anything a human medic could do. Still, the thought of cutting my arm open and pouring a cupful of my blood into Valin's mouth just to see if it did something to the bastard crossed my mind as I stood there under the ivy strands' soft glow.

It was eerie to see the face I only caught sight of in a mirror. I recoiled then, mostly astonished to find an elfin staring back at me, but then the memories resurfaced, foggy with pain and red with blood. His face… Tanic's and Valin's hovered over me, the stuff spun from nightmares and lurking in every shadow. I knew those hands intimately, having those long fingers work themselves under my skin to separate large expanses of it from my flesh. The things they poured into me—*shoved into me*—lingered. He and my father were the reason I wore the Wild Hunt clan's mark on my back, why my shirts sometimes caught on the ripple of scars flowing down from my shoulder blades toward my hips.

"Are you ready to go home, little brother?" Valin's words were laden with magic, Unsidhe fluid and powerful, calling to my blood and ordering my will to bend to his. Old commands were woven into his cadence, pounding through my mind to grab at my soul, seeking out the cracks I'd healed over since I'd escaped their grip. "Hopefully there'll be enough of you for Father to play with, but I can't make any promises. It's a long trip, and, well, we have a lot to catch up on. So, make it easier on yourself and come here. You won't like it if I have to come get you."

The net of his words stung—verbal barbs meant to hook me in—but I'd broken free of his hold—of their hold—since we'd first tangled. The Unsidhe magic slithered off of me, coursing down my spine and whispering off into the nothingness behind me. Only a slight smarting of the binding remained, coupled with a bit of sickness threatening to close my throat. I swallowed hard and it was gone, washed away with a bit of spit and laughter.

"Didn't you learn last time you tried that crap?" I cocked my head, returning my brother's smirk. "You have no power over me."

Valin did another sweeping arc, keeping his back to the rock columns I'd spotted in the main chamber. His eyes narrowed, a bit of fire lighting their depths, and the sulfurous scent of his intensifying magic crept across to tickle my nose. He was going for flash, hoping to cow me into some kind of submission with a bit of light and crackle, but most of that was for show. I'd felt the real thing, seen and felt it worked on me with little more than a crook of Tanic's fingernail into a part of my body, my bones tearing out of my flesh inch by inch until I screamed myself raw.

"Why haven't you gone crawling back to Tanic?" I studied his expression, wondering if I wore my anger as openly as he did. "Or tried to have an alliance with Bannon? You didn't mind being second-in-command to Tanic, so why not her? Or won't she let you feed her people to your ainmhi dubh?"

"Your mouth's gotten smart. I can't wait to break you of that." He cocked his head, studying me much like Newt did right before he tried to bite my nose off. "I think I liked you better when you could only mewl and whine like a dog. Maybe that's the first thing I'll do with you. Cut out your tongue."

"I'd say one of you should grow a beard so I know which side of the mirror you're from, but since both of you are pieces of crap, it wouldn't do any good." Kenny's voice—*Dempsey's voice*—rang out through the caverns, the crenulated walls catching his words and echoing them back at me. "I got him here. Now pay up."

"As soon as I'm done here," Valin murmured, shooting me an unreadable look. "Your wants aren't as important as my needs."

"Pick this shit up later. Right now, I want to know where my money is." Kenny limped out from behind one of the columns. I brought my Glock up, steadying my aim to his center mass. Startled, he took a step back, hiding behind one of the larger rocks, but I could still see his head. "Can't believe my brother ruined his life for you. Jesus, if you weren't worth a hell of a lot of cash, I'd pop you myself, but your brother here wants to skin you himself. Waste of meat, that's what you are."

"Humans." Valin strolled closer to Kenny, putting himself between me and the man I'd followed down the rabbit hole. "They bleat and squeal so much. Almost makes you wish you could turn them off." He turned slowly, laying his hand on Kenny's shoulder, squeezing down hard. "But then again, I can."

I couldn't have stopped him if I tried, and I knew better. I'd seen what the Unsidhe flesh shapers could do to their own, what they could do to a human, and I'd still let him get close to Kenny. Pulling my aim off of Dempsey's brother, I angled it toward mine. Kenny's eyes went blank, staring out into nothing, and he slumped under Valin's touch, weaving back and forth on his feet.

"Get your hand off of him, Valin," I warned. "This is between you and me."

"Nothing is just between us, brother." His smile returned my warning, a threat woven heavy with pain and agony. "This one needs to be shoved aside for now, because I think it's going to take a long time to break you, Ciméara, because you have forgotten where you belong—beneath my foot and writhing on the floor."

Valin's fingers twitched, and Kenny began to topple forward, the skin around his mouth stretching and moving to cover his lips. The sheath rippled, shifting quickly, and by the time Kenny hit the ground, his mouth was buried beneath a thin layer of skin, his lips forming an obscene bulge beneath the shaped flesh. His nostrils flared and fought to suck in air, and I took a step forward, intending on slicing apart the suffocating skin. But Valin's hands came up in a sharp warning.

"He can breathe, little brother, and he's out of the way." Valin stalked closer, keeping his body angled slightly away from me, minimizing my target. "If he's really lucky, I'll still pay him once I'm done breaking you. Or I might just kill him. No sense in paying for something I've already gotten my money's worth from. Now, are you ready to come home with me, Ciméara, or are you going to make this hard on both of us?"

"Probably hard on you, at least," I conceded, sighting on Valin's shoulder. "Because I'd rather eat a whole bitter melon pulled out of the devil's ass after he's eaten bad Chinese food than hand myself over to you and Tanic. Now, get away from him and call it a day."

For a brief moment, I thought Valin was considering his options. I should have known better. Instead, the asshole was laughing at me, a chuckle building up inside of his chest, rusty and creaky from lack of use. Shaking his head, my brother finally let a whimper of a chortle escape, breaking the thin set of his lips.

"You don't want me to hurt this one, because he's your dead master's brother, is that it?" Valin spared Kenny a glance, not bothering to mask his disgust. "Does he look like him? Is that why you want him alive? So you can hand your leash over to him?"

"Don't try that shit with me. We both know the real reason you need to drag me back to Tanic is because you're afraid he'll decide it doesn't matter which brother he has on the slab. What does it matter to him if it's you or me? We're all alike in the dark and bloodied." I returned Valin's laugh, watching his eyes narrow. "Last chance, Valin. Walk away. Take your daddy issues and find another rock to crawl under so he can't find you. I don't want to shoot you, but I'm also not really all that against it. I owe you a hell of a lot of payback."

"If you were going to shoot me, you would have already. Instead, you—"

I shot him.

Grazed his right upper arm really, but that was on purpose, taking a good chunk of meat off his muscle and drilling it into the rock behind him.

The boom of the Glock seemed to shock Valin the most, but then his face rippled with a blend of anger and pain, a tart sour smoothie of emotion he couldn't quite swallow. Staggering back, he ended up against a broad jut of rock rising up from the cavern floor, its spire dotted with various peeks of vintage holiday lights on a string poking up out of its surface.

He grunted in Unsidhe, a string of hot molten words I didn't know, but he sure as hell wasn't wishing me a happy birthday. Leaving a smear of blood behind on the spire, Valin staggered to the right, using the rock to brace himself.

"Never been shot before?" I bared my teeth, shoving as much contempt as I could into my voice. "Never bring magic to a gunfight, brother. You've got to touch me to hurt me now, and if there's one thing you will never do, it is lay hands on my flesh again."

"I have other magics, Ciméara." Valin stumbled again, distancing himself from Kenny's twitching body. It was getting difficult to keep an eye on them both, so I shifted, drawing closer to Dempsey's brother while holding my aim steady on Valin. "While you spent your time being skinned and peeled, I had centuries of learning how to craft the ainmhi dubh."

"Yeah, I've seen your black dogs." Shrugging, I shifted closer still. "They're crappy pieces of work, brother. Held together by the shittiest of spells and fall apart pretty easily. You wasted your time. Maybe basket weaving is more your style. Or flower arranging. Better yet, maybe you should take those flesh-shaping skills you're so proud of and become a dentist. Lots of money in braces. Humans like straight teeth."

I debated drilling a hole into Valin's other shoulder, mostly to make him stop talking. I didn't know how this was going to play out, and while the rage in my gut screamed for me to plant a piece of hot lead in between Valin's eyes, some part of me couldn't quite squeeze the trigger. Maybe it was because I'd lost so much, or perhaps it was a hard, sour truth that we'd both suffered under Tanic. Both of us were victims in our own way, shaped by Tanic's cruelties to dance to his tune. I'd been honest when I taunted Valin about returning to our father only to find himself being the one strapped to Tanic's worktable.

The Lord Master of the Wild Hunt did not tolerate or excuse failure, no matter who it was. There was a reason he was universally feared among the elfin, the stuff of nightmares woven into legends told in whispers with terrified glances at every lurking shadow.

"Oh, my time here in this hellhole hasn't been without its own rewards. I've learned something very important. You're right. Father's ways definitely do not suit me." Valin's free hand—the one not clutching his wound—sparkled with sickly green threads. A flesh shaper couldn't heal themselves. Something about the energy being a loop, drawing on its own

159

source nullifying the spell, but that didn't mean Valin was powerless, and I'd be a fool to think otherwise. "You see, brother, Tanic turns mammals and birds or sometimes warm-blooded reptiles if he can find ones large enough to shape. What you've met before, the cats and others I've crafted, including the one I sent north with you to scent you out, those were all just toys, experiments to see how far I could push their flesh."

"Pele wept, you talk a lot." I got even closer to Kenny, relieved to see his chest moving up and down as he lay facedown on the cavern floor. "Were you always like this? Or did you just get so lonely being yourself that you've got to chatter like a demented flamingo?"

Valin took another step back, drawing free from the rock he'd been leaning against. The blood he left behind smeared wide, a muddy brown under the ivy walls' shimmering blue light. He was bleeding a lot, more than I'd have thought for a grazing wound, and I wondered if I'd misjudged and hit him deeper than I'd thought.

"Oh, that tongue of yours is going to be cut out with a rusty knife, brother." His smirk flickered, much like the fireflies still weaving about in the main chamber. Then it strengthened, curving up over the echo of my face. "I've discovered the cats in this area aren't to my liking, but oh, the cold-blooded, those have become my favorite creatures to shape. You see, Ciméara, coming here has truly made me stronger, a true Hunt Master in my own right. And I have you to thank for it."

I smelled its musty scent before I saw it, a powdery medicinal tang slapping me in the face long before I heard the shush-shush-click of its legs skittering over the rock-laden floor. It slithered up, a dark slinky monster before Valin had ever laid hands on it. But infused with Unsidhe magics and my brother's wicked intent, the creature resonated malice, its carapace bristling with spikes and dotted with dark, oozing lichen.

There was no denying its ancestry, a denizen of the deep caves and a feared predator in its own right, but shaped by Valin's dark crafting, its long, segmented body clicked and whirred, its mandibles dripping with acid strong enough to leave small craters in the cavern's rocky floor. I'd faced off a cave centipede before, and in its natural state, the bastards were hard to kill.

It resembled nothing like any ainmhi dubh I'd ever seen, and I'd skinned more than a few in my time. Hell, I'd *been* skinned by more than a few even before I picked up my blades and guns to take their pelts, and none of the Hunt Masters' creations I'd encountered were as creepy as this one.

Its chiton was the bog-standard dead blue-gray of any other undead monster dragged up into life by a twisted Unsidhe flesh shaper, but that's where any similarity ended. Its textured armor portions sucked up any light, tiny spikes clustered like buckshot scattered over its length. The smoother parts of its chiton were crackled with dark lines, their curves pulsating when the creature moved.

Nearly ten feet long and bristling with legs, the mutated insect's head wove about, its glowing red eyes dulled under the blue. Its jaws snapped, antenna flexing about, and it seemed to be searching, its airborne talons waving while its rear legs scuttled its massive body forward. It stunk even worse up close, like the bowl of fermented aphids and borscht larvae someone once served me on a run, and my tongue recoiled down my throat, gagging me to avoid getting any of the creature's rankness in my mouth.

The bug-and-beet bowl was probably one of the worst things I'd ever eaten, and I'd spent a good portion of my life before Dempsey digging through ainmhi dubh shit looking for any scrap of meat or bone they didn't digest so I could have something in my belly.

This creature looked like that meal tasted.

"What in Dante's Hells were you thinking, Valin?" I took the Glock off of Valin, aiming for the ainmhi dubh's head.

The black dog—insect—moved even closer, scenting the air. I couldn't see Valin. He'd disappeared behind the rocks, but that was probably more to avoid becoming his own monster's prey than to hide from me. It was blind, driven up to a brighter light than it was used to, or maybe the transformation process stole its sight, but either way, it shifted carefully, hunting me down.

A gunshot rang out just as the creature found me. One of its fore antennae blasted up into shards, steel-hard carapace chunks flying out to pelt my face and shoulders. Throwing myself over Kenny's slack bulging body, I fired at the ainmhi dubh, and its head careened to the right to find the other shooter. Then I tracked my Glock over to where the bullet came from.

It was enough of a flinch to give the ainmhi dubh the opening it needed to strike at my legs.

Its mandibles snapped down on my left boot, cleaving off a good portion of its heel. I retaliated, kicking it firmly between its sightless eyes.

They were milky, and the now-sharpened chunk of leather-covered wood heel struck its mark.

The stench was as acidic as the fluids now gushing from its sliced-open domed eye, splashing over Kenny's unprotected arms. I backpedaled, shoving his squat, corpulent body back with my shoulders, kicking at the floor to move both of us out of the ainmhi dubh's next attack. Another shot rang out, clipping its head, and I took the distraction to get Kenny as far behind the rocks as I could. His chest jerked up and down, and a froth began to pour from his nostrils in a foamy spittle clogging his air passages.

"Shit. Shit!" I reached for my knife, leaving the Glock within reach, and tried to slice apart the stretch of skin across his mouth. Yet another shot rang out, and I shouted over the echoing report, "Best be someone on my fucking side of things!"

"Kai?" Cari called out. "I'll keep the thing pinned down. Let's get the hell out of here!"

"'Bout time you showed up!" I shoved at Kenny again, getting him under an outcropping, but too much of him remained vulnerable to the creature's scalding fluids. "What the hell took you so long?"

"Dumbass Malone! That's who was shooting at us. Or at the asshole we were chasing. Asshole thought he was helping. You need to kick his ass when we get out of here. Boy's got it bad for you." She sounded like she was getting closer, but it was hard to tell with the bouncing echoes. "Hold on. Let me see if I can draw that thing off of you."

The centipede dove down again, its massive head glancing off the rocks, but its wedged forehead was too broad, smashing against the sides of the gap above us. The boulders leaned in on each other, forming a partial arch and blocking off any bites, but its spit still seared down to Kenny's cheekbone when it splattered over his face. Swearing, I tried to shift the man around, looking for any angle to protect his flesh while working to open up his mouth.

"Get your witchy ass over here!" I yelled over the creature's furious keening. "He needs help I can't give."

The knife edge was sharp enough to pare a single strand of hair, but I didn't know if opening his mouth with it would help him breathe or start him bleeding to death. Above us, the ainmhi dubh battled the rock, creating a muddy gravel mixed in with its burning saliva. Hunching over Kenny's body was the best protection I could give him, but my leathers weren't going to survive much more, and the sting of the damned thing's dripping eye on my skin hurt more than its spit.

Twisting about, I stopped trying to pry Kenny's mouth open, leaving the tip of my best knife embedded into the slit I'd made through Valin's handiwork. The serrated blade's blood runnel seemed to leave enough of an opening for Kenny to breathe, and the foam pouring from his nostrils seemed to have ebbed down to a trickle. Grabbing at my Glock, I wedged myself into the gap and fired, hitting the ainmhi dubh with as much firepower as I could. A slip of a shadow moved in on my left and I shifted, giving Cari room to get to Kenny. But where the necromanced cave centipede burned me hot, the purring voice in my ear left me cold down to my soul.

"Hello, brother," Valin whispered as he crouched over me, his hand closing down over mine. "You *did* say the only way I could hurt you was to touch you."

Eighteen

I THOUGHT I remembered the pain clearly.

Gods, I was wrong.

The cavern faded, leaving me in the middle of a darkness I couldn't see out of. I lost Cari's voice. Even the hiss of the ainmhi dubh's spittle hitting the hard rocks disappeared. Kenny's labored breathing became my own, my lungs trapped in an endless cycle of struggling to pull in fresh air, anything untainted by the metallic boil of my blood moving through my veins toward my left hand.

"Do you feel that, brother?" Valin hissed into my ear, intimate and cloying. "Can you feel the iron in your blood coming to my touch? How does it feel? Like you're on fire?"

He probably could sense everything Dempsey had done to peel our father's handiwork from my body. All of the rebar taken out from under my skin, the staples pulled out from between my vertebrae, and everything else they'd shoved into my flesh, chaining me to their spells and power. I'd been their vessel, the crucible for their blood magic, and each word hammered into my marrow bound me closer. Dempsey spent the rest of his lifetime pulling out every bit of their evil that he could reach, but he couldn't get it all.

Not after gods knew how many years of their torture, and certainly not without a fight from me.

The bits and specks left in me were gathering, pulled together into a hot stream of fire through my blood by Valin's magic. My fingers shook, cramped around the Glock and pinned to the rocky ground while Kenny's convulsing body twitched under me. I couldn't get enough air, my lungs pressed flat in my chest, but my heart pounded, a frantic screaming beat echoing in my ears. A splash of heat on my head shocked me only for a brief moment, the ainmhi dubh's mandibles snapping futilely in the tight gap above me, but the pain was brief, a fleeting ping in the rising ocean of torture splitting my nerves apart.

And my brother—damn his eyes and soul—chuckled a deep rolling laugh between the Unsidhe spell he was crafting to pull the iron particles in my blood toward my hand.

"This will take me longer than if you still had our Clan's mark under your skin, but I'm willing to wait." Valin twisted his palm, grinding my fingers together, and something along my hand shifted, splitting open my flesh. "Do you feel that? The poison gathering under my touch? Should I have it go through your heart first, or maybe through the lace of your lungs so you spit blood up every time you exhale?

"Have you forgotten how much power I have over you? Even without Father, I can bend and break you with a few words and my touch. You were created to be nothing more than a repository, a hoard of magic held in flesh and bone until it's needed. Everything else you think you have is a lie. Your life? That Sidhe Lord? That human family you think you have? None of it is real. Nothing more than a dream from eating ainmhi dubh vomit. Once I get you back to the Clan's holdings, it'll be cotton floss whispers through the eternity you've earned yourself."

The skin along the sides of my fingers moved, curling outward and splitting apart. Valin pressed down again, shaping my flesh slowly, merging the meat of my hand until my joints grew rigid. This was an old game, one he'd taken a sadistic delight in when I was young and trapped in a cage under our father's worktable. It was agony, made torturous by the calling of iron to my imprisoned hand. My skin grew hot where the iron gathered into the streams in my blood, long streaks of purpling scarlet forming as the particles thickened and snagged on my arteries' walls. He would pull together as much iron as he could, poisoning my flesh until it rotted from my bones, then send it back through my body, aimed at an organ or sometimes even my brain, killing my thoughts and sentience until I healed from the cataclysmic destruction he'd created in me.

There was less iron in me now—not enough to do what he wanted and certainly not enough to render me mute and brain-dead, but he could still make me wish he'd killed me.

Pele knew I'd prayed for that fate more than a few times as soon as I'd discovered from watching them kill others that it was an option at all.

My far three fingers were fused, knitted together with pieces of skin and flesh. The Glock was slippery from my seeping blood and sebum. I tried to grip it, to pull out from under Valin's forceful press, but the moving iron through my body crept a tangle of pain through all of my joints, and I couldn't get anything to respond properly. My knee jerked when I tried to angle my elbow away, and my hips rolled back against Kenny's weight, unable to twist my torso away from Valin's reach.

The pain stole my reason, or maybe that was the iron working its way through the gray pudding in my skull, but the edges of my vision were going black. My hand throbbed, swollen to nearly three times its size. The splits were severe—chasms really—and following the lines of where my fingers used to be. With my index finger and thumb still free, Valin shifted, covering the unaffected digits. His magic followed, bringing with it the iron, pain, and poisoned blood. The pounding in my chest skipped one beat and then another, stuttering and faltering in its fight against the metal filaments pooling in its depths. I was going to lose consciousness soon if I didn't do something.

I just couldn't move.

"Fuck this," I muttered in Singlish, feeling the coarseness of the language on my tongue. It was tart and sharp, drowning in human flavors, as pungent and layered as the world I lived in. "And fuck you, brother."

The knife in my other hand shook as I brought it up, and my shoulder screamed with the effort of lifting the blade. Maybe it was years of living with Dempsey, or maybe my hatred for what they'd done to me, but the momentum of my arm falling back down had adequate thrust to drive the knife into the space above Valin's collarbone. It didn't go in deep. I didn't have enough strength to do more than let it sink under the weight of the weapon and my hand, but the tip buried deep enough to catch the flesh.

It was all my knife needed.

The keen edge I put on my blades to skin ainmhi dubh and the knife's weight did its job as my movement slid the weapon in. It slid easily through his skin, cutting through everything in its way until the guard nearly touched his chest. Gasping in pain, Valin grabbed at the hilt and pulled it free of his flesh, anger carving his face into our father's features.

Raising my knife up over his head, he growled, "I'll be taking your eyes out for that, little brother."

A bullet tearing through his shoulder took care of Valin for me, punching him forward in a splash of hot blood and shrill screaming, pulling Valin's weight off of me while he scrambled for cover.

There was too much blood for the ainmhi dubh to stand, firing its hunger. It raged above us, acidic spittle raining down on us in a shower of sparkling pain. Valin kicked at Kenny's belly, rolling him forward and sending me sprawling, my swollen, iron-filled hand flopping uselessly over the Glock. I heard something hard and metal hit the ground, my knife falling from Valin's hand. It bounced or rolled, I couldn't tell which, but either way, it landed next to my right thigh, well within reach.

"Kai! Tell me that wasn't you I shot!" Cari called out. I nearly couldn't hear her over the ainmhi dubh's hissing. "Because if it was, I'm really fucking sorry! You guys look alike in the dark. From behind. Shit, that sounds really crappy."

Twisting about to get at Valin was painful. My hand was too heavy to move, and each nudge I made rocked the swollen tissues, sending the iron slush in my blood into a swirling wash of agony. Fighting through the pain, I rolled over and cursed up a blue streak when I found the crevice behind me empty except for Kenny's flailing body. Valin was gone, leaving behind only his blood, a lot of pain, and a giant warped centipede bent on snapping my head off.

If I didn't have a head-munching bug and a bloated, unconscious Kenny to deal with, I'd have chased after him and beaten the shit out of him for what he'd done to me.

"Always running away, you damned bastard. You're going to have to face the music some time, brother. Can't run forever." I stared down at my useless hand with its forged-together fingers, purpled swollen skin, and an ocean of iron floating in it. "I'm good! Kenny's not. I've got to get this thing off of him so you can take a look at him. Just don't—"

She plugged another couple of shots at the ainmhi dubh, dimpling its weaving head, but its chiton deflected them, sending the bullets bouncing about the rocks around me. Swearing under my breath, I huffed through another wave of pain.

"Don't shoot at it!" I finished, shaking my head. "We need a cannon or something!"

"Let me see if I can draw it away," she shouted over the creature's babble. "I've got some cover. Maybe if both of us can hit it, we can take it down."

I didn't have a lot of hope for that plan, but I was willing to give anything a try. Healing from the acid was going to take some time. My skin crackled where the splashes hit me, inconsequential stings compared to my hand. My heart was settling down from its overclocked pace, but the iron lingered where Valin had put it. Moving my fingers only made the pain worse, and each time I shifted my hand, my nerves took shots of hot electricity, thickening my saliva and creeping tingles across my skin.

"Hey! Bug!" Cari's shouts ricocheted around the cavern about as much as her bullets did against the ainmhi dubh's head, but either way, the damned thing didn't seem like it was going to budge. "Getting closer. Maybe it's deaf and needs to smell me or something."

"Don't get your head bitten off, because not like I can superglue it back on and tell your mom it's fine." I did a quick check on Kenny. He was still struggling about, but the small slice I'd been able to put in the skin covering his mouth seemed to have helped him at least get some better air flow. If Cari didn't get over to him soon, no amount of hedge-witch healing would be able to help him. My link was unresponsive, too far underground to get any signal, and we'd need to head up top to call for a medic. "Because I sure as shit can't drag you up those rocks. Not with my hand like this."

He didn't look good. The ainmhi dubh's saliva hadn't hit him as much as it had me, but where it had, the flesh was black and still smoking about the edges as the acid continued to eat away at his skin. I spit at some of the larger spots, rubbing at them with my hand in the hopes it would at least dilute the corrosive fluids.

"You'd crap yourself if you knew I was doing this to you," I muttered, examining my work. I couldn't stay in the dubious shelter I'd found, not if we were going to stop the chittering menace. And since its attention seemed to be all on me, I was going to have to be the one to draw it away from Kenny. "Well, that's just going to have to do, because right now, I've got a damned giant botched termite to kill. Stay here, asshole. And if you see Valin, bite him for me."

My hand hurt like hell. It throbbed and danced about while I struggled to get up onto my feet. The loss of blood made me woozy, uncertain about where things were. With my depth perception a bit fuzzy, I turned and slammed my knitted-together fingers against the boulder closest to me, splitting the skin open even further, and my tortured cry was enough to spark the ainmhi dubh's interest in me once again.

Throwing up wasn't an option, but my stomach didn't seem to have been notified, because it twisted, screaming its intent up my throat. The taste of bile on my tongue overwhelmed the insect's musty odor, but only for a split second. Biting down on my reflexes, I staggered out, blood dripping from my useless hand, its dull maroon color now beginning to stretch back up my wrist in long streaks. I was too warm—hot beneath my leather jacket—but I couldn't risk shedding it. It was the only protection I had against the creature, and considering it fed itself by scooping out chunks of flesh into quivering scallops it could fit into its mouth, I wasn't going to take the chance that I'd be able to outrun it.

"Come on, you screwed-up thing," I choked out, leaning against the boulder with my shoulder to steady myself. I had another gun and a couple more knives on me, including a Ka-Bar for up-close work if I needed it, and right about now, I needed it. Drawing the blade took more out of me than I wanted to confess to, but eventually I got it free from its sheath. Taking a deep breath, I tossed out, "Okay, Odin. If you end up pulling me in after this, can you please make sure Ryder takes care of Newt? Sure, he's no raven, but he's all I've got. Pele, just... a fire spout wouldn't go unappreciated either, but I understand if you can't. Not exactly your neighborhood."

Lunging forward, I screamed at the top of my lungs at the ainmhi dubh, hoping to startle it into rearing back. I could fit what I knew about giant mutated centipedes on an eyelash, but we'd reached a do-or-die moment. Spotting Cari across the cavern, I wove forward, stumbling over rocks with my unresponsive feet, my sliced boot heel making my already screwed-up progress even worse.

My dripping blood left splotches over the rocks and ground, mimicking the kind of painting stupid people paid stupid money for. The churning gore in my belly threatened to add to the palette, but I had to get the ainmhi dubh clear of Cari and Kenny first. I had one thing to do before I could collapse, and if I were lucky, I could make it to the tight cluster of columns before the damned insect snapped me in two.

I didn't have high hopes for that. It wasn't the fastest black dog I'd ever faced, but it skittered and moved in jerky quick leaps. Even as partially blind and deaf as it appeared, it could still scent me out. How could it not? I was chumming the air like a severed swordfish head being dragged behind a speedboat hoping to draw out a sea serpent. Only the rocks couldn't smell me coming.

Keeping one eye on the ainmhi dubh and another on the ground was difficult—impossible really. I hit more rocks than I avoided, mostly small ones, but a good-sized boulder caught me in the knee, and the cursed bug probably felt the swear words pouring past my gritted teeth. It turned slowly, its head bobbing up and down, then stepped tentatively toward me, one of its many wiggling pointy legs landing smack dab in the middle of a blood pool.

Its scream shook the cavern, startling a cloud of sunrise bats, their translucent wings singing out waves of cut-glass discordance as they swarmed through the long space, sweeping up toward the hole in the ceiling. The fireflies fled before the burnt orange and dusk yellow airborne mammals, the pixies swirling outward, ignoring the giant weaving centipede to cling to the ivy-covered jagged crevices at the outer areas of the caves. If I'd not been bleeding out iron and blood, I'd have stopped to soak in the sight of their flashing bodies tucked into the darker blue illuminated plants—a seascape sculpted from light and sweeping shapes—but I had a death to attend.

I just wasn't sure if it was going to be me or the ainmhi dubh.

The centipede began thrashing, its leg smoking where it touched my blood. It tipped to the side, sliding through more drops, and then tumbled forward when it slid over a larger pool, the first joint of its segmented front leg buckling under. The leg's chiton cracked along the tip, spiderwebbing up over the initial bend, then continuing up to the pale stretch of its tibia.

Unable to find this new threat, the ainmhi dubh stumbled about, snapping its powerful mandibles in the air, hoping to strike out at whatever was breaking it apart.

"Got to be the iron." Bracing myself for what I was about to do, I took a long hard breath, glad Dempsey had pounded into my head the importance of keeping my knives and brain sharp. "Okay, you demented foul bastard, here's hoping this works."

I took my blade and sliced open my hand, going as deep as I dared, and sent a prayer to every god I laid down tribute to that my wild idea would work.

Already swollen to the point of splitting my skin, my hand didn't take too kindly to being carved apart like a Thanksgiving turkey. I dropped down to one knee, taking the rocky hit to my joint with a graceless tumble. Another slice down and the flesh gave, soaking my skin and threading down my wrist when I raised my hand up.

"Okay, time to play tag, asshole," I growled at the ainmhi dubh. "Just like your daddy did to me."

Its belly was low enough for me to smear a wide swath of my blood across its carapace. A few missteps forward brought me right up against the damned thing, and from there, I painted whatever I could reach. Some of it was splatters from my throbbing hand, while most of it was long smudges of poisoned blood across anything I could reach. I'd dropped my knife as I went, but at the moment, it didn't matter. The creature convulsed and shook, trying to fight off the acidic reaction of its creation and the iron-infused blood I was using to break down its hard armor.

Out of the corner of my eye, I spotted Cari kneeling over Kenny, her back to me and the ainmhi dubh. Some small part of my Stalker training reminded me to kick her ass for turning away from the greater threat in the area, but mostly, I was focused on getting as much blood on the creature as I could. It was smoking and crackling with each pass I made, unable to back away from me as its limbs slipped through my blood, compromising its already breaking legs.

Oddly enough, my hand was feeling better and some of the pain eased off, or at least the iron-fueled bits. I was suddenly very aware of the slices I'd made into my own flesh, and the too-sharp-edged agony was practically a relief. My stomach no longer felt like I was about to have it crawl up over my tongue, and the ainmhi dubh was beginning to smolder, its belly and chest starting to show thick black cracks through its chiton. It smelled, probably worse than any black dog I'd ever encountered, but nothing a good shot of whiskey couldn't take care of.

"Let's do this." I fumbled at my shoulder holster to get my other Glock out, still unsteady but stronger than I'd felt when Valin left me on top of Kenny. Raising my gun, I sighted on the widest smear I'd left on the creature's body and pulled the trigger, sending a hot screaming round right into its chest.

It fought its death in a pitched fit, pieces of its chiton falling off in crumbling chunks. I had to stumble to avoid the small sea of acid gushing out of its widening wounds, but I kept firing, taking advantage of its shattered defenses. It seemed to hiss and writhe for an eternity. Then Cari grabbed my waist, pulling me away from the damned thing before I could empty another magazine into it.

"Come on, we've got to get clear of this thing." She shoved at my side, ignoring my hiss of pain. "Kenny's dead. Probably was dead as soon as Valin touched him. The bastard turned his blood into something corrosive.

No way anyone but an elfin could have survived that. Sure as hell not him. Let's go."

"Got to make sure that thing's dead first," I argued, ejecting the empty mag and reaching for another tucked into my rig. Slamming in the new magazine, I balanced myself against Cari. "Can't let it go. It's an ainmhi dubh in the middle of the city. It survives this and lots of people are going to die. Do the job, Cari. Do it until we die."

She left me to stand on my own and pulled out her weapon. The little girl with her curly hair in pigtails hardened away until only the hibiki-Stalker remained. Sighting on the ainmhi dubh, she braced herself into a shooting stance. "You go high, Gracen. I'll go low."

"Watch your feet. Blood's going to eat you just like the rest," I warned her and began firing, aiming for the lengthening cracks.

I couldn't think about Kenny, or even what Dempsey might or might not have sent him. Whatever he knew about the original contract to extract me from Tanic was lost, and the only thing that mattered at the moment was killing the monster my brother left behind.

The ainmhi dubh's mandibles fell, severed from its head by a few of my shots. Its head reared back, and I took the opening it offered, sending the last of my magazine into the gaping empty mouth and straight into its fevered, rotten brain—or whatever was left of it after Valin corrupted it. Thrashing, it went down hard, and it nearly wiped Cari and me out as it fell. Its carapace began to fall off the soft bits hidden beneath it. There wasn't much there, mostly goo and acid, but there was enough to make us run.

Firing again, I hit something vital, because without warning, its head exploded and we were pelted by a hail of searing heat and insect shards. The sounds it began making were frightening, the anger and magic fueling its existence slowly unraveling, leaving behind only the creature Valin warped. Its color bled out from under its fragmented exoskeleton, turning it ashen as it began to empty its fluids over where we stood.

"Go on," I scolded her when she hitched her arm around my waist. "That hits me, I'll survive it. You won't."

"Can you just shut up and run?" She pulled at my torso, finding each bruise and welt along my side. "That thing's going to bring the roof down on our heads. Let me help you, damn it."

Its final scream was horrific, startling even the pixies from their hiding place. They swarmed around us, battering our heads as the creature sang its death keen. We fought over the rocks to get to where we'd come in, leaving my brother's creation behind. The bats left a trail of guano for us to follow, making it slippery to climb the rocks leading up to the building, and more than once, I caught Cari before she tumbled back over me, her flailing feet scoring a few hits against my cheek.

The fresh air was nice, and I collapsed on the building's rotten floor, grateful to be clear of the centipede's foul odor even as wafts of acrid smoke drifted up from the hole, its death filling the chamber below with its gassy stench. I hurt everywhere, and I didn't want to even guess what disgusting thing I was lying in, but the pain was good, cleansing in a way. Or at least it was until I tried to move. Then all of the torturous agony flooded back into my body, and I had to rethink my decision to survive the ainmhi dubh instead of simply letting its gushing fluids take me down and leaving me to die in its stink.

Cari poking at my still-swollen-and-tender hand brought me back to reason.

"Get any of that thing's blood or spit on you?" I groaned, pulling my hand up.

"Nope. Not a drop. Come on, we've got to get that taken care of." Always a bossy thing, she poked again, frowning at me when I told her to drop dead in Cantonese. "Listen to me. I looked. At Kenny."

"Yeah, I know. That's what I sent you to do," I said, sitting up, and was relieved to discover a dirty tarp beneath me instead of anything organic and growing. "You told me he was dead, but I swear to all the gods, it looked like he was breathing. I thought he was alive."

"Probably the chemicals changing in his system. Moving his guts and lungs about." She shook her head. "But that's not what I'm saying. I'm telling you I did a quick look. A hibiki look."

I tried to wrap my mind around what she was saying, and maybe the pain was making it hard for me to think, because I couldn't understand a damned thing. "What are you talking about? That takes forever. And peyote. Not to mention me or someone else stupid enough to do it chewing it all up and spitting it into your mouth with some worm-rotted tequila."

"Not for this. It was a single question. Just a slit across his eyes and a dip of my finger into the fluid there." She stroked at my hand, and I knew she was wishing she could do something for me, but human magic was nearly useless on an elfin, much less a chimera like me. "Mom taught me that a long time ago. Never thought I'd use it. Didn't think it would really give anyone anything, but it did what I needed it to do. It gave me an answer.

"I needed to see if he'd gotten anything from Dempsey. That's what I scried. I couldn't do anything else for him, so I figured I might as well do something for you." She sighed, then looked up as a thin thread of pixie fireflies spiraled above us. "Dempsey didn't send him anything. Ever. Just money to live off of, and not even a lot of that. I don't know what to tell you, Kai, but it looks like whatever you were hoping to find is lost forever."

Nineteen

CARI GAVE me about half an hour of arguing before she finally relented and dropped me off at my warehouse, promising to deliver the Scout back to Jonas once I got inside. Trying every angle, she cajoled, scolded, and threatened, but the day had already worn off any patience I had left, and my temper rose quickly, shutting her down before we got out of the understreets.

"At least let me come inside and help you," she said, pulling up into the warehouse's driveway. The puppy-dog-eyes trick she learned as a kid was deployed once again—a wide soft gaze and a flutter of lashes—but as much as I loved her, I needed to deal with everything without any coddling or fuss. "Kai, you're hurt and—"

"I'm going to be fine, mija," I murmured, leaning over to kiss her on the cheek. She grumbled under her breath, a mingled spit of Mexican and German she could have only learned from her mother, but eventually she sighed and nodded. "Get rid of the Scout and go home... or go to the Court and have a few drinks with Alexa. Don't worry about me. I've got this."

I waited until she pulled away and was down the street, the Scout's crimson rear lights fading off when she made the turn to get onto the freeway. Then I activated my link. Standing beneath the stars, I weighed the possibilities for the rest of my night, turning over everything I'd learned since Dempsey's death and scraping at who I thought I'd been.

Because, while everything I thought I'd known as a solid truth pretty much turned out to be a lie, the people and who I made myself was still as solid as the moment I stepped out onto that faraway lava field to go chase fire-assed chickens off a ledge.

The city lights drowned out the stars, and the moons hung over the horizon, nearly all crescents and coy behind a layer of frothy clouds. A hint of sugar lingered on the breeze as the *malasada* bakery a few blocks away kicked up its early evening fry. My stomach was still tender, but the eggy bread scent was a delectable whisper on the wind. Scrubbing at my face, I winced at the barely healed-over skin along my cheeks, sensitive from where the ainmhi dubh's acidic kiss left its mark.

My hand was nearly done healing, much quicker than I'd thought it would, but Cari put forth a theory that I'd pretty much lanced it like a blister and most of the iron Valin called to its swollen flesh had oozed out onto the cavern and on the ainmhi dubh. My three fingers were still fused, but it was mostly skin, a thick webbing holding them together rather than flesh. I could move each independently as far as the skin would stretch, and if I liked swimming, I imagined it would be a great way to power through the waves pounding the bay's shoreline.

Since I didn't submerge myself into water all that much, I was looking forward to getting the use of my hand back. Studying the webbing, it seemed easy enough, something a bit of booze would help with, and since I'd already had that on my evening list of things to do, I could take care of my hand while I did it.

Oddly enough, my warehouse home looked the same as I'd left it, a tall two-story brick square with steel rolling bay doors hiding the garage space I'd built up and its heavy wood door with its Celtic knotwork and glass inserts gleaming despite the faintness of light around it. An oil stain on the cement driveway looked too much like the blood I'd smeared on the centipede we'd killed, and I stared at it for a long time, wondering where I was going to go next in my life.

Worn down to the bone, I drank in the sight of my city, glad I'd made San Diego my home. After years of crawling over the long SoCal freeways, looking for monsters to kill, whiskey to drink, and a warm body or three to keep me company for a few nights, I found myself more than content to stand on the doorstep of a place I'd made my own.

Even though it was time I took one of the largest, scariest risks I would ever take in my lifetime.

"Okay, Ciméara, got to stop just surviving. Valin was right. Everything you're living's an illusion. Time to jump in and do something." I stared down at the communications bracelet on my wrist as if it somehow held the answers to my universe. Maybe it did. Either way, I wasn't going to know unless I finally did something about where I was going and what I wanted. "You've killed dragons, for Pele's sake. This isn't going to be any different."

A few button pushes and my link rang up, only to be answered before the second burble ended. I kept my eyes on a helicopter angling in to land on Medical's tallest tower, its blades whirring about, chopping through the air to bring in a life to be saved. The voice on the other end was strained, eager to know I was alive, perhaps, or just tired of waiting. I wasn't sure, and I sure as hell wasn't going to ask.

Not now at least. Maybe not ever. It all depended on how things worked out.

"I'm home," I said softly, hearing a heavy sigh of relief through the speaker. "At my place. Why don't you head over here. And oh, don't forget to bring my cat."

I WAS down about a fourth of the whiskey bottle when Ryder came through my front door.

After stopping long enough to put Newt down and then attend to my cat's caterwauling about the empty food bowl on the kitchen floor, he finally stalked through the warehouse to stand in front of me with a bag in one hand and a look of horror on his face.

To be fair, I'd just taken a deep swig of whiskey, picked up a pair of pinking shears, and snipped through the second bit of webbing connecting my ring and middle finger together as he walked up.

There were a lot of things in my life that gave me pause. Most of them came with fangs or claws, with the worst ones having wings as well, but seeing Ryder's face drain of all color definitely made me stop and contemplate the world for a moment.

"I didn't know elfin *could* turn green." I picked up the knife I'd balanced over a glass container filled with candle wax, its wick burning bright and high enough to nearly touch the blade lying across the rim. "Hold on a second. I've got to do this before the skin heals together again. Seems like webbing likes to stay webbing. Surprised all of us aren't sea elves cavorting in the ocean or something.

"Then again," I murmured, thinking about the raging waters off of the shoreline and the creatures living in a briny world no one really knew. Laying the hot steel against my sliced-apart skin, I bit back the hiss jerked up from my belly at the searing pain and blew away the rising wisp of acrid steam coming off the sealing flesh. "Maybe there used to be sea elfin and they got eaten by everything nasty in the Underhill waters or they've gone deep into the trenches, happily living their lives until the Merge hit, and now they're stuck with giant squid and angler fish."

The pain was a clean one, a kind of sharp, raspy ache followed by a sense of relief as it edged back into a dull throb. I chased the sear with a shot of whiskey, wiping away the thickness on my tongue from the sudden shock of the quick cauterization and the smell of my own skin being grilled under a blade I used to skin ainmhi dubh. Newt screamed from the kitchen, probably interested in whatever I was cooking in the living room, but I shushed him with a cutting retort he probably dismissed with a twitch of his whiskers.

"What in Morrigan's name are you doing?" Ryder croaked out, unsteadily gripping the couch arm, then sliding over onto the seat next to me. "And *why* are you doing it?"

I often forgot how insulated Ryder's world was, and a little bit of my resolve crumbled, eaten away by a slap of doubt. Shaking it off much like Newt'd done to me, I brandished the blade, then placed it back over the candle to heat up again.

"Valin did this. Well, he did a lot of things, but this is kind of what's left over," I said, picking up the snips, snicking the blades to make sure I hadn't gotten anything caught on their edges. "I'll tell you about it while I finish this up."

"Stop." Ryder placed his hand on my wrist, holding me still before I could make the next cut. "Don't… for gods' sake, don't do this to yourself. Or at least don't use that knife to seal the wound. I brought some salve with me. Cari called. Told me you were hurt but… this is beyond hurt, Kai. This is—"

"Yeah, not the worst he's ever done to me." I shrugged. "Hell, nothing compared to what Tanic's done. I mean, I give Valin credit for thinking on the spot, but it's all rinse and repeat of times back in the cuid Anbhás homestead. This time I was able to get myself out of it… with Cari's help. Owe that girl a lot for pulling my ass out of the fire today, I can tell you that."

I waited until he dug out the salve infused with Sidhe healing and probably a little more than a few tablespoons of fragrant oils. It glistened and sparkled, a bit of glitter in the gloom next to the rebar knots resting on the old steamer crates I used for a coffee table. The iron tangles were a reminder of what my life'd been like before Dempsey, and after they'd been pulled out of my back, I'd twisted them about in a bonfire, then placed them in the middle of my home. They'd become something my friends often picked up, running their fingers over the bumpy surfaces, the same textured rods that once shaped the black-pearl dragon wings sculpted into the scarred skin on my back. Ryder hated the sight of them and probably wasn't going to like what I had to tell him about Kenny, Valin, and the ainmhi dubh that my brother dragged up from death to hunt me down.

It took longer for the salve to work than the knife, but I could tell it was easier on Ryder. The snips did the job quick enough, and the whiskey was beginning to taste sweet. That could have been because Ryder'd joined me in drinking, his mouth on the bottle's rim adding a bit of sugar to the slap of booze when I drank after him, but that was probably all just in my mind. He listened as we waited for the salve to work, ignoring everything around us, including my cat, who'd found something with a bell to bat around the floor, its incessant jingle guaranteed to wake the dead if I left him to it during the night.

While the glittery potion slowly knitted the cuts shut, I told Ryder everything, including what Cari dragged up out of Kenny's corpse.

"So Malone was the one who shot that kid?" he finally asked, leaning on his knees and watching the flame dance about in its glass prison. "What's going to happen to him?"

"The cops took him in. As soon as he realized he'd hit the kids, he hurried over. Well, as much as he could hurry over, because he's still kind of banged up from pancaking in the parking lot. But by the time Malone got there, I'd already gone after Kenny," I explained. "He'd spotted us at the marketplace and figured I needed protection or something. Damned kid really can't aim for shit. He was trying to nick Kenny in the leg or something to slow him down. Malone's dangerous as he is. I dropped Samms a line to see if he'd be willing to take the kid in as an apprentice. Samms might be an asshole, but he's a good Stalker. If anyone's going to scrape off Malone's rose-colored glasses, it'll be him."

"Is Cari okay?"

"Yep. Right as rain." The snips were in my hand again, and Ryder stared at the webbing connecting my ring and pinkie finger. "You can look away. Only takes a little bit to cut it apart. Just blink really long, and it'll be done before you know it."

"Why are you doing this? By yourself, I mean?" Ryder gestured in the general direction of Balboa and the Southern Rise Court. "There are healers there who could at least do this for you. Even if you won't let them do magic on you, they could—we could go up there now. Or in the morning. You said it doesn't hurt. Why are you—"

"Because tonight, when I make love to you, I intend to be able to use all of my fingers to coax you with, lordling. I want to run my hands through that golden hair of yours and feel it on my skin. I want to be able to stroke you and not have my pinky finger dancing about because it's attached to the one next to it. So yeah, that's why I'm doing this," I said softly, making a snip through the stretch of skin between the first two joints. "Why am I wanting us here? Now?

"Think about it, if one damned kiss made the place grow like mushrooms after a thunderstorm, imagine what the hell's going to happen once we finally do this?" Nodding toward where the Court lay on the mesas above downtown, its spires reaching up for stars it could never touch. "The first time I'm with you, I want it to be between us. No Court, no one else but you, me, and hopefully a cat with a belly full enough he won't bother us for at least eight hours so I can do everything I've ever dreamed about doing to you. Just tell me… yes or no. Because I'm tired of just breathing. I want to have the taste of you on me, on my tongue, in my hair, and if you're not ready for that, it's okay. I can wait."

Luckily I didn't have my finger anywhere near the shears when Ryder twisted his hand into my hair. I let myself be pulled in close until our mouths brushed, and he whispered into my parted lips, "If you think I'm not going to say yes to you, then you've not been paying attention, *áinle*. For someone who makes his living watching the shadows, you do *not* see the things that are right under your nose."

I NEVER got the last bit of skin snipped. It was everything I could do to get the salve on the first cut I'd made before Ryder hooked his fingers into my hair and pushed me down onto the couch. Something hard dug into the small of my back, probably something Newt dragged up into the cushions, but I wasn't going to complain. Not with the stretch of Ryder's lean body on me and the concentration I needed to pull his clothes off without tearing anything.

Since I wasn't so great at the not tearing anything, I resigned myself to having to make sure the pants I gave him in the morning were at least clean.

"Are you sure about this, Chimera?" Ryder lay on my bed, dragged up the stairs with a bit of persuasion and a lot of kisses meant to steal his breath. They'd worked, or at least they looked like they did, judging by the rough pinkness of his lips. Naked, he was a sheath of golden shades against the black sheets, his eyes as bright and vivid as spring breaking through a dismal winter. "Because as much as I need you, it would kill me to know you're not ready for this. For us. Because once we start this, I'm not going to let go. And you know how long our kind live."

He wasn't the only one who couldn't breathe.

"Never been more sure about this in my life," I murmured, resting on my knees at the end of the bed to drink in the sight of him. There was a fear in me so great I nearly couldn't speak, but to appreciate the gift of Ryder in my life, there on my sheets, wasn't something I could let go by in silence. "I can't tell you I'm great at this. Relationships and you—you need them. So—"

"We'll work it out, áinle," Ryder murmured, reaching for me. "We shall definitely work it out."

We started slow, exploring each other until all I could taste was popcorn green tea, vanilla, and Sidhe. I found a spot where he couldn't stand my teeth dragging across his skin—a sensitive triangle along his hip and then its twin on the other side. His fingers and tongue traced my scars and tattoos, and he sighed over the marbled, puckered ribbing on my back and stroked at the ink down my thighs and hip.

He was sleek beneath me when we joined, his back glistening with sweat and his lower lip clenched between his teeth while I took my time with him. Ryder pushed up to seat me, nearly breaking my vow to prolong every enjoyable moment. So I bit the tip of his ear, burying my face in a tangle of metallic gold hair, and chuckled.

"We have all night, lordling," I whispered, using the tip of my tongue to trace down the scallop of his ear. "You're the one used to living forever. You'd think you'd be the one with patience."

His link chimed once from its resting place on the milk crate I had beside the bed, then again, falling into a syncopated dance beat only a stream of messages could make. He went to grab for it, but I stopped him, lightly sinking my canines into his forearm.

"Could be important." His plea was soft, carrying with it the weight of a Sidhe Lord with a new Court and a lot of responsibilities. "Let me at least look."

I waited while he scrolled through, then took the thin gold bracelet from his hand, not looking at the screen. "Anyone dead? The girls are okay?"

"No," he said, making a halfhearted grab for the link. "And yes, they're fine. The Court is—"

"Far enough away and well enough to take care of their own shit for right now," I told him, tossing the link toward the pile of mostly whole clothes on the floor. "Right now, it's just us, remember?"

The slivered moons were our only company when we finally touched our own stars, hitting the zenith of our bodies' peak after hours of teasing and love. I wasn't sure who'd fallen first. In the end, it didn't matter. I plunged down into the sweetness of our blood's aria, succumbing to the enticing melody he'd offered me from the moment we first met. It was nearly too much, carrying me away from everything other than the bed I shared with a Sidhe Lord who had more heart than common sense.

Inside of me, something shifted, something unfettered I'd not known existed. It reached for Ryder's soul, his heart, and entwined me through them. I felt him with every breath I took in, had his touch warming my skin even as his fingers left me. I wrapped my fingers around his, my palms pressing the backs of his hands down into the mattress when I took him over the edge, following close behind with every bit of darkness in me fleeing under the light he'd brought with him. Ryder clenched and pulled me in. We were tangled and wrapped around each other until we were slick against each other's skin and I smelled of his Sidhe scent, happily drowning under his touch.

We crested, then reached for each other again, holding back sleep and the night until our bodies ached and our limbs were too heavy to move, and even then, as we collapsed onto the sweat-dampened sheets, our fingers brushed wherever we could reach of the other and I couldn't seem to catch my breath, not caring if I ever did.

The silence around us was only broken by our heavy breathing. Then Ryder finally whispered, "I love you. I needed you to hear it. And I don't need to hear you say it in return, but I needed *me* to say it."

I traced circles across his palm, then turned over onto my stomach to peer out through the fall of black-and-purple hair covering most of my face. He did me the favor of pushing it back, tucking a large hank behind my notched ear, and then ran his fingers down my still-damp cheek.

"I think you do need to hear it." Arguing the point, I continued, "I don't know if what I feel is love. I'm not a poet. I'm not going to think flowers and sweets when I see you. I'm sorry for that. But what I can tell you is that I'd die for you. I'd avenge you. I'll defend you and yours, and hell, I'd even do it for free, which says a lot, because I'm a mercenary bastard who kills monsters for a living. If you'll have me in your life, then I want to be there. But if ever you don't, tell me, and I won't darken your world anymore. That's the best kind of love I can offer you. That I'll be here when you need me, and I'll tell you when I think you're full of shit."

"I expect nothing less from you, Chimera." Ryder chuckled, the shimmery specks in his eyes flickering with amusement and the moonlight coming through the windows above the bed. "And I was going to suggest sleep, but right now, I think I've got better things to do with you than that."

Epilogue

NEWT WOKE me up. Nothing said get out of bed louder than a tiny pointy-toed angry cat who looked more goblin than feline walking across the tender bits of your body while screaming about his empty belly. I left Ryder to his sleep, glad one of us could chase the morning under the covers, and dragged myself up to stumble down and get the cat his tribute. Once the tuna-and-egg slop hit his bowl, Newt discarded me like so much trash, and I gathered up my aching limbs to shove them and whatever they were left attached to to stand under a hot shower, angling the spray heads so nearly every inch of my body could be pounded by the hard streams.

As reluctant as I was to scrub Ryder from my body, I needed to or I'd get nothing done except to crawl back in bed and make my body ache more. And as I pulled my oldest pair of jeans up my legs and over my ass, I felt every twinge my overstretched muscles made while I moved.

"*Iesu*, I've got to wash those sheets once he wakes up," I muttered, discovering the bit of webbing I hadn't been able to cut split at some point during the night and healed correctly. "Not that I remember the last time I changed them, but screw it, I haven't been sleeping here much, anyway."

The day broke gray, and I'd missed it, but whatever clear skies there'd been were gone, leaving a cloak of mist and dreary light behind. I got a good view of the fogged-over shoreline from the stretch of windows along the back of the warehouse, and the cat dogged my footsteps once I brought a cup of coffee into the living space. The big block engine I'd hung on a mount was surrounded by the boxes Jonas had dragged over from Dempsey's Lakeside double-wide, packed up and forgotten when Razor moved into the place. I'd put off digging through the old man's stuff while he'd been alive, and now that he was gone, it seemed wrong to be leaving his life to sit like garbage beneath a chunk of metal I couldn't find a home for.

"Okay, old man, let's see what there is of you in there." I dragged one box over, then another. Sitting down on the couch, I stared at the boxes, then grabbed the smallest, shoving aside the knotted rebar with a cardboard corner as I set it down on the shipping crate. "Guess I'll start here."

There weren't many—only seven—hardly enough to hold Dempsey's character and sure as hell not enough to speak for the man he'd been. Quite a bit of Dempsey's things were over at Jonas's place from when he'd gone there to live, and what was left at the Lakeside house had been mostly stored-away things. I'd already taken his weapons home, cleaning what was usable and glass-casing the guns he'd gotten back before the Merge, most of them antiques and untrustworthy in the field.

The first box was odd, tidbits of clothing and a chewed-through blanket. I didn't know what to make of what I'd found until I reached the bottom of the box and found a length of iron chain with a clip attached to a ring soldered to the end of it. Staring at the thing like it was a snake coiled to bite me, I grabbed at the blanket again, recognizing it as something Dempsey used to wrap around me in the beginning of our lives together. I'd been feral, attracted to the red stars quilted into the heavy blanket, and I'd fallen for the flash of color every time he'd come near, only to be captured in it until I calmed down enough to trust him.

"Should have pulled my teeth," I grumbled at my dead mentor. "Would have been easier on you."

"Not every solution requires pulling teeth or cutting off body parts," Ryder called out as he came down the stairs. "Sometimes it's better to gain small steps than take huge leaps."

"Said the guy who wouldn't let me cut my fingers apart so I could make them work better before we fell into bed." I nodded toward the kitchen. "There's a thermos cup of hot water in there for you and a bunch of those frou-frou teas you like. Bags, not leaves, so don't get too excited."

"The fact that you even thought to have tea for me warms my heart." From the sounds Ryder made in the kitchen, I guessed he found the tea. He walked back out, holding the lid from the sealable cup against its side while he swished a bag of leaves around in the hot water. "I hurt everywhere."

"Yeah, well, that happens sometimes," I remarked, carefully placing the blanket and everything else back in the box, then setting it aside to deal with later. The next one was a bit heavier and larger, so I shoved at the crate with my foot to make room on the floor in front of me. "Good to see you found the clothes I left."

"I thought I was doing well enough until I moved my right arm. Shoulder stings as if I'd landed on a bag of wasps." He hissed as he sat down, giving me a baleful glare when I glanced at him. "I love you, áinle, but you *bite*."

"You knew what you were getting into," I reminded him. "When have I not bitten? Move your knee so I don't hit you with the flap. Never know what Dempsey thought to save, and with our luck, it'll be some cursed mechanical bird with a thirst for Sidhe blood."

The papers on top were Dempsey's retirement portfolio from SoCalGov and the resolution of his Stalker license. I'd have thought he'd have burned them as soon as he opened them, but instead he'd shoved them aside, much like I'd done with what he'd used to bring me home. The rest of it seemed to be odds and bits from his Stalker career—loose pictures of kills with friends I knew and many I'd never met. There was a leather jacket folded up at the bottom, broad in the shoulder, with a tearing bite taken out of the upper left sleeve, about the size of my teeth span when he'd first found me.

"Oh, I have a matching one of those on my right shoulder." Ryder grimaced, reaching for the jacket to hold it, then examining the cleanly cut mark. "Yep, exactly like that. With those canine points too. Imagine that."

"Shut up. You didn't complain at the time, so you don't get to now," I grumbled back. "Okay, what's this, then?"

The package was soft-sided, a large brown envelope stuffed to the gills and held together by yellowed packing tape. Dempsey's strong handwriting was faded, the black marker he used now a soft gray against the manila paper, but the name and address were still legible—a long-demolished motel in New Vegas and a room number scrawled out under Kenny's name.

"I'll be damned." Reaching for the knife I'd used to cauterize my skin, I muttered at Ryder, "Bastard never mailed it. No wonder Cari's witchy magic came up empty. Kenny never got this because Dempsey never sent it. He must have shoved it in here when we were moving to San Diego and thought he'd shipped it off."

I didn't want to see my fingers trembling, but they had a mind of their own, and it was hard to hold on to the knife. Ryder leaned in, his thigh against mine, and he nudged my shoulder, wincing as he moved.

"No matter what's in there," he murmured, "it'll be fine. It won't really change anything."

Taking the package from me was easy enough. Getting it open was hard. The tape was gummy and the fabric threads running through it fought my blade, too sticky and old to be sliced clean even with a sharp edge. He finally wrested it open and the package burst apart, eager to breathe and vomit up its contents after years of being held in by a corset of plastic and glue.

Something triangular went bouncing across the area rug, a dried, withered bit Newt made a beeline for as soon as he saw movement. I pounced first, barely making it in time to grab at the folded-over scrap before my cat dug his teeth into it. An enraged mewl rumbled from his tiny throat, his chest puffed out and his tail bristling, ready to fight me for his prize, but I flicked a belled stuffed mouse out from its hiding place next to one of the boxes and he bounded after it, distracted and happy.

"Huh." I pulled myself back up onto the couch, examining what I had in my hand. "I'll be damned. Well, I'm sure I am, but it's definite now."

"What is that?" Ryder recoiled, much like he'd done when he found me snipping my fingers apart. "That looks like—"

"Yep, fits right in," I said cheerfully, holding my hair back as I fit the piece into the notch taken out of my ear. Except for some looseness from years of drying and a bit of growth, the triangular bit was a perfect match. "Looks like this is what Dempsey was given to sniff me out with. Like a puzzle piece. Find the elfin this fits to. Better than a glass slipper."

"Some paper, looks like a contract, but there's no names," Ryder commented, spreading them out on a box lid. "Only numbers, like a code and money amounts, higher if you're alive, and when he needed to be in SoCal to get his money. They gave him six months to find you and bring you over."

"Took him a few," I admitted. "I wasn't very cooperative."

"No, I can't imagine you were. You're not cooperative *now*," he drawled, rolling his eyes at me. "*This*, now, this I know."

The large square piece of silk he slipped out of the broken package was dull, as worn from age as the tape, or perhaps even more. Speckled with brown spots I suspected were blood, the silk's cobalt hue faded toward the edges, leached to a robin's-egg hue from water damage. It was double-sided, plain on one, but when Ryder turned it over, I saw an elaborate sigil of a silvery white dragon picked out in shiny threads, the colors shimmering when he ran it over his hand. There were bits of blue and green worked into its ridges, a fierce Asiatic draconian face captured in mid snarl. It was a simple sweep of floss, beads, and silk, more of an impression than a true rendering, but the sight of it left me perplexed.

"A Clan sigil." Ryder caught my confusion with a glance. Then, figuring I needed more of an explanation, he continued, "Something like this is given to a child at birth, or when they're named. It's a formal welcome to their House. Their Clan. I recognize this one. It's a dead Clan. The Xishari. I just don't know why Dempsey had it."

"You know a lot about dead Clans?" I turned the bit of mummified flesh over in my fingers. "And how the hell does a Clan die? Everyone of that bloodline bites the dust?"

"Or if there's one left and she renamed herself, making a new Clan." Ryder brushed the square out, spreading it over his thigh. "It's considered to be ill luck to be the last of a Clan, especially if they've all fallen in battle. That's what happened to the Xishari. Everyone was killed after the Last Great War with the Unsidhe. Before the Merge. Only Sebac remained, so she set aside her blood name and formed her own Clan, the Sebac. That's how I know about the Xishari. She was the last of her Clan and then the first of her own. It's a part of our family history. There are a few dead Clans, but this sigil, I know very well. It's a cloud dragon. It was their mark."

"Huh." I mulled over what he said, scratching at the dragon scale under my skin. After a moment, I held the bit of my flesh Dempsey meant to send to his brother and turned it over so Ryder could see the Xishari sigil inked into the triangular slice. "Then explain to me why it was tattooed onto my ear and why Tanic cut it out."

RHYS FORD is an award-winning author with several long-running LGBT+ mystery, thriller, paranormal, and urban fantasy series and is a two-time LAMBDA finalist with her *Murder and Mayhem* novels. She is also a 2017 Gold and Silver Medal winner in the Florida Authors and Publishers President's Book Awards for her novels *Ink and Shadows* and *Hanging the Stars*. She is published by Dreamspinner Press and DSP Publications.

She shares the house with Harley, a gray tuxedo with a flower on her face, Badger, a disgruntled alley cat who isn't sure living inside is a step up the social ladder, as well as a ginger cairn terrorist named Gus. Rhys is also enslaved to the upkeep of a 1979 Pontiac Firebird and enjoys murdering make-believe people.

Rhys can be found at the following locations:
Blog: www.rhysford.com
Facebook: www.facebook.com/rhys.ford.author

BOOK ONE IN THE KAI GRACEN SERIES

RHYS FORD

BLACK
DOG BLUES

*"Heart-pounding action, dramatic betrayals,
and creepy backstories"* — *AudioFile Magazine*

The Kai Gracen Series: Book One

Ever since being part of the pot in a high-stakes poker game, elfin outcast Kai Gracen figures he used up his good karma when Dempsey, a human Stalker, won the hand and took him in. Following the violent merge of Earth and Underhill, the human and elfin races are left with a messy, monster-ridden world, and Stalkers are the only cavalry willing to ride to someone's rescue when something shadowy appears.

It's a hard life but one Kai likes—filled with bounty, a few friends, and most importantly, no other elfin around to remind him of his past. And killing monsters is easy. Especially since he's one himself.

But when a sidhe lord named Ryder arrives in San Diego, Kai is conscripted to do a job for Ryder's fledgling Dawn Court. It's supposed to be a simple run up the coast during dragon-mating season to retrieve a pregnant human woman seeking sanctuary. Easy, quick, and best of all, profitable. But Kai ends up in the middle of a deadly bloodline feud he has no hope of escaping.

No one ever got rich being a Stalker. But then few of them got old, either, and it doesn't look like Kai will be the exception.

www.dsppublications.com

RHYS FORD

MAD LIZARD
MAMBO

The Kai Gracen Series: Book Two

Kai Gracen has no intention of being anyone's pawn. A pity Fate and
SoCalGov have a different opinion on the matter.

Licensed Stalkers make their living hunting down monsters and
dangerous criminals… and their lives are usually brief, brutal, and thankless.
Despite being elfin and cursed with a nearly immortal lifespan, Kai didn't
expect to be any different. Then Ryder, the High Lord of the Southern Rise
Court, arrived in San Diego, and Kai's not-so-mundane life went from mild
mayhem to full-throttle chaos.

Now an official liaison between the growing Sidhe court and the human
populace, Kai is at Ryder's beck and call for anything a High Lord might
need a Stalker to do. Unfortunately for Kai, this means chasing down a
flimsy rumor about an ancient lost court somewhere in the Nevada desert—a
court with powerful magics that might save Ryder's—and Kai's—people
from becoming a bloody memory in their merged world's violent history.

The race for the elfin people's salvation opens unwelcome windows
into Kai's murky past, and it could also slam the door on any future he
might have with his own kind and Ryder.

www.dsppublications.com

BOOK THREE IN THE KAI GRACEN SERIES

RHYS FORD

JACKED
CAT JIVE

"Kai...tough, scrappy, outcast, snark-monger extraordinaire." — Gail Carriger, Author of *The Parasol Protectorate Series*

The Kai Gracen Series: Book Three

Stalker Kai Gracen knew his human upbringing would eventually clash with his elfin heritage, but not so soon. Between Ryder, a pain-in-his-neck sidhe lord coaxing him to join San Diego's Southern Rise Court, and picking up bounties for SoCalGov, he has more than enough to deal with. With his loyalties divided between the humans who raised him and the sidhe lord he's befriended and sworn to protect, Kai finds himself standing at a crossroads.

When a friend begs Kai to rescue a small group of elfin refugees fleeing the Dusk Court, he's pulled into a dangerous mission with Ryder through San Diego's understreets and the wilderness beyond. Things go from bad to downright treacherous when Kerrick, Ryder's cousin, insists on joining them, staking a claim on Southern Rise and Kai.

Burdened by his painful past, Kai must stand with Ryder against Kerrick while facing down the very court he fears and loathes. Dying while on a run is expected for a Stalker, but Kai wonders if embracing his elfin blood also means losing his heart, soul, and humanity along the way.

www.dsppublications.com